Somewh

Somewhere Like This

Pat Arrowsmith

First published 1970 by W H Allen & Co. Ltd
This edition and preface first published November 1990 by
GMP Publishers Ltd,
P O Box 247, London, N17 9QR, UK

world copyright © 1970 Pat Arrowsmith

Distributed in North America by
Alyson Publications Inc.,
40 Plympton Street, Boston, MA 02118, USA

Distributed in Australia by
Bulldog Books,
P O Box 155, Broadway, NSW 2007, Australia

British Library Cataloguing in Publication Data
    Arrowsmith, Pat
    Somewhere like this.
    I. Title
    823.914 [F]

    ISBN 0-85449-143-0

Printed and bound in the EC on environmentally-friendly paper
by Norhaven A/S, Viborg, Denmark

Preface

I have been in prison eleven times - twelve if you count my virtual gaoling in 1945 for breaking out of Cheltenham Ladies' College and going on the town on Victory in Europe Night - for which crime I was confined as a moral invalid, more or less incommunicado in the school sanatorium for a month or so. It was good training for what was to follow...

My eleven sentences (totalling over two years inside) have been for opposing either nuclear weapons, the Vietnam war or the deployment of British troops in N. Ireland, and on one occasion of law-breaking on a picket line. I have been in three English prisons, a Scottish one, a Bangkok jail and an aliens bureau in Greece. Amnesty International has twice adopted me as a prisoner of conscience - actually managing to get a week off one of my six month sentences: a reward for my handing in a useless (to me) bunch of keys I found in the garden.

My prison experiences have included being forcibly fed (I have twice been on hunger strike, winning out on both occasions), being kept in virtual solitary confinement on Rule 43 for weeks on end in a dungeon-like punishment cell for taking part in a small sit-down strike by members of the prisoners' union I helped to set up, and escaping from prison.

I have managed to do some useful things inside - like assembling a collection of prison drawings and writing poems, a novel (*Jericho*) and the draft of *To Asia in Peace* (a book about a non-violent mission to S.E. Asia). I was allowed on one occasion to have a copy of *Somewhere Like This* (written between prison sentences) sent in to me. As I was refusing on principle to work I was earning no pocket money with which to buy sweets, so I lent the book to fellow inmates for a toffee an hour. The general verdict was that it was too true to prison life to be interesting!

Although this book is fiction, not autobiographical (political imprisonment does not feature in it), nevertheless it reflects the social scene I myself observed and experienced in prison in the mid-sixties when a fairly rigid butch/fem type of lesbianism was the order of the day in Holloway. Later the pattern changed and half the dykes inside ceased to be quasi-fellows.

The book's title is intended to imply that in some ways prison life is the same as life outside: if you are nice, people (screws and cons) are nice to you in return; if you are well behaved, life can be reasonably tranquil; if, however, you step out of line, you can be in for real trouble - as I found out to my cost...

I

LORRY SHIFTED UNCOMFORTABLY IN HER SLEEP ON THE
unsprung bed. She was really called Florence, but had decided a year
or two ago to become Lorry. She was happier that way.

It was summer time, so she was not precisely cold; but the bedclothes
lay too lightly upon her, and the sheets were too short. Presently the
continual unaccustomed scratchiness of blanket against the skin of her
feet woke her. Early though it was, a checker-board of sunlight played
on the shiny wall alongside the squat barred window. The outline of
each square followed the contours of the uneven stonework beneath the
bright blue paint. Lorry, lying flat on the bed (for the narrow bedclothes
came untucked if she rolled over on to her side), looking up at the
familiar criss-cross pattern, remembered abruptly where she was, and
was immediately filled with rage and, at the same time, a sense of mild
relief.

The top of her mind seethed with anger over the injustice of what
had happened—not so much the injustice of her arrest (getting arrested
was just a normal, not infrequent occurrence in her life); rather the
injustice of fate in having planted a totally unexpected noisy terrier in
the house, which otherwise they would have burgled with impunity.
She caught herself actually muttering aloud with anger as she thought
of all they had stood to earn from the job, but for the dog.

Then briefly—very briefly—she recalled the humiliating experience
of the day before: how Pete, Greg and she had all been driven off in a
'meat safe' from Bow Street to the Scrubs. They had never before
actually taken her to the Scrubs. They had never before actually taken
her to the wrong prison, but this time they failed to discover she was
not Lorry but Florence until she was standing before the MO, naked,
absurd, and more bitterly ashamed than ever before in her life of her
hateful female chest, which she stuck out truculently in an attempt to
conceal her embarrassment. There had been roars of laughter and

I

the sort of ribald cracks she herself was apt nowadays to make about women. One male officer had actually given her a teasing slap on the buttocks. She had turned quickly, all set to give him a good kick in the balls, but the other two officers had just managed to restrain her.

When at last they had got her to Collingwood, quite late the evening before, and had handed her over to the officer on duty with some other crack about there being no female underwear at the Scrubs, she had almost, for a moment, felt as if she were home again. Glancing round at the familiar network of railings, wire and spiral staircases, as she marched away from Receptions to Admissions Wing, she had felt both caged and safe.

Now, as she lay in bed, she heard, down at the end of the wing, a tremendous jangling and clattering as the heavy door was unlocked and the prison officers' footsteps reverberated on the stone floor. The bell would soon ring, and the usual first day's routine start. Lorry's rage dissolved as she lay on in bed wondering what work she would be given, whether any officer in charge of a job knew she was back in and had asked for her yet, and, above all, whether there was going to be anyone she might fancy on her wing this time.

About ten minutes after the bell rang, she got out of bed and studied, with extreme distaste, the clothes allotted to her. Nowadays, she never wore women's clothes except when she was inside. She had given them up three years ago after she had first visited the Golden Arrow in Paddington, and had seen all the women there in full drag—dressed exactly like men, just as she herself had for years wanted to be. There was only one consolation about having to put on feminine knickers and the baggy green dress: everyone else in Collingwood, butch, fem or straight, had to do the same.

The most degrading thing of all was putting on the white, thickish ladies' knickers instead of the men's pants she was used to. And these were the worst sort of knickers—voluminous, the unelasticated legs reaching half way down her thighs. She would have to get hold of a smaller pair with elastic in the legs, which she could pull right up so that they looked more like a pair of briefs.

She would not of course use the roll-on suspender belt for her stockings. She had managed to persuade the girl in Receptions the day before to give her a bit of elastic to make into garters. The girl had been easily persuaded. A suggestive wink followed by an engaging grin had been enough. Lorry had not even had to bribe her with one of the two cigarettes she had managed, by a fluke, to smuggle through Receptions in her bedroom slippers. On the contrary, the girl had offered her a roll-up. One glance at Lorry's cropped head, and the fourteen-year-old cheeky expression she had assumed three years ago along with the boys' clothes, had been enough to convince her that here was someone worth cultivating.

Lorry pushed the brassière under her mattress and pulled the roll-on over her head and down round her chest in order to make it look as flat as possible. She wished she had some sticking plaster—still, the roll-on was the next best thing. With great reluctance, she put on the dress, carefully leaving the top button undone to make it look more shirt-like, and rolled the elbow-length sleeves up as far as they would go. As it was still early, it was cold within the heavy stonework of Collingwood. However, in order not to conceal her businesslike sleeves and forearms, Lorry decided not to wear the matted, over-washed bottle green cardigan (which was in any case far too short). She pulled on the nylon stockings carelessly, indifferent to whether or not they laddered, and rolled them neatly over the garters so that they almost looked like knee-socks. This was not strictly allowed—but it was often possible to get away with it. Finally, with relief, she put on the one item of clothing she did not despise: the black, boy's lace-up shoes. She briskly straightened her bed, then sat on the edge of it waiting for her cell to be unlocked.

2

EARLIER THAT MORNING, THE BUZZING OF MISS HEWSON'S alarm clock incorporated itself into her dreams and almost failed to wake her. Luckily it just succeeded in penetrating into her consciousness. Had she overslept, Miss Whittaker would have been left on her own to cope with breakfast on G Wing, and she herself would have been severely reprimanded by Mac when she came on duty at nine o'clock. She would, in fact, have been just as sharply reprimanded as any of the prisoners ever were—perhaps more so. Mac was on the whole tougher with her juniors than with the prisoners, with many of whom she seemed to forge a bond of affinity.

This was both puzzling and aggravating. Surely she ought to treat her colleagues, even if junior, better than a bunch of criminals. Then guiltily Miss Hewson remembered that it did not do to think of the misguided, unfortunate women in Collingwood as criminals. They were social misfits to be helped and guided. And that was the trouble: Mac, who had been years in the prison service and held all the old-fashioned ideas (believed in punishment and hanging, scorned the new-fangled Group Counselling), seemed able to get on friendly terms with the toughest prisoners—hardened old tarts and callous Borstal-bred youngsters.

She, on the other hand, had been influenced by articles and radio programmes on the rehabilitative work sensitive prison officers could perform. She would like to have trained as a social worker had she had the necessary academic qualifications. Yet during the two months she had so far been in Collingwood, she had failed to make genuine contact with a single prisoner.

The common impression about prisoners—anyway the impression she had always previously held—was that they lived in a state of perpetual hatred and dread of their strict bullying wardresses. In fact it was she who was afraid of the prisoners, rather than they of her.

She always allowed herself five minutes between hearing the alarm and getting up. It was a pity she did, for she invariably spent this brief period thinking gloomily about the difficulties and dreariness of the day ahead.

This morning, she looked dispiritedly round at her small bedroom, with its chilly pale blue and grey distempered walls and fawn linoleum-covered floor. She was housed in the annexe, a prefabricated building, supposed to be temporary, but which had in fact accommodated junior officers, in its frigid, barrack-like atmosphere, for several years past.

As Miss Hewson stared at the one ink-stained mat by her bed, and at the shiny, cheap-looking furniture, it struck her that she was not much better off than the prisoners themselves. Her room was scarcely larger than a prison cell. There was only one chair in the room—an unwelcoming, tightly-stuffed, straight-up affair, which always seemed to reject her when she tried to flop back exhausted into it after standing for hours on duty. When, very occasionally, another officer dropped in for a chat or cup of tea last thing, she had to sit on the bed—just as the prisoners did in their cells when they visited each other.

There was hardly enough space for her belongings. She could only with difficulty cram her clothes into the cupboard, and there seemed nowhere to put her books and radio.

Miss Hewson looked at her clock and saw that her five minutes were up. She got out of bed reluctantly yet purposefully, washed, then put on her neatly-pressed uniform, which at first she had been so proud of, but which she now regarded with distaste. By six-thirty she was just in time to join Miss Whittaker and set off to unlock the women on G Wing.

3

MAVIS'S DREAMS RESOLVED THEMSELVES INTO A HUGE lump of dread, which gradually lowered itself overpoweringly on to her brain, as though some great weight were descending from the ceiling. The sense of undefined apprehension became fear, then terror, as the immense lump seemed to turn into a lid round her skull and slowly start to crush it. She screamed, or strove to, or so she thought. In fact she merely gasped, but the strain and panic woke her.

As soon as she looked round the minute room, its scanty furniture only dimly discernible in the halflight (it was two in the morning), she knew where she was. She licked her lips thoroughly, almost scrubbed them with her tongue. This was something she had done all her life at moments of stress—although sometimes her action was misconstrued as a flirtatious gesture. It was a way of reassuring herself that she was still alive. If her lips felt moist, all was well: she was herself, an individual in her own right, vital and with her own thoughts and notions. If they were dry, she felt she was only the shadow of a person. All kinds of half-buried feelings were revived, associated with the most unpleasant occurrences of her life.

The terror, if not the precise recollection, came back to her of the time when she was three, when some man—her father probably—had thrown a beer bottle at her mother, making the blood stream down her face.

Subsequent fears and miseries also recurred: the frantic feeling of being killed, of having her life-line snapped, the morning the two ladies came and drove her and her sisters away from their mother in the basement flat to a strange brick village in the country, full of strange children.

Dry lips conjured up a melée of other half remembered, similarly panic-stricken feelings from her childhood—which was not far away in any case. For although she was married herself now and had four young children, she was still only twenty-three. Seen at certain moments, she looked considerably older, more like forty-three, her small-boned, well formed, pale face beneath the fluffy blonde hair looking careworn and suddenly angular. At moments of gaiety, however, she looked dainty and young, almost like a pretty fifteen-year-old.

But licking her lips this time did not help. The sense of terror remained; and, although it no longer felt as though her skull were being compressed, she fulfilled the intention of her dream and gave a loud yell. But the yell gave her no satisfaction. It did not seem to reverberate or carry, but was muffled and cut short, so she thought, by the heavy, screw-studded door.

The apparent futility of her scream, and the sight of the forbidding door, turned her waking terror into acute claustrophobia. She screamed out again, then again and again. Her lips were dry as paper. Her yells were just puffs of cotton wool blown out uselessly against the massive door, stone walls, and cave-curved ceiling. But the more futile her yelling seemed, the more frantic she became. She felt buried alive. She jumped out of bed, rushed at the door, and banged it till her fists smarted.

In the darkness she made out a bell, and was for a moment relieved.

6

After all she was not irretrievably buried and cut off from the rest of the world. She pressed the bell. It wobbled. As she could not hear it ring, and assumed it was either broken or a hoax, she irrationally pressed it again. Nothing happened.

Her panic returned, combined now with terrified fury. She pressed the bell again and again viciously. She yelled repeatedly, oblivious of the growing hoarseness of her voice. She broke the skin of her fists through beating against the studded door. It became of paramount importance that, since she herself could not get out, at least some sign of herself, some noise, should penetrate the thick wood and form a life-giving bond with the outside world.

So she picked up her metal wash-basin and clashed that against the door; then the tin jug; then the empty chamber pot; then, these not proving effective, the wooden chair. She bashed and bashed it against the unrelenting door, which seemed to become a person, an aloof, unyielding, omnipotent person—like the magistrate in court the day before, or like Miss Roberts, the approved school headmistress of her girlhood. Mavis was hitting Miss Roberts again and again in the face as she hammered the door with her chair.

She seemed to have been banging and yelling for a long time. She was becoming exhausted. Then her dream started to recur: the room was gradually shrinking; the walls and ceiling started to close in around her. Soon they would become the nightmare helmet round her skull. She collapsed on the floor, licked her lips again in a final, frantic effort to ward off disaster, and stretched out her arms feebly to try to push back the encroaching walls.

Then a sudden glare of light dazzled her. It was, she thought, her moment of death. She sank back flat on the floor, sobbing and shuddering, as Miss Philips, the night duty officer, switched on the dim cell bulb and cautiously opened the door.

'Well well, what's all this now?' she said heartily—for she was quite a good-natured woman, who did not like to see prisoners or anyone else in deep distress. Turning to the young officer with her, she said: 'Let's see if we can get her straightened out ourselves and not call over for Sister. I hate to see them sent over to that hospital and given the needle the moment they get in. It always makes them worse, not better.' Turning back to Mavis, who was crouching on the floor sobbing and gasping,

7

she resumed: 'Now then, duck, let's get you back into bed. It's not that bad you know really, once you get used to it. Come along, Miss Thomas, let's get her back in.'

Between them they hoisted Mavis, now quite limp, to her feet, and set her down on the edge of the bed.

'Get her a cup of tea, Miss Thomas, that'll put her right,' Miss Philips said. 'You know where the tin is—top side drawer of the desk.' She put Mavis's cardigan round her quaking shoulders, sat squarely on the bed beside her and repeated: 'Yes, duck, you'll find it's not so bad once you get used to it. There's good and bad in here, just like anywhere else. First night's always worst.'

Mavis did not reply, but her sobbing gradually abated. Miss Philips's rousing but quite kindly tone dispelled the nightmare. The cell became a room again and no longer a shrinking box closing in around her. The sudden flood of dull light had been like a breath of air to a suffocating person. She remained disorientated for a few moments however, oblivious of where she was, unconcerned who the person sitting beside her might be. It was enough that she was no longer shut into a tiny, dark room by herself.

She licked her lips again, and this time they stayed moist. Her paralysed mind began to re-awaken. Faint thoughts started to tingle in her brain, almost like numbed fingers coming back to life. Searching for something to latch on to, they gradually focused on some of her immediate troubles. Haltingly, sitting staring at her feet, talking more to herself than to Miss Philips, she mumbled in a sob-choked voice:

'It's my little Doreen—and the boys. I don't know what they'll do to my Doreen. And Ron's only a baby still . . .' Her voice tailed off.

'Oh, they'll be all right,' Miss Philips replied with bluff reassurance. All the mothers in Collingwood were constantly worrying and weeping about their children. 'The Council will look after them, I daresay, and take them off to some nice country house at the seaside where they'll have a grand time . . .'

'They'll take them away from me. I won't never see them again,' Mavis mumbled. She buried her face in her hands and rocked to and fro despairingly on the bed, re-living in her mind the concoction of misery recalled by her own removal from home as an infant, and her recent removal in the police van.

'Well, perhaps you need a good cry. It may help put you right,' Miss Philips responded, and gave her a slight pat on the back.

Miss Thomas returned with the tea. Mavis gulped it down, still not raising her eyes from the ground, then obeyed the two officers and got back into bed. Miss Philips stood looking speculatively at her for a moment, then turned to Miss Thomas and said:

'It's the claustrophobia you know—it's that what gets them like this. Especially the first night. Some of them never seem to get over it, but for some it just seems to be the first night—being locked up in a strange place for the first time. But they get over it once they settle down and get used to it. I think we'll leave this one's door ajar tonight.' Turning back to Mavis, she said: 'Now I'll leave your door open just a crack so you don't feel so cut off. But don't go telling the P.O. or I'll be on report to the Governor—won't I, Miss Thomas?' and she gave a slight chuckle to try to cheer Mavis up. 'Well, goodnight, and see you get off to sleep now,' she concluded. And she and Miss Thomas went downstairs again to the office.

Reassured by the crack of light, soothed by the tea, and exhausted after her bout of terror, Mavis soon fell asleep. She did not wake until her cell door was abruptly pushed open, and a cold-voiced officer announced that it was breakfast time, and she should have been up and dressed twenty minutes ago.

4

JAN WAS SITTING ON THE GROUND FLOOR OF G WING. She was depressed, suffering from that over-fed yet undernourished feeling that nearly always followed the heavy, unappetizing Collingwood dinners. There might be meat, but it was invariably leathery, gristle-riddled and tasteless. It was swamped in mud-brown gravy, and submerged beneath a sodden mass of over-cooked cabbage and a great bank of powdery potato. Nor were the puddings as a rule any better. Today's

9

had been typical: a great wedge of treacle-soaked suet pudding, the greasy remnants of which were still cleaving to Jan's palate.

Collingwood meals might not seem quite so bad to the others—more what they were used to anyway, Jan thought, glancing round the circle of women sitting having their after-dinner gossip before resuming work. After all, the majority, unlike her, were working-class women, who did not go in for fresh fruit, salads, and the delicate foreign dishes which she appreciated.

Her gloom was enhanced by the surroundings. The brightest sunshine was always dulled by the grubby upper windows of the wing. It was further chilled by the heavy stonework, on which, even in summer time, the light lay only in tepid patches. Today, not being sunny at all, the wing was grey and toneless, like a vast dim cavern. All the small attempts to brighten it up—the repainting of the iron bars in a heavy yellow, the tantalizing display of travel posters on the walls, the cage of budgerigars at the far end—seemed futile. If anything, by very contrast, they increased the dreariness.

Ignoring the chatter going on around her, Jan looked up through the wire safety-netting at the distant roof. She did not feel caged in. On the contrary, she felt, at that moment, a mild sense of agoraphobia. The arched roof seemed furlongs away, like cathedral vaulting in the twilight. She felt as though she were an insignificant, unnoticed speck of humanity, lost in some huge, impersonal arena.

She stared down the length of the wing. So pallid was the grey light filtering in, that the wing seemed immeasurably long, the far end only faintly discernible. Then she became a grain of dust caught in the gloom of an interminable corridor—the endless corridor of life. For that was how life, anyway hers, just then seemed.

She had three years of prison ahead of her. For three years her days would be drab and monotonous. She would be a nobody, lost in a crowd of nobodies. She would be deprived of the things she most valued and enjoyed. Parts of her personality would be suppressed. She would shrink.

And this was not the first time Jan had been inside—it was the fifth time. On every previous occasion, she had done quite a long stretch. The diamond smuggling, then forgery, had been followed by the safe-breaking fiasco, and that by man-slaughter through dangerous driving. This time, she was in for straight larceny. In a fit of aberration, it now seemed to her, she had got into an empty, unlocked Cadillac parked in Grosvenor Square, and simply driven off. If, at that particular juncture, she had happened to see a Mini-Minor, she would not have dreamt of stealing it. It was the magnitude and potential speed of the Cadillac that had appealed to her—it was what she had needed just then. So now she was back in Collingwood for the fifth time. A life of unalleviated tedium stretched before her. She had spent fifteen years in prison so far. She was forty-one.

Jan felt too bored and depressed even to read the paper. As she fiddled desultorily with it, dog-earing and un-dog-earing the left-hand corner, she half listened to the conversation going on around her. Beryl Hunt, a heavy, determined woman, clicking her knitting needles emphatically, was announcing in a loud undertone to the woman beside her:

'So I turns round and says to the judge, "Sir," I says—and he was lucky to get called Sir—"I'm going straight back to my solicitor." And you know who he is?—represented Magnus Drake in the famous Harley Street trial—and so I says to him, "Just get my appeal heard in one week's time—just one week mind—or I'll take the case right up to the High Court. I'll see my M.P. and get it to the House of Lords, that's what I'll do." ' She paused dramatically, glanced up from her knitting at the woman beside her, then resumed, 'And do you know what he said?—"Mrs Hunt," he says—'

'Yes, and do you know what they had the nerve to say to me last Tuesday?' broke in the woman beside her, who had not been listening. 'They actually had the bloody nerve to go and say I had no right—no *right* mind!—to say my own kids were not to be let go to that cousin of his—and she's not just his cousin, mind. There's more going on there . . . And that I had no right—me a tax payer an' all—to have them go to St Dunstan's. So what do we pay taxes for at all is what I'd like to know. So I says to them, "Look," I says . . .'

But Jan did not care what the woman had said, for she had heard it all countless times before and knew that half of it was untrue anyway. So she tried to close her ears to the talk going on around her. Shielding her face with the paper, she attempted to concentrate on world affairs. The conversation droned on around her with the monotony of rising and falling waves.

Suddenly there was a jangling of keys as the wing door was unlocked. Jan glanced up from her paper and saw one of the Admissions Wing officers usher in a new prisoner.

'Here you are, Miss Hewson,' she called down the wing, 'here's another one for you—an old friend back.' Lorry came in, and Miss Thomas clattered out again.

Jan watched Lorry walk purposefully down the wing to the office, holding a bundle of clothing propped on her shoulder as though she were a sailor. She studied her with interest, her boredom immediately dispelled. She was always glad when a newcomer arrived—who knew how she might turn out? So far, this sentence, they had all been disappointing. Jan had been hopeful about a newcomer called Maud at first, but her hopes had soon been dashed. Butch though Maud had looked with her cropped hair and sideboards, she had turned out to be a phony: someone who had come in in woman's clothes. She had been overheard in Receptions announcing she intended to go butch this time in order to get a girl friend who would keep her in fags. Once she had heard this, Jan lost interest in her. Rob, who had arrived soon after, had almost immediately found herself a girl friend, so she had been no use either.

Perhaps this new butch, however, would prove to be the genuine article, and would show an interest in her, Jan thought hopefully, as Miss Hewson accompanied Lorry up the spiral staircase to the top landing. She was pleased to see that Lorry was allotted the cell next to hers which had recently fallen vacant.

A few minutes later, Jan saw Lorry come out of her cell dressed for work in shirt and dungarees. She had evidently been put on an outdoor job, or on the painting party. If she was going on painting, then they would both be in the same work party. Dressed like this, her hair cropped like a boy's, you would never have taken her for a girl at all, Jan thought happily.

Lorry clattered noisily down the metal stairs. When she was almost at the bottom, she gripped the hand rails and nimbly leaped down the last four rungs. Then, to counteract the tom-boyish exuberance of her jump, she sauntered leisurely across the flat towards the circle of seated women. She did not enter the circle, but paused on the edge, slouched against a table, her hands thrust deep in the pockets of her dungarees,

After a moment or two, she pulled out the tin of tobacco and cigarette papers given her by the fat woman on Admissions Wing who fancied her. She rolled a cigarette, lit it, and puffed ruminatively as she inspected the group of women seated before her. They were mostly heavy and middle-aged, and, at first glance, did not look a very promising collection—although the slim, youngish brunette over by the record-player had possibilities. She did not notice Jan at all, watching her surreptitiously from behind her paper.

It was the first time Miss Hewson had been on duty alone during the dinner-hour. She knew it ended officially at half-past one. The trusties, who wore red arm bands and helped the officers with minor supervisory jobs, were also supposed to leave the wing at half-past one, accompanied by the women they conducted to the jam factory, phone shop and work rooms. In fact no one ever began to make a move until twenty to two at the very earliest.

Sitting up in her glass office at the far end of the wing, Miss Hewson looked nervously at her wrist-watch. It was between ten and a quarter past one. She dreaded the moment when she would have to announce it was time to set off to work. It never struck her that the women might set off on their own accord.

Miss Hewson liked being in a position of authority, yet she disliked giving orders for fear of being disobeyed. She dreaded having to try to deal with defiant prisoners. This all had something to do with her schooldays when she had longed to be made a prefect but had not been sure how she would have coped with the situation had she achieved her ambition. For in those days, she had been a quiet, plump girl, neither particularly clever nor good at games. As a prefect, she would probably have been derided and defied by the juniors. Luckily, perhaps, she had never been put to the test. Now she was a prison officer, she had the chance to prove to herself that she could keep order and command obedience. Yet she thought she wanted the prisoners' confidence rather than awe and respect. If only she could relax and joke with them, and be popular like Miss Whittaker.

She glanced again at her watch. It was now a quarter past. Could she muster up enough courage to venture forth down the wing and try to mingle with the women in a natural way for ten minutes or so?

13

Perhaps she should attempt to have a brief quiet talk with one of them and so establish a helping relationship with her.

She delayed setting off for a moment or two as she studied herself in the small mirror above the desk. Whyever shouldn't she be able to make friends with these people and be liked and respected by them, she wondered fleetingly, as her twenty-two-year-old, neat-featured face looked back at her. After all, she was reasonably pretty, if not exactly spectacular—much prettier, as well as slimmer, than she had been in her schooldays. There was nothing alarming about her face or appearance generally; neither, however, was there anything immediately engaging about it. The lively fieriness of her hair, and the carefree sprinkling of freckles all over her skin, were contradicted by the precision of her compressed mouth, with its long upper lip, and the strained, rather staring look in her eyes beneath the pale, almost invisible brows.

She straightened her already straight tie, and fingered her hair pointlessly for a moment before the mirror. Suddenly she felt she was being watched. She turned abruptly and was embarrassed to see she was being observed closely from a little down the wing by that disconcertingly boyish girl who had just arrived. Once again, she glanced at her watch. Then she left the glass office, closing the door carefully behind her.

She went resolutely down the wing, striding rather than walking, to where the circle of women were seated chattering. Dora, she noticed, was sitting in silence a little apart from the others. It would be easier to start talking to her than to break into any of the conversations going on. So she crossed over to her (walking diffidently instead of striding, now she was approaching her destination), and perched awkwardly on the arm of the dingy, knottily-intestined armchair in which Dora was sitting. She tried to appear nonchalant and at ease, but managed to look —as Jan sitting not far off noticed—exceedingly stiff and awkward.

Dora was lounging in the chair smoking, with a glazed, faraway look in her eyes.

'A penny for them, Dora,' Miss Hewson said, squeezing her compressed mouth into a jolly smile.

Dora regarded her bleakly. Just then she was absorbed in thinking about her husband and the woman next door. She had scarcely noticed

14

Miss Hewson settling on to the arm of her chair, and hardly heard her question. She unglazed her eyes, focused them on Miss Hewson, and said:

'Do you know if we've got the pictures this Friday?'

'Yes, and I think it's a very good one this time—"Oliver Twist",' Miss Hewson replied, out to sound as cheerful and encouraging as possible. She was puzzled and disappointed by Dora's prosaic response to her question. She had hoped to draw her out—get her to say something personal.

'Never 'eard of it,' remarked Bett, the young brunette by the record player. Another voice commented scornfully:

'That's a children's film. What they want to go and show us children's pictures for, Miss Hewson?' Without waiting for Miss Hewson to reply, the woman turned to Beryl Hunt and continued indignantly, 'That's what's the trouble with this place—all this talk about reform and making good and adjusting and all that shit, then they go and treat you just like you was a bunch of fucking kids all the time.'

Miss Hewson did not know what to say. She did not want either to agree or disagree. So she looked at her watch and was relieved to see it was now just on half-past one. It was time to stop talking and get the women off to work.

'Now then, girls,' she said, briskly, she hoped, rather than brusquely, 'time for work now.' She raised her voice for the benefit of those still upstairs and called out, 'Work time everybody please.'

Beryl looked up from her knitting with indignant surprise.

'Oh no, Miss Hewson,' she stated emphatically, 'we don't start work till a quarter to. It's only half past now.'

Miss Hewson fingered her leather belt nervously. The thing she dreaded was happening. She raised her hand from her belt and scratched the side of her neck, which always tingled at moments of stress. Then she glanced pointlessly at her watch yet again. Imbuing her voice with all the firmness she could muster (making it sound sharper than she had intended), she repeated:

'It's time you all went to work now.'

Jan decided to be helpful. She laid down her newspaper.

'The position is, Miss Hewson,' she explained, 'that while officially we are all supposed to set off for work at one-thirty, nevertheless no one usually makes a move until a quarter to. We are not really expected to, you see.'

Her superior, painstaking tone put Miss Hewson on her metal. Jan's upper-class accent always irritated her—Collingwood inmates had no right to sound so educated or ladylike. And it was not as though Jan were a spy or political prisoner or anything like that. She was just a common thief like the others. Furthermore, her very courtesy made her more remote and inaccessible than the other prisoners. Jan was not someone she could ever hope to help or advise. So she glared as sternly as she could at her.

'Never mind what you usually do, Carruthers,' she said, 'it's what you *should* do that matters. A rule's a rule, and the rule is that you go to work at half-past one. Anyway, I don't know how any of you women think you know what the time is, seeing you haven't got watches.' Glancing again at her own, she lied, 'It's now nearly twenty to, so kindly hurry up.'

'Well, I'm not moving till a quarter to,' said Beryl, clicking her needles fiercely. 'I'm not budging for a silly bitch like her,' she added in a deliberately loud aside to the West Indian woman next to her. 'Who does she think she is anyway? Only been on the wing a few weeks and thinks she can run the place.'

'Rars cloth woman,' the West Indian muttered ominously.

Beryl was echoed by the others; and after a few moments there was quite a chorus of protest.

Miss Hewson stared at the circle of women. She was desperate now to be obeyed, yet dazed with fright and uncertain of what to do next.

Jan watched her with interest. She was enjoying the scene. It relieved the tedium; and she was always amused by the flounderings and *faux pas* of tactless new officers. Their mistakes gave her a feeling of superiority. In a way, she was proud of her own many years' experience of Collingwood life.

If only she could just make one of them move it would be something, Miss Hewson thought. It might get the others mobilized. She decided to reason with Beryl, despite her previous protest, as she was the wing Red Band, therefore something like a school prefect.

'Come along, Hunt.' she said, sounding jolly again, 'you're the Red

16

Band, so surely you should be setting a good example to the others.'
But Beryl merely replied flatly:

'I'm not going to work a moment before we've got to.' With pursed lips and creased forehead, she concentrated on her knitting. Miss Hewson could see she was immovable as a rock. Suddenly she caught sight of Lorry. There was a possibility, surely—a new girl on the wing.

'You, Harrison,' she said, pointing at Lorry and almost shouting, 'you're working in the garden, so you don't have to wait to be fetched. You can go straight out on your own now.' And she marched down to the wing door, unlocked and opened it with a clash, and stood waiting beside it, apparently expecting to be obeyed. She stood stock still, stiff and erect, like a well-groomed sentry, but her neck, Jan noticed, had flushed bright pink. Miss Hewson stared at Lorry, every muscle of her body, every nerve in her brain, tense with effort to will her to walk down the wing and out through the door.

Lorry took a deep breath on her cigarette stub, then deliberately broke rules by stamping it out on the stone floor instead of in an ash tray. Sticking her hands in her pockets, she surveyed the ring of faces, now all turned expectantly towards her. She had the chance of making a striking initial impression: of filling them all with admiration, and launching herself as the most popular, desired person on the wing. And she had a choice of responses: either to give Miss Hewson a cheeky answer or totally to ignore her. She decided to do the latter. Turning to Bett, the promising brunette, she drawled in her most affected, boyish voice:

'Baby, that sure is a crazy hair cut you've got—real kinky. I really dig that.' Bett giggled coyly, and someone remarked with a chuckle:

'Kinky's the word. You've said it mate!' Rob glared at Lorry, all set to do battle for her girl, but Miss Hewson intervened:

'Harrison,' she repeated, 'you Harrison'—and her voice roughened hysterically—'come along immediately. And you're not to stub out your cigarette on the floor—I could put you on report for that.'

Lorry turned slowly towards Miss Hewson and said:

'You just fucking put me on a fucking report then.' And everyone burst out laughing, except Jan, who merely smiled dryly.

Miss Hewson's neck flamed. She took a few steps towards Lorry, looking as though she might hit her, or at least try to drag her to the door. Then, abruptly realizing that she had no idea why she was approaching Lorry, nor what she would do when she reached her, she stopped short and stood still, flummoxed with rage.

'Anyroad,' Lorry resumed scornfully, 'it's me can put you on report—get you a fucking white sheet. Telling me to go off to work on my own. It's not allowed. I'm not a fucking Red Band. Fucking cheek. I'll tell the Chief.'

At this, Miss Hewson felt more muddled than ever—did she really know the rules herself? But increased confusion only added to her rage. She went right up to Lorry, took hold of her forearm, her fingers digging painfully into the flesh, and started trying to pull her towards the door.

' You fucking prat! You fucking let go my fucking arm! I'll get you for this,' Lorry shouted at Miss Hewson, striving to stand her ground and free her arm. But Miss Hewson was stronger than she looked, and Lorry could not easily liberate herself. Her face became contorted with rage as she struggled. Miss Hewson managed to drag her a few feet. Half of Lorry's mind boiled with such fury that she aimed a blow at Miss Hewson's face with her free arm. The other half of her mind was suddenly filled with misery. The gradually-accumulated tension and wretchedness of the past day or two reached bursting point. All at once tears were running down her face, and she was sobbing and gasping as she struggled.

Miss Hewson ducked to avoid Lorry's blow. Involuntarily she recoiled and let go of her. Lorry lurched back a step or two. Then, still choking with sobs, she glared at Miss Hewson in fury and shouted hoarsely:

'I'll kill you for this, you filthy cunt!' She clenched her fists and squared up, obviously intending to hit Miss Hewson straight in the face.

Jan decided to intervene. If Lorry actually struck Miss Hewson, she would probably be despatched to a punishment cell, or to the hospital for observation. Jan wanted to get to know Lorry better. Besides being promisingly boyish, there was something endearing about this outburst of rage, even about the accompanying tears. Jan did not like children. Her one daughter, now aged fifteen (unwanted product of a brief, unwise marriage), was brought up by Jan's own mother. Traces of childishness in adults, however—especially women—moved her. Laying aside her paper, she got up from her chair and said:

'Look, stop it. You'll be sorry later.' She approached Lorry from behind, caught hold of her round the waist, and tried to twist her away from Miss Hewson.

Lorry was taken by surprise. Deflected from hitting Miss Hewson, she immediately struck out at Jan. She managed at close range to give her quite a hard punch on the chin. Jan at once slapped her. Soon both women were fighting each other viciously. Lorry was by now so frustrated and furious that she was glad to be hitting out at anyone. Jan was so enraged that Lorry had turned on her when she was only trying to help her that she slapped and clawed at her frenziedly.

Miss Hewson, once she had recovered her equilibrium, realized she must stop this instantly. But she did not want to re-enter the fray herself and get all scratched and battered trying to separate the women.

'Go it, kid!' Bett shouted, presumably to Lorry. 'Let 'er 'ave it. That's the way.'

Excitement was mounting. Unless the fight were soon stopped, it might turn into a general brawl. Miss Hewson glanced helplessly at the other prisoners. They were all watching the fight intently, some almost avidly.

'Come on, Hunt,' she shouted in desperation at Beryl, 'you're a Red Band. Help me get these two separated.' Then, without waiting for Beryl's response, she went over to the struggling couple and began to make ineffectual attempts to part them.

She was doing this—making futile, stabbing, clutching motions with her arms at one woman then at the other, breathless and gasping with panic-stricken determination—when the door opened and Mac, the P.O., entered the wing.

Mac's years of Collingwood experience told her at once what was happening. Without a moment's hesitation, she boomed out in a loud, authoritative voice:

'Carruthers, Harrison, stop this at once!'

They were both taken by surprise. As they paused, Mac descended on them. She forced herself between them, and managed to restrain Lorry without much difficulty.

Miss Hewson stepped back and watched, exceedingly humiliated.

'I'm surprised at you, Carruthers,' Mac said, looking sternly at Jan, '—and at you too,' she added, swivelling round to face Lorry, 'carrying on like this the moment you get on the wing. Silly little fool.' She scrutinized Lorry for a moment, more with interest than indignation. Then, with a sudden faint smile, she turned back to Jan.

'Oh I see,' she said, now sounding a trifle quizzical, 'so it's like that is it. Well, that's a funny way to go about it, Jan. I was wondering when you were going to start getting going again. You didn't let so much grass grow under your feet last time, did you?'

This cryptic remark puzzled Miss Hewson. Also she was baffled by the kindly sarcasm of Mac's tone. Surely she should be storming at the women. To her indignant astonishment, Mac then turned abruptly to her and said briskly:

'Now, Miss Hewson, let's get all this lot off to work before we get a broken nose on the wing on top of everything else. And you're very late—they should have started work ten minutes ago.' In three minutes Mac had them all rounded up and despatched to their respective jobs.

5

MAVIS WENT ABOUT IN A DAZE DURING HER FIRST FEW days in Collingwood, hardly aware of her surroundings or fellow prisoners, obeying orders and doing what was required of her as though she were clockwork. It had been like this to begin with at approved school; and further back too when she first arrived at the children's home. It was as though the abrupt sundering from home and family had killed her and set her wandering in Limbo.

The nightmare and acute terror of her first night did not recur, but she suffered from mild claustrophobia all day. She was oblivious of her surroundings because her mind was completely dominated by worried thoughts about her children—particularly Doreen, her four-year-old. She was for ever engaged in an exhausting effort both to envisage her children as they were at the moment, and somehow to communicate with them. Her mind was perpetually and painfully stretching out to reach Doreen; but always in vain, because here she was, enclosed within massive stone walls, through which her thought waves could not penetrate.

Mavis believed in thought waves and telepathy. Her favourite aunt had been a spiritualist, and used to impress her, as a child, with accounts of mediums getting in touch with people 'on the other side', reading minds, curing diseases by the laying on of hands and the like. But, strive though she might, Mavis felt incapable of reaching Doreen. Mavis looked pale, strained and morose. As she responded only in monosyllables to any attempts at conversation with her, the other women soon gave up and ignored her. During her spare time, she would retire to her cell and lie face down on her bed, not weeping or sulking, as the others who saw her thought, but once again stretching the muscles of her mind taut in a vain endeavour to reach her children.

If only she could at least get out of doors a bit more. She was not keen on fresh air and exercise; but if she were not cooped up in a building practically all day, it might be easier to achieve contact with the children. Even though high brick walls surrounded the Collingwood garden and yards, if she were outdoors, her thoughts might be able to vault over the walls and escape to Doreen and the boys—perhaps be met half way by their thoughts. This could never happen so long as she was securely locked away in the wing or Work Room.

The daily half-hour exercise period was too brief to be any use. Her mind needed longer than this to make the arduous journey to Doreen. She was always tired out by the end of exercise, even panting slightly, exhausted by her mental efforts rather than by any expenditure of physical energy.

Miss Whittaker, standing guard over the exercise ground, noticed Mavis and was puzzled. At lunch one day, she remarked to Miss Thomas:

'You know that McCann—thin pale little bit of a thing in for G.B.H., first offender—well it's funny how she is on exercise. Just moons around on her own at a snail's pace, even slower than the others, but she'll come in at the end all puffing and blowing like she's just won the half mile.'

'She's a bit of a nut case,' Miss Thomas responded, 'raised hell her first night. Right round the twist she was, screaming and bashing her cell door. We thought at first she was having a smash-up. She should have gone to the hospital really, but Miss Philips was on, and you know what she is about the Hospital.'

'That sort should get as good as they give in my opinion,' commented an elderly officer. 'A good old taste of the birch wouldn't do them any harm.' Miss Whittaker and Miss Thomas both disagreed, but did not like to argue with a senior officer. They changed the subject.

As Mavis was thin and pale (but actually quite wiry), she had been assigned to the Work Room rather than to one of the heavier jobs. On the whole she was glad of this—although she would rather have been in the garden. The Work Room jobs were monotonous and un-demanding, requiring the minimum concentration and effort. This meant that Mavis was able, while at work, to continue focusing her thoughts on Doreen.

Most of the women in the Work Room were busy assembling plastic dolls' furniture for an outside firm; or else making red and blue knicker-bockers for miniature teddy bears. But Mavis, being a newcomer, was put on to the duller job of sewing mail-bags, along with one or two other women whose knickerbocker output was considered too low even by leisurely Collingwood standards. She was glad not to be making toys—that would have been unbearable. Fortunately she liked sewing; so now she sat on a bench at the long back table, stitching up the sides of the coarse green mail-bags with as much automatic care and precision as if they had been the cotton frocks she used to make for the approved school annual sale of work.

Sometimes the radio blared out the latest pop hits; sometimes it did not. It made no difference to Mavis: she neither listened to the music nor to the conversations going on around her.

There were only two other women on Mavis's work bench. They were from a different wing, and appeared to be friends. Mavis made a point of not sitting too near them so that their incessant chatter should not disturb her and interrupt her thought waves.

Across the aisle dividing the Work Room slumped a huge, ungainly woman, who seemed as unsociable and engrossed in her own thoughts as Mavis. She sewed the seams of her mail-bags with immense, straggly stitches (which she was usually made to unpick), muttering to herself as she worked. Every now and then, her muttering became murmuring. Most of the time, she was conducting an imaginary dialogue with her absent daughter. Now and again, she would pull the skirt of her dress right up, exposing the great pallid wedge of blue-veined thigh flesh protruding between the grip of her too-tight stocking top and her knicker elastic. She would then start pulling and fiddling with the stray pubic hairs that encroached down the inner sides of her thighs, until, after a few moments, she was either reprimanded by the officer in charge, or got tired of the distraction herself and resumed her clumsy sewing.

But for several days, Mavis noticed none of this. She remained insulated in her private world of striving to meet Doreen.

Then one day a third prisoner seated herself on the back bench. This meant Mavis found herself sitting closer than usual to the other pair of women. She was still too wrapped up in her own thoughts to overhear their persistent conversation. All at once, however, she was jerked back into her immediate surroundings.

For no apparent reason, the slumped woman across the aisle, who had been muttering more loudly than usual that day, suddenly rose from her seat and shouted loudly:

'Oh fuck it all!' Then she subsided muttering again, pulled up her skirt and started fiddling with her pubic hairs. Everyone in the room stared at her, then turned and sniggered at each other.

Miss Whittaker, on duty in the Work Room that day, was too accustomed to irrational outbursts to be perturbed.

'Now then, Polly,' she called down the room, sounding amused rather than ruffled. Then she came over to Polly, saw what she was doing, promptly pushed her offending hand off her thigh and pulled down her skirt, saying, 'Really, Polly, there's a time and place for everything you know.' Everyone laughed. Then she looked at Mavis, who was sufficiently disturbed by Polly's outburst to have turned to see what she was doing.

Mavis's expression was glazed and remote, almost unfocused. Miss Whittaker recalled her dreary meandering round the exercise ground.

'Well, how are you getting on, McCann?' she said bracingly. 'We don't get much of a squeak out of you, do we? Let's see how your work's getting on.'

But Mavis's sewing was impeccable. Miss Whittaker could think of nothing further to say except:

'That's excellent. No one's going to lose any love letters out of that bag.' She paused, then added in a jolly tone, 'You should give old Polly Do-Little here some sewing lessons.' Mavis gave her a faint, vague smile, but still said nothing. Miss Whittaker was not sure she had even heard her; so, after saying: 'Keep on with the good work then and you'll get a rise,' she gave up and returned to her table at the far end of the room.

However, Polly and Miss Whittaker between them had disturbed Mavis and halted her thought waves. Unwillingly, almost unwittingly, she began to overhear Polly's muttered monologue.

'Come 'ere me darling. No, over 'ere, Agnes. No, your Dad's not going to 'urt you. If 'e so much as lays an 'and on you I'll do 'im . . . No, Agnes, you ain't a going to. No girl o' mine's ever gon a do a thing like that . . . Now see what you've gone an' done, you wicked girl—gone an' let the kettle boil over . . . Oh fuck 'im. Oh fuck 'em all . . .'

The rambling and muttering struck a chord in Mavis's mind. Here was someone else whose thoughts were focused on her daughter. Indeed, they were so rivetted that evidently she imagined her daughter was present. Mavis was filled with admiration. If only she could get so close to Doreen that she actually believed they were physically together again.

And there was something familiar—disagreeably familiar—about part of what Polly was saying: the part about her Dad's not laying a hand on her daughter. But why should it be familiar? Tom, her own Doreen's father, was not in the habit of beating or ill-treating the children. He was not interested enough in them to bother. There was something about Polly's monologue that reminded her unpleasantly of her own childhood. She was baffled, but she felt that Polly and she must have something basic in common. It might be worth while getting to know her better.

So, leaning across the aisle towards Polly, she did something she had never done since entering Collingwood: she tried to open a conversation. In a hushed, breathless voice, she said to Polly:

'Your Agnes, is she fair or dark? My Doreen's dark. She's four.'

Polly stopped muttering and looked at Mavis in surprise that rapidly turned to blankness.

'Don't know any Agnes,' she answered hoarsely; then turned slightly on her bench so that now she had her back to Mavis. She resumed her muttering, only this time Mavis could not distinguish what she was saying.

Mavis returned to her sewing crestfallen. She tried to concentrate on Doreen and launch her thought waves towards her again, but could not do so. Then she began, for the first time, to listen to the chattering pair next to her.

'You see, Vi,' one of them was saying in a confidential yet audible tone, 'my Jack's been inside too. Never told no one before, because, you know how these women are—set of bleeding old chatterboxes. Always slagging each other. You can't keep nothing private like. Well, Jack's was a frame-up, see—just like mine. Down Cable Street in this place we always go Saturday nights. And there was a bloke got stabbed, all carved up. Streaming down with blood he was, and my Jack, he sees who done it, but he isn't going to let on like is he? Real sucker, my Jack. It's a woman, see. So when the cops come there's no one left there but my Jack and a couple of other blokes who swear he done it, even though they'd seen plain as daylight 'twas this other woman. Well, so that's what's got him three years—G.B.H. An' all for nothing. He won't even speak about it now. Why, back last summer at Butlins—'

'Yes, they're all alike,' the other woman butted in. 'Get you every time. Now just take this what happened to me . . .'

Mavis's attention soon veered away from the conversation. The moment the first woman mentioned the stabbing in the pub and how her husband had got charged with G.B.H., Mavis was back in the 'Duke of Edinburgh', Wordsworth Street ten days ago, re-living the whole scene.

Tom had been out late as usual, ostensibly working overtime—although almost certainly he was pub-crawling with his mates, very likely getting off with all sorts of women at the same time.

25

Usually Mavis stayed at home in the evenings, keeping an eye on the children, half watching television, and doing nothing in particular. But that night her sister Amy and her husband had come over and persuaded her, for once, to leave the children on their own.

'After all, they're in bed and asleep, aren't they? They'll come to no harm,' Amy had assured her. 'It's time you got out a bit, Mave, with that good-for-nothing husband of yours leaving you all by yourself night after night.' Mavis had been feeling more than usually bored and depressed that evening on account of Tom's absence. She had allowed herself to be persuaded.

Even so, all evening in the pub, her agreeable sense of freedom and defiance had been marred by anxiety over the children. Doreen sometimes woke up at about half-past nine or ten and called out to her, or came downstairs. She didn't very often, still, she did occasionally. So from about nine o'clock onwards, Mavis had found herself growing steadily more uneasy, trying to stave off uncomfortable speculations about what Doreen might do if she did wake up that night, come downstairs and find her out. She grew edgy. Amy had said:

'Oh do stop going on and on licking your mouth like that, Mave. You'll make your lips all sore, and it looks queer.' Mavis had retorted tartly:

'Queer yourself. Look who's talking—you with all your lipstick right up to your nose to try and make your lips look fatter!'

'Well, if that's how you feel . . .' Amy had replied crossly, and had turned away to talk to her husband.

By now, Mavis was deaf to the chatter going on around her in the Work Room. She stretched her legs tensely before her under the table as she recalled what had happened next that night. She saw again the short, gingery, quite ordinary-looking man who, at about a quarter to ten, had wandered over to her as she stood in the crowded pub a little apart from Amy and her husband. After staring at her for a moment or two, he had asked the stock question:

'Haven't I seen you somewhere before?'

His appearance—the ginger hair, his shortness and weediness, the continuous single line of his eyebrows and the moulding of his mouth and chin—had been sharply and disagreeably familiar. He must have reminded Mavis of some hateful person from her past—her father possibly, or one of her uncles, or even perhaps some social worker or magistrate who had caused her so much misery by getting her dragged away from home. There were a lot of hateful people he might have reminded her of.

Mavis licked her lips hard and bent her knees with a crack beneath the Work Room table as she experienced again the incomprehensible anger roused in her by the man—anger quite out of proportion to his silly question. This anger, mixed with her guilt and anxiety over the children and despondency about Tom, had made her respond in a surprisingly loud voice:

'You clear off, you. Who are you anyway. Don't you come messing round me, you dirty git, you!'

She had spoken so loudly that most of the others in the bar had turned to see what was going on. The stranger was amazed at first by Mavis's fury. Then, assuming she was drunk, he became amused. He had patted her on the shoulder and said in a maddeningly soothing tone:

'Now now, duck. Just you take it easy now.'

For a few seconds, Mavis's mind again blazed with the uncontrollable rage ignited by the man's touch. Staring before her with a fixed expression, muttering slightly now, like Polly across the aisle, she heard herself screaming at the man:

'You filthy dirty pig! You bastard! Take your filthy paws off me— sod off!' And she felt herself again vibrating with the sudden uprush of fury, as violent as it was puzzling, then stoop down, wrench off the pointed jade-green court shoe, and, before anyone had taken in what she was doing, bash the stranger in the face again and again with the stiletto heel. After a second or two, as the blood had begun to ooze, then trickle and stream down his face, her own fury had drained out of her.

She could hardly remember what had happened next. By the time they had come to take her away, she had been stunned, blank and bewildered. And now here she was in Collingwood with a three-year-sentence for Grievous Bodily Harm (the man had nearly died). She never had discovered whether Doreen had woken up that night and found herself abandoned. She had not seen her since.

Mavis was re-living this scene so intensely (although she never stopped her precise, clockwork stitching) that she did not hear her name called out by Miss Whittaker, together with about eight others. Miss Whittaker repeated her name questioningly; but it was not until one of the two chattering women beside Mavis had nudged her and said:

'That's you isn't it, love?' that she took in the fact that she was required to leave her work and go off somewhere with a Red Band.

For a moment she was filled with dread. Was she being sent for to be given some bad news about Doreen or one of the boys? Perhaps Doreen had discovered she was out that night and had done something terrible; or possibly all the children had suffocated in bed? She was relieved when she discovered she was going somewhere with a group of prisoners.

The Red Band explained, as she conducted them across the garden, that they were off to the Clinic for a medical examination. This sounded innocuous; but as they were all waiting outside the Clinic in a small barred lobby, a little like a cage, Mavis was filled with alarm by the remarks of some of the others who had been through all this before.

'Real butchers, they are,' a fat blonde woman said with relish, proud to be an old-stager. 'Pull you apart. Fair tug at you, like you was just an old piece of elastic.'

'Well, that's all they do think of you in here,' another woman responded gloomily. 'Might just as well be an old sock for all they care.'

'Like butchers, did you say?' a young girl who looked about seventeen added. 'Butch you mean. They *like* doing it—specially that Dr Green. She's bent. Last time she just stared and stared at me like she'd like to . . .'

Mavis gathered that it was to be no mere chest-tapping examination. She sat silent, licking her lips repeatedly. In the end she was asked to go in. The doctor was quite matter-of-fact and did not display an unhealthy interest in her person. Nor was she rough with her. As for the actual intrusion into her body—she was surprisingly indifferent to it, just as she had become indifferent to Tom's intermittent entries.

After the VD test, the Red Band led them over to the main prison and up one of the narrow, spiral staircases to the top gallery of F Wing. They went along the slate-flagged corridor to a small room, which was in fact two former cells knocked into one. There were three rows of desks in the room, a blackboard, and a table at one end, behind which

28

sat a youngish woman, dressed, not in the military-style navy-blue officers' uniform, but in a pink twin-set and fawn skirt, garnished with a pearl necklace. She beamed at them as they entered.

Mavis wondered vaguely who she was. In addition to the prison officers, there always seemed to be droves of women in mufti roaming round Collingwood.

'Hello—what a lot of you there are today! I only had four last time,' the woman said, still beaming at them. The way she greeted them they might have been a Sunday school outing. 'Beryl, get a few more desks in from next door, can you please?' she said to the Red Band. Then, as they were all settling down, she went on, in an almost confidential tone, as though for some reason she were telling them an important secret:

'My name is Miss Canister.'

Once they were all seated, Miss Canister, in a slow, carefully explaining tone, continued:

'Now, I have asked for you all to leave your work this afternoon and come over here to me for a little while as I would like you to do one or two little experiments—they are rather like games really. I expect from time to time you have all done things like this at parties.' She smiled at them sweetly.

Mavis's vagueness was dispelled. She even forgot for the moment about Doreen, and became aware of what was going on around her. For there was something disquietingly familiar about Miss Canister. She did not immediately recognize what it was, yet it roused her in some way. She stared at Miss Canister apprehensively, not for one moment believing that they had been removed from work merely to play party games.

'Now,' Miss Canister said a trifle more briskly, 'I want to show you what I would like you to do. First I shall give you each a little booklet' —and she distributed a pile of slim, limp-covered books, which, at first glance, appeared to be reading primers for six-year-olds.

'If you turn to page one,' Miss Canister announced, 'you will see three pictures, each of them numbered. What I should like you to try to do is to see which two pictures match, and then, using the sheet of paper and pencil on your desk—which I should like you each to put your name and number on first please—write down the two numbers of the matching pictures, leaving out the number of the picture that doesn't

29

match. For instance'—and now she picked up a piece of chalk, crossed
to the blackboard, and, speaking very slowly indeed, enunciating with
great precision as she illustrated her point on the blackboard, continued,
'here are three little pictures, just to show you what I mean.' And she
did simple sketches on the board of a cat, a dog and a house. 'These,'
she said, 'are not actually in the booklet, but they are like the ones that
are in it, and will show you what I mean. These, you see, are a house,
a dog, and a cat.'

Someone sitting behind Mavis tittered and murmured:

'Shouldn't like to 'ave to live in that 'ouse. Fucking falling over, it is.'
And someone else said:

'That ain't no fucking cat. It's a fucking rat.'

'Pussy, pussy, pussy—who's for a bit of pussy? It's just what I could
do with right now,' contributed a heavy, masculine-looking woman.
'Why not draw a plate with your pussy, Miss, 'stead of a house?'
But Miss Canister, unruffled by the giggles, continued in the same
tone:

'So you would write down one and two, the numbers of the cat and
dog, wouldn't you? which are alike because they are both animals,
aren't they? and leave out three, the house, because it is a thing and not
an animal.'

She turned round from the blackboard to face the women again; and
the same voice that had criticized the drawing of the house asked:

'Please, Miss, is this the Eleven Plus what we're doing?' Still
undeterred by the giggles, Miss Canister smiled with great kindness at
the questioner and replied:

'Well of course it isn't exactly, because you are all older than eleven,
aren't you? However, you are right, it is a little similar. We would like
you to attempt these tests in order to know what work you will be
happiest doing while you're here.'

'But we're working already, aren't we?' a woman said crossly. Others
joined in:

'Happy, by Jesus!—is that what they've gone and got us locked away
in here for?'

'Bleeding cheek, I call it, making us do the Eleven Plus.'

Still unperturbed, but now adopting a brisker, more businesslike
tone as she glanced at her wrist watch, Miss Canister said:

30

'Well now, I want you to see how much of this booklet you can get through in twenty minutes, then we'll move on to the next part.' Her tone quelled the sniggers, and everyone set to work on the test, except an elderly woman next to Mavis, who leaned across to her and whispered:

'Don't you do it dearie. I wouldn't. She's a head shrinker—that's what she is. What they want is to get to read your mind so's they can control you.' She sat idle at her desk until Miss Canister caught her eye and said:

'Now don't worry if you can't quite do them all, and don't try to hurry. But I should like everyone to have a try.' At that, the woman began doodling idly on her sheet of paper. Glancing across at her, Mavis could see she was not doing the tests at all, but instead a crude sketch of a couple having intercourse.

The moment her next door neighbour whispered to her, Mavis understood why Miss Canister was faintly familiar. She had encountered various people like her before during the unpleasant episodes of her life: welfare workers, the lady at the Child Guidance . . . This made her worried about the test. If she did badly, who knew what unpleasant consequences might follow

She had not recovered from re-living the scene in the 'Duke of Edinburgh'. She was still shaken by the sharp, painfully realistic recollection of her violence there, and what had led up to it. This, together with her disquiet about the test itself, kept her thoughts anchored in the present. For once they did not veer off on a vain quest for contact with Doreen. At the same time, her nervousness lest she do badly in the test made her moidered and unable to concentrate properly.

Most of the test seemed fairly simple, yet she made slow progress. Confronted with pictures of a strawberry, an apple and a pear, she took a long while before deciding to match up the apple and the strawberry, as they were both red, and pears usually green or yellow. She was less than half way through the book when Miss Canister announced:

'I should like you to hand back those booklets now, please, so that we can move on to the next part. Never mind if you haven't quite finished them all. This is not an examination, and accuracy is just as important as speed.'

Mavis was puzzled. If this was not an exam, what was it? When she found that the next part of the test was to match up different patterns—squares, circles, interlocking curves, speckled oblongs and so on—she knew that, whatever Miss Canister said, they *must* be doing an exam. She distinctly remembered having done something similar in the Eleven Plus. So, evidently, did someone else, for one of the previously-complaining voices said querulously:

'This *is* the bloody Eleven Plus. Why do they give us this to do? We may be a load of bleeding cons, but, Christ, we aren't kids!'

'You will find,' Miss Canister responded evenly, 'that although the first part of this test may be simple, and, as you say, could be done by eleven-year-olds, nevertheless it gets harder as it goes on. Indeed'—and for the first time a slight note of asperity entered her voice—'I shall be quite surprised if any of you are able to complete this test in the half hour allotted for it.'

She was quite correct as far as Mavis was concerned. Matching pairs of recognizable objects, such as bicycles, prams and watering-cans, was much less difficult, she found, than discovering points of similarity among the geometrical figures now confronting her.

She had felt nervous and flustered enough doing the earlier part of the test. Now her anxiety mounted to panic as she thought of the minutes ticking away while she peered with blind confusion at the complex diagrams before her. She licked her dry lips again and again. Miss Canister no longer seemed just disagreeably reminiscent of some welfare officer from her past. In Mavis's mind, the ingratiating smile slowly turned into a leer. Latching on to what the woman sitting beside her had said, Mavis thought of Miss Canister as a real head-shrinker: someone with the power gradually to compress her skull and crush her out of existence.

The claustrophobic terror of her first night in Collingwood started to recur. She had done only four or five of the initial very simple tests when a film seemed to develop over her eyeballs. They felt as dry as her lips. Her vision slipped askew, and she seemed to be staring, half blind, through a fluffy cloud at the unfocused maze of circles, lines, squares and lozenges. Intermittently the cloud cleared a little, but then the patterns danced and wavered. The dots became sparks, the lines and curves streaks of light. She was dazzled, and presently closed her eyes. She felt as if Miss Canister's hands were cupped round her head, squeezing. However, the pressure was abruptly removed when Miss Canister's real voice broke the silence:

'I'll have these booklets back now, please, if someone would be good enough to collect them for me; and then we'll move on to the last part.'

Mavis opened her eyes again. The cloud disappeared and everything reverted to normal.

'Now,' said Miss Canister, 'I should like to test your powers of self-expression. I'm going to pass round to each of you a sheet of paper on which you will find a list of unfinished sentences. You will understand what I mean when you see them. All I want you to do is to finish them off in any way you like. There is no right or wrong way of doing this,' she added reassuringly, 'it is just an opportunity for you to write down whatever you want—whatever first comes into your head when you read what is written on the paper.'

This did not sound nearly so difficult as matching up pictures and patterns. It struck Mavis as strange that they could write what they liked, and that there should be no rules or correct answers. But she was so relieved to be given something comparatively easy to do that she did not stop to speculate about the purpose of the exercise.

Nor, apparently, did anyone else. They all bent over their papers and began to write, including the woman beside Mavis, who up till now had done nothing but doodle and make pornographic sketches.

This part of the test seemed so simple that Mavis actually finished it before time was up. As she swiftly completed the unfinished sentences, her mind automatically returned to Doreen and all the thoughts and memories associated with her. She did as Miss Canister had advised, and for the most part wrote down the first thoughts that entered her head as she read the words on the paper. Only once or twice did she stop to wonder whether what she wrote might displease or shock Miss Canister.

'The happiest moment of my life was . . .' she finished off with the words, 'when I saw my little girl again'—thinking as she wrote, not of the past, but ahead to the time when she was released and would see Doreen again.

The next half sentence ran, 'What I remember most about my child-hood is . . .' and Mavis promptly wrote, 'Dying', then crossed it out and substituted, 'Being driven away'. But 'The thing I am most afraid of is . . .' made her pause for a few moments. For some reason, it never occurred to her simply to invent a fictitious fear. Automatically she was falling in with Miss Canister's plan and trying to complete the sentences truthfully.

She thought of the man in the 'Duke of Edinburgh' and how he had unpleasantly, almost alarmingly, reminded her of someone else. At the same time, she half remembered her father. So she wrote, 'Men who—', then could not go on, as she did not quite know what it was about men—or these particular men—that had frightened her. Then she remembered how the blood had run down her mother's face once when her father had thrown something at her. At the same time, she recalled the wounded face of the man she had struck in the 'Duke of Edinburgh'. So she crossed out 'Men who' and wrote just 'blood'. But ending off the sentence with such brevity was surely inadequate, and would indicate that her powers of self-expression were very limited. She crossed out 'Blood' also.

Glancing at the next unfinished sentence, she found it read, 'The thing that sticks out in my mind most about my parents is . . .' This seemed the appropriate place for referring to the blood, so she finished this one off, 'Him throwing something at her and the blood all running out on her face.'

Returning to what most frightened her, she then put 'Spiders', because they did; but again felt this was insufficient as it was only one word. So she crossed this out too; then suddenly found herself, almost unwittingly, writing down, 'Seeing her again.' She did not quite know why she wrote this. The pencil just seemed to write the words of its own accord.

She then completed the rest of the sentences quite briskly, without any second thoughts. To prove her powers of self-expression were good, and counterbalance any bad impression she might have made earlier by writing down only one word, she now did her best to make the sentences as long as possible. For instance, after 'What I most like to do in my spare time . . .' she added, 'Doing housework, going shopping, minding the children, watching television, talking to the neighbours and reading.' She felt quite proud of this achievement—it should prove what good powers of self-expression she had. And for 'Things I don't like doing . . .' she put, 'Washing up, sweeping, mending, going for long walks and' (recalling some dreadful compulsory choral classes at the approved school) 'singing.'

She sat still at her desk for a few minutes after she had finished. Then she peered surreptitiously at what the woman next to her was writing. After 'What I most like to do in my spare time . . .' she had written, 'You know bloody well you stupid cow, same as everyone else, a bloody good fuck.' For some reason Mavis was shocked.

'Well now,' Miss Canister announced a few minutes later, 'I think time is up. If someone would just collect the papers . . . And thank you all for coming along and co-operating.' Mavis was surprised—so she need not have done the test at all if she had not wanted to? As they were conducted back to their wings, she wondered uneasily if she had written the wrong things in the last part: should she have just invented a lot of things and not tried to be accurate?

Mavis soon forgot about the test, and reverted to her constant, frustrating struggle to reach Doreen. Then, a couple of days later, as she was sitting silent at the tea table, oblivious of the chatter going on around her, her thought waves were abruptly interrupted by a familiar voice behind her saying her name. She turned and saw Miss Canister standing smiling at her.

'Oh Mrs McCann,' Miss Canister repeated—and Mavis was surprised and instantly suspicious to hear herself addressed for the first time in Collingwood as 'Mrs'—'I wonder whether you could possibly just spare me a few moments please?—no, no,' she added hurriedly as Mavis, a half-eaten slice of bread and jam still on her plate, automatically rose from her seat. 'Finish your tea first. There's no hurry.'

Mavis subsided onto her chair again. She took another mouthful of bread and jam, embarrassed by the knowledge that Miss Canister was standing close to her, watching and waiting. The masticated lump of unappetizing, thinly-spread bread seemed to turn to plasticine in her mouth, and would not go down her throat however hard she tried to swallow.

She had been sitting chewing for minutes on end, it seemed, before it occurred to her to try to rinse the bread down with a mouthful of tea. She took too big a gulp, and choked. Seeing this, Miss Canister discreetly withdrew a little, turned to a woman she knew at another table, and exchanged a few remarks with her. Now Miss Canister's back was turned, Mavis quickly and surreptitiously spat the slimy, still unswallowed lump of dough into her handkerchief. Forcing a thin smile on to her face, she said to Miss Canister:

'I'm ready now.'

'Ah good,' Miss Canister said enthusiastically, turning back to her. 'We will go upstairs to my office then. I shan't keep you long.'

'Do take a chair,' Miss Canister said, as soon as she had seated herself behind the desk. Mavis sat down obediently, hands folded in her lap, waiting resignedly for the worst to befall. Miss Canister made a great show of rustling through a sheaf of papers in a big file on her desk.

'Well now,' she said as she continued rustling, 'I found your papers in the little test we did the other day most interesting.' She stopped, then repeated a trifle ruminatively, 'Yes, most interesting.' Then abruptly she looked up from the papers and directed a broad encouraging smile at Mavis, who was instantly dazzled, as though sudden torchlight had been shone in her face.

'I wonder,' Miss Canister enquired, her voice now hushed and intimate, at the same time magnetic, 'if there is anything on your mind?'

Already disconcerted by Miss Canister's smile, Mavis was now dazed and bewildered by the unexpected question. In any case, it was too general to have any meaning for her. She could remember no time in her life when she did not have innumerable things on her mind. Presumably this applied to most people. So she did not reply, but merely looked blankly at Miss Canister, who, forcing her voice to an even greater depth of intimacy, and injecting it with a heavy dose of sympathy, tried again:

'There were one or two little things in your papers—especially your last paper—which made me just wonder whether perhaps there were certain matters you might be rather especially anxious about?'

She paused expectantly, the smile now infused with a searching look. Indeed now only Miss Canister's mouth was smiling; her eyes were serious and probing. Mavis was more or less aware of this; and it increased her suspicion of Miss Canister. Instead of drawing her out, as intended, Miss Canister's manner silenced her.

Mavis made no reply. She could think of nothing about which she was not anxious. But there seemed no point in pouring out all her worries to Miss Canister, who was nothing to do with her, and presumably could do nothing to help her. They both sat in silence for a moment or two, Miss Canister still with the searching, smiling look directed at Mavis, who continued to look back expressionlessly. She licked her lips, then lowered her eyes and stared down at her hands fiddling with a button on her dress. She knew she was supposed to say something.

Eventually, the prolonged silence, and the knowledge that Miss Canister was still scrutinizing her, forced Mavis to look up. She opened her mouth in order to attempt some sort of response, then closed it again, as she could think of nothing to say.

'Yes,' said Miss Canister encouragingly. So she opened her mouth again, and found herself mumbling:

'Well, it's a lot of things really. There's so much to worry about . . .' Her voice tailed off. She was barely audible, but Miss Canister was gratified to have received any response at all.

'One or two little things you wrote in the last part of the test,' she pursued, 'were particularly interesting. For instance'—and now, to Mavis's relief, she looked back at the papers on her desk and started to rustle them again—'I noticed that for your chief childhood memory you wrote "dying", then crossed it out and put "being driven away". Very interesting.' She ended on a questioning note, and raised her head again to fix Mavis with the stimulating smile. As Mavis did not reply, she added, 'Perhaps, as a child, you had a serious illness and nearly died, but don't like to think about it any more?'

This time she had her facts wrong. Mavis felt indignant.

'I wasn't never nearly killed in my life when I was little,' she said so defensively that Miss Canister, noting with interest that 'dying' had turned into being killed, was immediately quite sure she had been.

'Ah,' she said expectantly, hoping to draw Mavis out more. But she was disappointed. The intentness of her stare, and the crystallization of her smile dried Mavis up again. Miss Canister resumed, 'So you think about being driven away in connection with your childhood?' and Mavis replied laconically:

'Always getting driven away, we was, to one home or another.'

'Ah,' said Miss Canister again, beginning to think she could see the link between this and dying. Perhaps there was also a link with the streaming blood that featured in Mavis's test responses. 'What about blood?' she asked hopefully '—you mentioned this twice.'

'No I didn't,' Mavis replied with surprising promptness. 'I crossed it out.'

Miss Canister's smile was now both so probing and encouraging that it seemed to be simultaneously a rapier and a rubber sink suction pad. But she got nowhere with Mavis, who did not want to tell her the unpleasant memories conjured up in her mind by the word 'blood'. Nor did Miss Canister achieve anything when she tried to elicit the feelings that had prompted Mavis to write, 'Men who', then cross it out, as the thing she was most afraid of.

Perhaps she should be more general in her approach, she decided. Mavis McCann was obviously a disturbed woman requiring some attention. But it might be wiser to try a general conversation about her affairs than to continue this apparently fruitless atttempt to analyse her responses on the emotional stability test.

Pushing the file to one side, she clasped her hands on the desk, and, leaning slightly forward, as though to diminish the infinite social distance between Mavis and herself, said with great interest:

'Tell me, Mrs McCann, a little about your family. You have four children, haven't you?—three little boys, one still quite a baby, and a little girl. That must be quite a handful to cope with!'

Miss Canister had evidently stopped probing, and was just being friendly; so Mavis's suspicion evaporated and was replaced by gratitude that here was someone in Collingwood who seemed genuinely interested in her children.

'My Doreen,' she replied quite proudly, 'gives me a hand with Ken and John and the baby.'

'Ah, so your little girl, Doreen, helps you,' Miss Canister said, relieved that at last Mavis was talking.

'Yes, proper little housewife, she is. I don't know what I'd do without her,' Mavis continued, adding after a slight pause, 'She takes a bit after me when I was little.'

'Yes, I see,' Miss Canister responded pensively, 'she's like you when you were a little girl.' Was she beginning to see a pattern? She remembered that for 'the happiest moment of her life' Mavis had written 'When I saw my little girl again'; so she tried tentatively:

'You must miss Doreen a great deal. Perhaps seeing her again is what you look forward to most when you get out?' She glanced briefly at the papers on the desk, and noted Mavis's curious response, 'Seeing her again,' to the question 'what frightened her most'. Would Mavis's answer now throw any light on this?

At last she had succeeded in saying the right thing. By demonstrating interest in Mavis's children, and sympathising with her over missing them, she managed to unblock Mavis. At once she received an almost incoherent rush of mixed feeling from her about Doreen: how she missed her; longed to see her again, and tried to reach her in her thoughts; how at the same time she dreaded seeing her because of guilt over having left her alone in the house that night; how, in some mysterious way, she almost felt Doreen *was* her—she herself when she was little; how frantic and frustrated she perpetually felt because she was shut away indoors where her thought waves were prevented from reaching Doreen.

Miss Canister listened attentively, taking it all in more or less, nodding at intervals, and occasionally interjecting a stimulating 'Ah' or 'I see.'

When at last Mavis stopped, Miss Canister looked thoughtfully at her for a few minutes. There was not much, that she could actually *do* for Mavis; still, she now knew a little more about her, and could pass on the information to others, who might or might not take her advice.

'Well,' she said finally, sounding brisk and businesslike, 'I must arrange for you to see Miss Davies, the social worker. You can talk to her about the children, and she will find out for you if they are all right and being properly looked after. Meanwhile,' she concluded, 'I see from a report that you suffer from nightmares and mild claustrophobia; so I will see what I can do about getting you transferred from the Work Room to some outside job where you will feel less shut in. I think perhaps you might be happier, more at ease with yourself, and less cut off from your children, if you were to work outdoors in the garden.'

6

After tea the day of her arrival, she hung about down on the flat, wondering what to do. Presently Bett drifted over to the record player and put on one of the latest pop hits. Then, closing her eyes dreamily, she started slowly to gyrate. Lorry decided she might as well lose no time pursuing someone on the wing, and Bett didn't look bad. She approached her with an ingratiating smile and said:

'Mind if I join you?'

Lorry started to dance opposite Bett, closing her eyes in forced ecstasy.

'Crazy song, I really go for it, don't you?' she was murmuring, when a hand fell heavily on her shoulder, and Rob, whom she had not seen approaching, said peremptorily:

'That's my bird. Hands off or there'll be trouble.' Her tone was so menacing and her expression so ferocious that Lorry decided not to argue and risk getting into two fights all in one day.

'Nackers, what's wrong with just having a dance? I don't like to see a bird without a partner,' she grumbled as she stopped dancing and drew away from Bett. 'Anyroad,' she excused herself, 'I've got business of my own—got to fix up my peter.' And she walked jauntily away, trying to look both blasé and purposeful.

As she passed Jan's cell, she noticed her through the half-open door, stretched out on her bed engrossed in a book. Should she stop and say 'hello'? She decided not to. It was up to Jan to approach her—it was she who had got into a fight with her, not the other way round. And anyway, what had made her join in the after-dinner battle with Miss Hewson? It had been none of her business. Could it have been that, in a funny sort of way, she had been trying to show she was interested in her? Lorry half hoped Jan might drop in on her in her cell—after all, they were next door neighbours. She did not, however. On the contrary, for the next few days she appeared hardly to notice her.

She even seemed to go out of her way to ignore and avoid her. Lorry was vaguely disappointed.

Nor was she any luckier at work. In the Laundry, on her last sentence, she had had no less than three girl friends in succession. The Laundry, run by two tolerant officers said to be that way themselves, had been ideal for love affairs: full of dark corners and large pieces of equipment behind which many prolonged, if somewhat uncomfortable, love scenes took place.

Lorry was pleased when she learned she was to be on gardening this time. It should be even better than the Laundry. She liked the prospect of a strenuous open-air job, and the garden, full of sheds, bushes and outdoor lavatories, should be just the place for conducting a love affair—especially as Miss Foster, the officer in charge, had a welcome habit of retiring indoors for lengthy tea breaks. Furthermore, as a gardener, Lorry could, at least during working hours, dress comfortably as a boy. By a lucky chance, she was, at the moment, the only Collingwood butch on a job which entitled her to wear a shirt and dungarees. This gave her a head start over all the others who had to do the best they could to look masculine in cotton dresses.

Her first morning out, Miss Foster set her to do some hoeing with one of the only two others at present in the garden. Lorry was delighted when she saw her fellow gardeners, two slender, corn-haired nineteen-year-olds—just the sort of girls who attracted her most.

As soon as Miss Foster was out of sight, Lorry propped herself on her hoe, rolled two cigarettes and offered one to her workmate, who accepted it with a grateful smile.

'When d'you go out?' Lorry asked politely—this being the stock Collingwood way of opening a conversation. The girl just smiled and nodded. Lorry, puzzled, repeated her question; but the girl smilingly shook her head and touched her mouth. After a slight pause, seeing Lorry's bewilderment, she managed to stumble out in a foreign accent:

'I no—not—can—I Finn.'

So that was it. Lorry made one or two further abortive efforts to start a conversation, then gave up. Neither this girl nor the other (also a Finn) could speak more than a phrase or two of English. Since, in any case, they were both due to be deported in a week or so, Lorry decided it was not worth while trying to pursue either of them.

During her first week, she was severely reprimanded by Mac twice, which was unfortunate. Lorry quite liked Mac, but knew from previous sentences that she could make life abominable for any prisoner she got her knife into. First, there was the telling off over the fight with Miss Hewson. Then, on Sunday, she got into trouble again.

Sunday dinner was usually the best meal of the week: a slice of fatty pork with the usual trimmings. But this time it was different. Everybody was grumbling, and Lorry decided to use the situation as an occasion for demonstrating bravado.

'Fucking terrible—only fit for pigs and screws,' she announced loudly, then ostentatiously got up from the table and marched out into the wing kitchen, where she tipped her plate of luke-warm, gristly roast beef and leathery Yorkshire pudding into the rubbish bin. She returned to her table, then, in sudden rage, picked up her pudding (sour rhubarb soaked in dust-flecked custard), and stalked over to where Miss Hewson was serving out behind the hot plate.

'Here, eat the fucking swill yourself, and I hope it makes you sick!' she shouted, and crashed the plate of pudding down in front of her. Chips of china flew in all directions, and Miss Hewson was thoroughly spattered with rhubarb and custard. She put Lorry on report to Mac.

'Now look here Lorry,' Mac said crossly to her that evening (unlike most of the other officers, she called the women on her wing by their christian names). 'Are you going to go carrying on like this your whole sentence? making a damned nuisance of yourself—and a fool of yourself too, if I might say so. I'm not soft like your Miss Foster, and I'm not going to put up with it. I'm not going to put up with it, Lorry.' She paused and glared at Lorry, who was too cowed to respond. 'I think you and I understand each other,' Mac continued 'and you know as well as I do that when I say I'm not putting up with it, I mean it. Now I know as well as you do that quite often you get a bloody awful dinner—so do we in the Mess too, I can assure you. If you don't like it, you don't have to eat it, do you?' Again she paused.

'Guess not,' Lorry muttered sulkily.

'No one's going to notice—no officer with any sense that is—' Mac went on, 'if you just don't eat something you don't fancy now and again. We're all human after all, and just because you're a prisoner it doesn't mean you've got to eat every damn thing that's stuck in front of you. But there's no call to go making all this hullabaloo, getting everyone on the wing all het up, and getting poor Miss Hewson's knickers in a twist—after all, she's only a new, young officer. . . .' She tailed off, perhaps regretting this last remark, then reiterated, 'getting everyone on the wing all het up—that's what I won't put up with Lorry. If you object to your food—and I can't say I blame you if you do sometimes—then you know as well as I do that the proper thing to do is to book for the Governor about it, or complain to the Visiting Magistrate—or even kick Hell out of the women who work in the kitchen if you like. But don't,' she ended ominously, 'go kicking up Hell on this wing, or I'll kick Hell out of you, Lorry. Believe me I will.' Lorry believed her.

A few days later, Lorry looked up from scrubbing her small, plain wood table top (it was Cell Clean-Up Night) to see Jan standing in the doorway watching her. Lorry was taken aback and at once embarrassed. How long had Jan been standing studying her? She blushed slightly. Jan saw and was amused.

'Got a light by any chance?' she asked as casually as she could.

'Sure. Got just about four left I think,' Lorry replied. She dug a match box out of her pocket, took out a match, and, having wiped a corner of the soapy table top, laid the match down upon it. Then, with a pin that she detached from the inside of her collar, she proceeded deftly to split the match-stick into quarters.

Jan watched her intently, liking the almost technical precision with which she worked.

'Thanks. That's fine,' she said. 'I'll call in and pay you back tomorrow.' She put the roll-up she was carrying between her lips, and leaned towards Lorry, who struck one of the match quarters and lit it for her. Jan half closed her eyes as, still leaning towards Lorry, she inhaled deeply. Lorry, watching her, felt gratified. This was what she liked: a woman approaching her for a light, and she being able gallantly to oblige. It had been a bad week. She was feeling bored

43

and despondent, ready for any diversion; so she was glad Jan had called on her.

She had been right about Jan deliberately ignoring her. Jan had made up her mind to play it cool: to watch and weigh up Lorry for a few days, and not jeopardize her chances by acting precipitately and risking making the wrong sort of approach again. She realized that her unwise intrusion into the fight between Lorry and Miss Hewson may have alienated Lorry for ever. Now she must act cautiously if she wanted to get anywhere with her.

After drawing on the cigarette, Jan threw her head back rather affectedly and released the tobacco smoke through her nostrils. Then she smiled at Lorry and remarked:

'Just about the only thing in this place that makes life tolerable, isn't it, smoking?'

Lorry grunted and looked at Jan warily. Pleased though she had been to light Jan's cigarette for her, she was not sure now that Jan herself was pleasing. She was too old to appeal to Lorry; and, close to, looked older than at a distance. At a casual glance, she could pass for twenty-nine or thirty but now, standing only a few feet away, she looked all of forty. Some white hairs were visible in the otherwise reddish colour-rinsed hair. A network of fine lines was etched in the dry skin of her somewhat bird-like, finely boned face; and beneath her eyes, blueish trouble grooves were clearly discernible.

Undeterred by Lorry's non-committal response, finding a certain surliness in her manner engaging rather than repelling, Jan pursued:

'Yes, life would be pretty well unbearable but for fags, wouldn't it?—except for the rare occasions one can get hold of some pills.'

Lorry wondered what she was after—first getting embroiled in a fight with her, then ignoring her, now making small talk. She replied cautiously:

'Well, it's what they want isn't it?—to give you a bloody time.'

'Mind if I sit down?' Jan asked. Lorry made a sweeping gesture towards the bed. She herself stood slouched against the table with her hands in her pockets, while Jan settled herself comfortably on the bed.

They were both silent for a few moments. Lorry felt shy and awkward. Making advances herself to younger girls came naturally to her,

44

but it was different with older women. She was apt to feel ill at ease, even though flattered, when they pursued her. It made her confused. Switching from being a young woman herself into being a quasi-boy in quest of girls had been a relatively simple reversal of the natural order; but she felt all at sea when, down at the 'Golden Arrow', older women, sometimes quite masculine themselves, seemed to want her. And there was something particularly embarrassing about Jan. Perhaps it was her well-bred voice and obviously upper-class background that all the years in Collingwood had failed to obliterate.

Lorry rolled and lit a cigarette for herself, trying to appear relaxed.

Jan was not hoodwinked. She could tell at once that Lorry was tongue-tied, and was secretly amused. Lorry was becoming more and more like an enchanting gauche boy every minute. Jan foresaw a fascinating time ahead—provided she played her cards right. She would slowly break down and penetrate Lorry's shyness, then draw her out, finally absorbing her until she was all hers. Once she had fully entered into and taken charge of her mind and feelings, then would come the moment for physical entry and domination.

She smiled encouragingly at Lorry, who decided it was time she volunteered some remark herself. But what could she say? Her usual slangy badinage seemed inappropriate—Jan slightly reminded her of a schoolteacher. At last she said gruffly:

'What job are you on?'

'Painting,' Jan answered easily. 'Not a bad job as they go in here. What about you?'

'Gardening,' Lorry replied laconically. Surely she should say something more, otherwise Jan would think her stupid and dull; but she could think of nothing to add.

Jan regarded her searchingly. There were two things she looked for in her fellow prisoners: straightforward sex appeal (usually, but not always, of the tom-boyish variety), and the ability to make conversation about general matters: to have ideas and interests that ranged beyond mere Collingwood gossip and personal problems. The trouble was, such people were rare. Jan spent her time on the lookout for them, but was usually disappointed.

Bev, a previous lover of Jan's, in for murder, had been an exception.

45

She read a lot and could talk intelligently on almost any topic, from football to ballet. Even more important, Bev had actually been able to listen to Jan and take an interest in what she had to say. She had shared Jan's passion for travelling. When not in prison, Jan contrived to spend much time travelling about the world (on the strength of a family inheritance augmented by the rewards of successful past burglaries). Bev had been fascinated by her descriptions of the different countries she had visited, of the luxury hotels and liners she had been in, also of the remote bush villages she had managed to visit. She had been a wonderful lover too, somehow able in a remarkable and acceptable way to combine dependence and independence in her relations with Jan.

Lorry looked a little like Bev. Was there any chance, Jan wondered as she sat studying her, that she might turn out to resemble her in other ways? Bev too had been gruff and clumsy at first. It had taken Jan weeks of patient effort to draw her out.

'What's it like in the garden?' she enquired.

'Oh, I guess it's all right,' Lorry answered, 'no worse than any other graft.' She could think of nothing to say about her job. There was a slight pause. Lorry knew Jan expected something more of her, so she added, 'Foster seems OK—bit of a nit though.'

Jan gave a barely audible sigh and looked away from Lorry. Perhaps there was nothing to Lorry but sex appeal; or, even if there was, drawing her out was probably going to require immense effort. Was it really worth it, she debated. She was six years older and that much lazier than when she had engaged in the difficult, tortuous process of penetrating Bev's wall of reserve. Should she just settle for a simple physical affair with Lorry? She might just as well get down to business right away and sound her out about the possibilities of bed.

As she sat, drawing lethargically on her roll-up, she glanced round Lorry's cell. Then, for the first time, she noticed the pictures Lorry had chosen to stick on her walls. They were not the usual sort—pin-ups of pop stars or exotic scenes from the Riviera. One was of the interior of a Nigerian bush house, from Sunday's colour supplement. It was anthropologically interesting rather than lush or escapist. Beside it was a simple black and white newspaper photograph of a swing bridge on the London docks.

Anyone choosing two such pictures must surely have a few interests beyond her own petty, personal affairs. Lorry might after all be worth cultivating. Jan decided to make the effort.

'That photo of the African hut you've got stuck up . . .' she tried. 'I noticed that one in last Sunday's paper too. Interesting, isn't it? So's your picture of the swing bridge.'

Lorry did not know why she had chosen the picture of the African hut. She had stuck up the swing bridge photograph because she thought it would add to her virile image: it was a tough, manly sort of picture to have on her cell wall.

'I like docks,' she responded, glad that her ploy had evidently worked. 'Always wanted to go to sea if I could have.'

Jan was encouraged. This sounded promising. She settled herself more comfortably on Lorry's bed, all set to embark on a long conversation about the joys of travelling. At that moment, to her extreme annoyance, the cell door was pushed wide open by Rose.

'Oh, so that's where you've got to!' Rose exclaimed at Jan in surprised indignation. 'I've been looking all over the wing for you. I never thought,' she added, staring suspiciously at Lorry, 'of looking for you here. Mind if I come in? And without waiting for an answer, she entered the cell, pulled the door to again, and seated herself on the bed next to Jan. She sat very close to her, almost proprietorily.

Rose was a comparative newcomer to the wing. By chance, she had sat by Jan at tea the day she arrived. She had attached herself to her ever since.

There was nothing pleasing about Rose. She had lank, shoulder-length hair, and a slight cast in her left eye. Her breath smelt, and her conversation had so far been exclusively about the boring intricacies of her appeal. The crime she claimed not to have committed did not appeal to Jan, who was not worried about hoisting, hustling, forgery, murder, or even (unlike most of the others) child neglect. But Rose's crime was writing libellous, anonymous letters which, in Jan's opinion, was thoroughly cheap, scruffy and undignified.

Jan had done all she could to get rid of Rose: tried to brush her off when she insisted on walking beside her on exercise; replied in monosyllables, and eventually not at all, when she intruded into her cell in the evenings and interrupted her reading—but all in vain. Rose was not to be dislodged. She just droned on and on about her appeal. The sole occasion so far when she had shown the remotest interest in Jan's affairs was when she had taxed her about the fracas with Lorry and Miss Hewson (which she had not witnessed as she was 'resting in cell' that day with a fake cold).

Jan could not tell what Rose wanted. Perhaps she just needed a listening post? On the other hand, there was a horrible possibility that she wanted an affair with her. She was apt to try to sit very close to her whenever she could. Once she had even nearly managed to get hold of her hand. Observing her now as she sat beside her staring suspiciously at Lorry, it suddenly struck Jan that Rose could be very jealous—dangerous too; poison-pen letter-writers always were.

Turning away from Lorry, Rose said all in a rush to Jan:

'Going to the pictures on Saturday, Janny?'—and Jan winced. 'They're doing some smashing film, Miss Hewson said. Forgotten what it's called. I'll bring some toffee, and you can share it. I know you spend all your earnings on fags. Do you know,' she went on, still exclusively addressing Jan, 'what my lawyer's gone and done now, the bugger. I've just got a letter from him and he says—'

'Do you like going to films?' Jan cut in, addressing Lorry and drawing away from Rose.

'Oh, I dunno,' Lorry replied; then won Jan's approval by adding, 'All depends what's on.'

'That's right,' Rose said, hurriedly and breathlessly, thrusting herself back into the conversation. 'Some are awful and some are marvellous. Do you remember, Janny, that awful one we saw the time before last? Real shit it was, all about some arty bloke, or poet or something who lived in one of those arty Hamstead houses. And there was Dora sitting next to me on the other side, burping all the way through—you remember, Jan?'

Jan was spared having to answer. The door was pushed open again. Miss Hewson stood on the threshold looking disapproving.

'You should all be cleaning your cells now. And anyway, you know it's not allowed to close your doors when there's more than one of you in the room,' she said, infusing as much severity as she could into her thin voice. 'And you're not to sit two together on a bed

48

either,' she added, doing her best to glare fiercely at Jan and Rose. 'You know the rules as well as I do.'

'Damn sight better,' murmured Rose with a silly giggle. Lorry expostulated:

'But we've finished cleaning our cells.'

Miss Hewson stood glaring at the three women for a few moments. She was not in a good humour—she seldom was. She was not at all happy in her job, yet could not seriously consider resigning so soon. It would be so feeble, so contrary to all the 'if you don't succeed . . .' precepts she had imbibed at grammar school and the church youth club. Besides, what would her father, a retired policeman, think if she were to hand in her notice? He had been delighted when she joined the prison service. Perhaps those who dedicated their lives to helping others should be prepared to suffer certain hardships themselves.

By now, she was, against her will, beginning heartily to dislike one or two of the women on her wing. At first, the prisoners had just been an amorphous crowd of disturbed people waiting to be cured. Then, by degrees, Miss Hewson became conscious of them as individuals—Hunt, for instance, against whom she bore a grudge for being so unco-operative over the fight with Lorry.

As she stood now in Lorry's doorway, looking at the three women, she realized with shame how much she disliked all of them. There was Jan, so high fallutin'; and Rose—everyone hated Rose. As for Lorry, she had disliked her from the start. She was for ever defying her and being rude to her. Also, she made her feel uneasy and embarrassed. Whenever Lorry looked at her, she felt she was stripping her naked in her mind's eye. And worse, Lorry stripped her mentally and emotionally. Sometimes, she reminded her of an exasperating schoolboy, for ever poking fun at her. At other times, she was a cruelly perceptive adult, skilfully seeking out her weak spots, then needling her unmercifully.

Miss Hewson fiddled with her tie, then glanced at her watch. She was in a quandary. No doubt they really had finished cleaning their cells. And was it a very heinous offence warranting a severe reprimand, even punishment, for two to sit together on a bed with the cell door pulled to? Would Mac think she was making a fuss about nothing if she

49

put the women on report? Her flushed neck started to tingle. She said as menacingly as she could:

'I could put you all on report for this, you know. And the Governor takes a very serious view of this kind of thing.'

She was giving herself time, as both Lorry and Jan could tell. Neither of them wanted to be put on report. Jan was afraid it might lead to prompt separation from Lorry, and Lorry did not want any more trouble at the moment. So they both decided to mollify rather than insult Miss Hewson. She was rather disconcerted when Lorry, instead of being defiant, adopted a little boy's pleading air.

'Oh Miss Hewson, be nice, be a doll, and let it go this time, please,' she said. 'We just pulled the door to without thinking really. We were only just sitting here having a gossip.'

Disliking the false subservience of Lorry's manner, with its objectionable flirtatious overtone, Miss Hewson was just starting to prevaricate:

'Well, but you're not allowed to forget prison rules, and anyway—' when Jan, guessing correctly that she had still not quite made up her mind what to do, interrupted:

'Look, but there are three of us in the cell, aren't there? I mean, those rules about two on a bed and keeping the door open are for when only two women are in there together, aren't they?—I mean, for obvious reasons.'

As she spoke quietly and rationally, Miss Hewson listened to what she said. Jan was probably correct—she had not thought of this. She had better not make an issue of the affair.

'All right,' she conceded 'we'll forget it this time. But you'd better all return to your own rooms now, and see it doesn't happen again.'

Jan and Rose meekly obeyed her. Miss Hewson returned to the office feeling defeated. She disliked Jan and Lorry more than ever.

7

MAVIS'S CHANGE OF JOB DID HER GOOD. SHE WAS A town girl, not keen on outdoor activity, yet here in Collingwood, she was glad to be in the garden. Now that she was alone for much of the day, free to wander about on her own in the open air, her claustrophobia evaporated. From the garden, her thoughts could fly unhampered to her children—although now they were free to do so, perversely they no longer needed to so much. In any case, she was rather less worried and uncertain about her children's fate than she had been at first. Miss Davies, the social worker, had told her they had gone to their grand-parents and were not, as she feared, locked away in some remote children's home.

In summer time the prison garden was quite pleasant, provided you did not raise your eyes too often to the grim, mock castle walls that rose up on every side, studded with row upon row of squat, sinister cell windows. The dreary grey courtyards between the wings were enlivened here and there with strips of grass and flower beds, which, at this time of year, were gay with geraniums and snapdragons. There were one or two reasonably large lawns, round which the women took their daily exercise in a straggly, shambling crocodile.

One of Mavis's jobs so far had been to trim the edges of two or three rose beds set in the lawns. She would stop work every now and then, and, for brief moments of delight, inhale deep breaths of scent. She found she quite enjoyed hoeing flower-beds, and sitting on banks clipping the long grass. The novelty of the job, together with the novelty of working outdoors in the sunshine, appealed to her.

For several days, she hardly noticed her fellow-gardeners, as they were all scattered about on different jobs. Miss Foster was quiet and unobtrusive. She merely explained what she wanted done, then vanished. She hardly seemed to care whether they worked or not. Mavis's workmates were not like prisoners at all. She could not imagine why the two Finns were there. Lorry was just like a jolly boy, and reminded her of her nextdoor neighbour's son. It was impossible to regard her as a woman prisoner, and to begin with, Mavis kept mistaking her for one of the male civilian workers who did maintenance jobs in the prison. Luckily, she seemed quite friendly and good humoured.

One morning Lorry tried to strike up a conversation with her as they were sitting in the garden shed waiting for Miss Foster.

'When d'you go out then, Mavis?' she asked in a kindly tone.

'Three years in August. I've got three years,' Mavis answered, finding she was quite pleased to be asked a personal question by Lorry.

'Oh that's rough—that's real rough,' Lorry said. 'They haven't any right to go shutting anyone away that long for anything, have they?' She smiled encouragingly at Mavis, hoping to draw her out; but Mavis just murmured hesitantly:

'No. No I suppose not. Suppose they shouldn't.' The conversation was cut short as, at that moment, Miss Foster arrived and sent them off to their various jobs.

Her comparative solitude and freedom out in the garden made Mavis more disposed to be sociable back on the wing. She became a trifle less withdrawn, less perpetually insulated in her own thoughts.

One evening, she got acquainted with Olive, the woman in the next cell to hers. Olive was a warm-hearted abortionist to whom everyone on the wing was apt to turn with their troubles. She was a good listener, so her Collingwood cell, like her Deptford flat, was a kind of social centre. Here she plied her callers with roll-ups, scrounged tea when she could, and gave sound advice.

It was about half-an-hour before they were locked up for the night. The cookery class, which Olive attended, was just over.

'Like a bit of pie, duck?' she said, approaching Mavis, who was standing in her doorway gazing vacantly down the wing. She looked at Olive in surprise, then said:

'Oh yes, yes, thank you very much.'

'Come in and visit me in my home then—come to dinner!' Olive went on; and Mavis, encouraged by her friendly joviality, followed her into her cell.

'Not exactly a banquet—still better than nothing. Beggars can't be

52

choosers, as they say,' Olive remarked, offering Mavis a slice of cheese pie. 'That's my Ted there,' she went on with her mouth full. She proudly indicated the photograph of a thirteen-year-old boy stuck in the corner of her mirror. 'You got any, duck?—I've got four. Four too many my bloke always says.'

'I've got four too,' Mavis responded. So Olive and she had something in common. This and Olive's hospitality led her to continue: 'Mine are called Doreen and Ken and John. Then there's the baby, Ron. Ken, he takes after his Dad quite a bit, but my Doreen's the spit an' image of me, they all say.'

For ten minutes or so, she and Olive exchanged notes about their respective children. Then a sudden influx of people into Olive's cell silenced Mavis and she retired to her own cell. Next day, however, she had a further conversation with Olive. After that, they chatted together at some time or another practically every day.

Mavis did not attend the cookery class; she went to Current Events. She never contributed to the discussion, for she was still too shy to speak in front of a whole group of people. One evening, however, towards the end of the class, she took everyone by surprise.

It was a typical class. Polly was sitting with her skirt pulled right up, fiddling with the pubic hairs that straggled down below the knicker elastic. In the Work Room, Mavis had never noticed her doing this. Now she did, and was shocked.

Mrs Crew, the elderly history teacher who came to Collingwood twice a week to take the class, was sitting next to Polly. Presently, she reached across unobtrusively to her and swiftly pulled her skirt down, saying in a quiet aside which only Polly was supposed to hear:

'I shouldn't do that if I were you, Polly. It isn't very nice, is it?' But of course all the others had noticed.

'Disgusting cow, isn't she?' remarked Anny, in for peddling pornographic literature. She glared censoriously at Polly; then, turning to Mrs Crew, said, 'Didn't ought to be on this wing at all, that one. Star Prisoner not in for soliciting, my arse! She should be over on F Wing with the other hustlers. Seen her peddling her wares down the Edgware Road for the past ten years. You dirty slag, you!' and she resumed staring at Polly. 'You don't have to go showing it all to us. We know what it looks like. We've got it too.'

53

Mrs Crew sighed. It was almost impossible to open a discussion about current events with these women.

Polly was saner than she seemed. Much of the time, she might live in a fantasy world, but a portion of her mind was always attuned to her surroundings. Her response to Amy was like an abrupt burst of rifle fire. Words exploding swiftly and harshly from her throat like bullets, she retorted angrily:

'Peddling—peddling what? Me peddling? Who's on about peddling and hustling? It's you're a fucking dirty peddling cunt, with your fucking dirty peddling post cards—'

The class was bound to break up in chaos any minute, Mrs Crew realized, unless she could quickly pacify these women and get them on to current events.

'Now, well then—' she cut in. 'That'll do, both of you. I'm sure Polly won't do it again, Anny. And now let's all—'

Anny subsided, muttering ominously. But then it was her turn to be attacked. At the moment she was the most unpopular woman on Star Wing. Her crime, involvement in a pornographic picture book racket, was considered dirty and beneath contempt by her fellow prisoners, in for clean, straightforward offences like fraud and breaking and entering. She was the wing scapegoat. And she did not now succeed in getting her own back by taking it out of Polly, because someone swiftly cut in on Mrs Crew:

'Old Polly's all right. She just don't know what she's doing half the time. It's that Anny. It's she's the piddling one. Talk about the pot calling the kettle—she's the one what's a dirty-minded effing so and so. You know what she's in here for?—she's in here for—'

'Yes well,' Mrs Crew interrupted firmly, 'you're all in here for something, aren't you?—or you wouldn't be here.' But it was the wrong response. An immediate chorus of, 'No, I'm not,' arose from several women at once, followed by an almost incoherent babble of indignant voices protesting innocence.

Mrs Crew sat back helplessly for a few minutes. She had better let them get it off their chests. Presently, latching on to something one of them was saying, she seized the opportunity of breaking in:

'Yes, Maggy, and what you say about your husband being off in Norfolk reminds me of something I read in the paper only today. I

54

wonder whether any of you saw it? If so, what did you think of it?—that piece about the haunted council house in Norfolk, where the tenants say they can hear footsteps on the stairs when nobody's there, and things move mysteriously about.'

At this, Mavis, who until then had been paying no attention, sat forward in her chair, listening intently.

Mrs Crew would rather have started a discussion on the Cold War or the Colour Problem, but with everyone so edgy and quarrelsome this evening, she was thankful to get them on to any impersonal topic. For a few moments there was quite a brisk debate about the haunted house —or rather a sequence of remarks, for no one listened to what anybody else was saying.

'How could they?' Maggy demanded. 'I mean, with science and all, how can things move around if you don't move them?' She looked disdainfully at Mrs Crew, who replied:

'I agree, it's very remarkable. There are a lot of things science hasn't fully explained yet—Linda please put your cigarette out. You know smoking isn't allowed during classes.'

'Oh please, Mrs Crew,' said Linda, a Young Prisoner, wheedlingly.

'No, Linda,' Mrs Crew replied, 'I have to keep the prison rules just the same as you, and *I* would get into trouble if one of the officers came in and caught you smoking.' Linda glared at her disbelievingly.

'Smoking's bad for the lungs—gives you cancer, don't it?' Anny volunteered.

'No it don't,' another voice countered; and Mrs Crew, afraid another quarrel was brewing, swiftly intervened:

'Yes, well, going back to this house in Norfolk. I wonder what the rest of you think about this? It's not the first haunted house that's received press publicity in recent years.' She was rewarded when a quieter voiced woman responded:

'Yes, there was this other one—a vicarage in Essex or somewhere. I read a library book about it. "Most Haunted House in England" or something it was called. Footsteps on the stairs and all that too.'

Mavis licked her lips. They were reassuringly damp. She opened her mouth, about to join in the conversation, but was prevented by Linda breaking in:

'Can I go to the toilet please?'

Mrs Crew nodded and sighed. This, of course, was just an excuse for going to have a smoke. Probably the discussion she had at last managed to start would again be disrupted. However, it continued after a fashion for a few moments.

'All a bleeding load of rubbish, lot o' cock, is what I say,' Anny announced fiercely. Just then, she needed to condemn everyone and everything. Ignoring her, the quiet-voiced woman resumed:

'My old Grandad used to see things like that—footsteps on the stairs and that. They lived in ever such an old cottage in Hampstead. Hundreds of years old. Lord of the manor let it to them, and they knew him quite well. He would call round and—' Again Mavis prepared to speak, but now an elderly woman butted in, addressing Mrs Crew:

'Did you see "The House that X Built", Mrs Crew? Lovely film that, all about an 'aunted 'ouse where a nun comes at midnight. Only it turns out she isn't no nun after all, and she gets raped like. Stewart Granger, 'e was in it.'

'Never did like Stewart Granger,' another voice volunteered morosely. 'Give me Cliff Richard any time.'

'Elvis for me. He's fab,' remarked another, countered by someone else saying scornfully:

'Oh you and your noisy pop singers!'

'Elvis ain't a pop singer, not a proper one,' a girl who looked about sixteen retorted, while, speaking at the same time, the quiet-voiced woman said:

'Now what I like's a nice opera. Something serious. Gilbert and Sullivan—don't you, Mrs Crew?'

But even this debate did not last long. Linda came banging back into the room. Ignoring Mrs Crew, she announced excitedly to the circle of women:

'Just guess what. *She's* back. Helen's back. I've just seen her, and she says she's had a crazy time—telly, radio on all day, heaps of flowers and chocolates and magazines, and her old man and the baby allowed to come and visit her every day—'

'Lucky devil,' someone broke in. 'I'll book for the M.O. tomorrow and see if they can't get me into St Mark's for me scrape a bit quicker. Back's playing up something terrible these days. I've been feeling that poorly lately, Mrs Crew . . .' And for some moments everyone talked happily about their various illnesses. Meanwhile, Mavis sat pensively with bent head. She had stopped listening.

Mrs Crew leaned back wearily in her chair, and again gave a slight sigh. The women revelled in discussing disease. There was no stopping them once they got started. They had to have at least ten minutes in which to pour it all out. She was relieved when the quiet-voiced woman presently said:

'Cancer's the most terrible disease, isn't it, Mrs Crew? I mean, it can't never be cured, can it?' Here was her opportunity for re-opening a rather more general discussion.

'Well,' she replied laboriously, 'that's only partially true nowadays. For instance, I heard on the wireless only the other day a doctor describing how cancer quite often *can* be cured if it is caught in time. I wonder—did any of you hear the programme? What did you think of it?'

'It's not all a bleeding load of rubbish,' Mavis abruptly announced. Everyone looked at her in surprise. She was a comparative newcomer to the class, Mrs Crew observed. She had barely noticed her before, as she never joined in the discussion. Puzzled, she responded:

'Well no, I agree, it's not all rubbish. As I was saying, this doctor on the wireless was explaining how it can now sometimes be cured.'

'My Dad died of it,' Anny remarked gloomily. 'That proves it can't never be cured. And he wasn't never a smoker nor nothing like that. Real clean living man he was.'

Mavis glared at Anny and stated accusingly:

'You said it was all a load of bleeding rubbish—spirits and communicating with The Other Side and telepathy and that.' Anny looked blankly at her. She had no idea what Mavis was talking about. Mrs Crew had, however. She was grateful to Mavis for getting them off illness and back on to a more interesting, impersonal subject.

'Oh yes,' she said, smiling appreciatively at Mavis, 'you've gone back to what I was telling you about that haunted house in Norwich. Yes, well I myself am rather inclined to believe there's more in Heaven and Earth—'

'And what's more,' Mavis interrupted, 'I've seen it myself. My Auntie used to take me up the Spiritualists, and there was folks there as 'd never seen you before could tell you all about yourself—like if you was

57

married and how many children you'd got. And there was a man once, you'd never believe it, could put you in touch with relatives on The Other Side.'

It was so unusual for Mavis to hold forth that everyone attended, albeit mystified by what she was saying. There was silence for a moment when she stopped, then Mrs Crew, nodding and looking intently at Mavis, responded rather lamely:

'That's very interesting, very interesting indeed.'

'No it's not. It's a load of bleeding shit like I said,' Anny contradicted scornfully. 'Anyone believes in fairy stories like that ought to have their head looked at.'

Anny was attacking something sacred and of fundamental importance to Mavis. For if telepathy were all nonsense, it meant that she could not possibly, after all, be in communication with Doreen and the boys. Anny had wounded her personally. She was enraged and astonished everyone by rejoining loudly:

'Shut your big effing mouth, you old prat. A lot you and the likes of you know about it!'

It was the first time Mavis had so much as raised her voice or disagreed in any way with another prisoner. Anny was momentarily taken aback, but soon recovered her equilibrium and shouted:

'Don't you go calling me names like that, you fucking slag. No one never spoke to me like that before in my life!'

'Call me an effing slag, would you?' Mavis screamed. She got up from her chair, rushed across the room, and slapped Anny in the face. Anny promptly slapped her back harder.

'Girls, girls, this won't do,' expostulated Mrs Crew feebly; but soon both women were battering each other with all their might, spluttering, gasping and intermittently shrieking loudly enough to disturb the P.O. and Wing Governor, closeted together in the office directly beneath.

They swiftly ended their confabulations, and hurried from the room, mounting the spiral staircase with as much speed as decorum permitted. In a matter of moments, the P.O. managed to separate the two women —but only just in time: the rest of the class was preparing to take sides and join in, while Mrs Crew fluttered helplessly round the struggling pair, beseeching them in vain to calm down.

'You know, McCann,' the Wing Governor said to Mavis in her office next day, 'we usually try and get as many of our Stars as we can out of Collingwood and away to open prison as soon as possible. I had hoped to be able to get you off to Cranham Court next week or the week after. In fact, Miss Canister strongly recommended that you should go as soon as possible. But now, after what happened in class last night, I don't very well see how we can send you there yet awhile. It's a privilege, you see, to go to an open prison.' She sounded sorrowful rather than severe.

'Yes, I see,' Mavis replied meekly. Not long ago, she would have been deeply upset to learn she had forfeited the privilege of going to an open prison. She had envied the women despatched there week by week from Star Wing, even though not all of them were keen to go. Cranham Court sounded so free and open compared with Collingwood. You could come and go in the grounds more or less as you pleased; and the building was a converted country house, not a gruesome, mock-medieval fortress. Being at Cranham Court would hardly be like being in prison at all. She would not feel perpetually confined, and her thoughts could roam freely.

However, since starting to work in the garden, Mavis had stopped yearning to go to Cranham Court. She was just beginning to get used to Collingwood, and was not anxious to be uprooted and transferred somewhere else where she would have to adjust to new conditions all over again. Life had just started to become bearable in Collingwood. There was Olive she could talk to, and there was Lorry in the garden.

8

LORRY WAS FEELING CHEERFUL AS SHE PUSHED HER mowing machine up and down the main lawn. She worked with care and precision, making certain that each stretch she mowed overlapped the last, and that she left behind no fringes or tufts of uncut grass. She attacked the scattered patches of daisies with particular vigour, gratified as the sharp blades neatly beheaded them. While she worked, she whistled the latest pop tunes.

Life was improving. She could tell she was one of the most sought-after women in Collingwood. People were taken with her. They liked her brush of cropped, sandy hair and her open-air face with its snub nose, rosy cheeks, cheeky grin and liberal sprinkling of freckles. She was a nice, healthy tom-boy—not like the other butches in at the moment, who greased and smarmed their hair (one or two even staining it with black boot polish), cultivated pseudo-sideboards, and had heavy, masculine faces belied by their high female voices. Lorry's voice, without being deep or gruff, had a rather boyish timbre.

She had soon become quite a well-known figure, brandishing her hose or pushing her mowing-machine over the Collingwood lawns. People passing by, officers as well as prisoners, exchanged remarks and greetings with her. Some stopped if they could for a brief chat. Occasionally, Lorry would slightly spray some passing prisoner with her hose. They usually took it in good part, for it was impossible to get very indignant with anyone who appeared so cheerful and jovial.

As she mowed and whistled, Lorry thought happily about her popularity. In many ways, life in Collingwood was better than outside. True, she had her own circle of special friends and acquaintances outside: the girls and men who went to the same gay clubs as she. But there she had to face the competition of many other lesbians, some of them exceedingly attractive. But in Collingwood, butches were relatively scarce, hence sought after in a way they never were outside, even in the gay clubs. She did not care whether the other prisoners desired her for herself because they were fem, or because they were simply ordinary women looking for an ersatz man. It was enough for her that she was generally popular.

Moreover, here she felt normal. Outside, however convincing her disguise, there was always the chance of people seeing through it. And even if they did not, she had the uncomfortable knowledge that they would despise and deride her, or worse, if they discovered that she was really a lesbian posing as a man. But in Collingwood lesbianism was not queer: it was taken for granted—even by most of the officers.

Lorry paused in her lawn-mowing for a moment as she watched the

F Wing women come out. She looked at them pityingly as they shambled round the big lawn in two's and three's—she, as a gardener, did not have to join in these degrading bouts of exercise.

'Hi there, Lorry. How long've you got this time?' someone called.

'Twenty years,' she shouted back merrily.

Then a girl broke rules by scurrying over the lawn to her.

'Lorry,' she said breathlessly, 'see that bird there?—blond bird walking back there with Maggie and Jose?' She indicated a hefty, unprepossessing woman, her hair a hard, yellow veneer over dead, dark grey.

'Yeah, what about her?' Lorry replied.

'She fancies you,' the girl went on, '—really gone on you. Name's Bessy Parker. But she's shy like—you know. Don't like to say it to your face. But the whole wing knows.'

'Crowther, get back off the grass,' shouted the harsh voice of one of the supervising officers.

'OK. Well see you later, Lorry,' the girl said hurriedly, and ran back to the path.

Lorry cautiously studied Bessy. She was not her type at all. Probably she was some housewife who had 'turned' while in Collingwood in order to make the best of whatever substitute male she could find. Even so, Lorry was gratified when the woman peeped at her and giggled as she passed. And she did not mind when a whole group of F Wing women started sniggering, nudging each other and whispering each time Bessy walked by her. She tried to appear indifferent. But, unattractive though Bessy was, she could not help glancing covertly at her now and then.

After this, every day, Lorry found herself automatically looking for a job to do on or near the big lawn at about eleven o'clock when F Wing came out on exercise. Bessy's passion was reported to be intense, and was almost her sole topic of conversation on the wing. Lorry enjoyed the sense of power she got out of knowing she could make or mar Bessy's day simply by withholding or deigning to bestow a faint smile on her as she went by.

A few days later, a Red Band slipped a note into Lorry's hand. It was from one of the kitchen workers—totally unknown to Lorry. In scrawling childish handwriting it ran:

61

'Daring Lorry, i sure do hope you dont mind me calling you darling honey but ive woched you and see as your the one for me please Lorry darling I relly fansy you and hope to go to bed with you your luvly smile and those freckles relly send me hoping this finds you as it leaves me. fondest love Mary. P.S. ime on H wing and ave got red air dont disapoint me darling ime waiting for your arnser nite an day.'

Lorry was pleased and intrigued, but did not want to commit herself to paper. She did not know how to reply to an unknown love-letter writer, who might be young and pretty, but on the other hand might be tough and ugly as an old boot. So next day, when the Red Band asked her whether she had an answer for her to deliver, Lorry said:

'What kind of a bird is she?—I mean, is she a blond or what? Is she bent?'

'She's Mary—Mary who works in the kitchen. You know—' was all the reply she got. 'Look, I must run now, or Sister'll do me. See you later.' And the Red Band hurried off, leaving Lorry none the wiser. So she still did not answer the note.

Next day, the Red Band slipped a small package into her hand. It was three cigarettes (real cigarettes, not roll-ups) wrapped in two or three squares of toilet paper, tied round with a bit of ribbon from the Work Room. The package contained another note from Mary, similar to the first. This was just the thing, Lorry decided, being kept in fags by some bird you'd never even met and owed nothing to—free fags with no strings attached. Mary must be encouraged. So she wrote her a thank-you note for the Red Band to deliver. It was brief and suitably grateful, yet non-committal. In her large, flourishing handwriting, embellished with plenty of squiggles, Lorry wrote:

'Dear Mary, Thank you very much for the cigarettes. I love smoking and am very greatful for them. I shall greatly enjoy smoking them, and shall think of you every time I do. Ever yours— Lorry Harrison.'

the signature was written larger than the rest and underlined.

Then there was Mavis. As soon as she had seen Mavis, Lorry was taken with her. She liked her pale, fluffy hair. Her neatly cut features, and a certain squirrel-like quality, as though she were perpetually poised, about to sprint off, reminded Lorry of a German girl with whom she had once had a brief, tempestuous affair.

She was even more struck by Mavis's expression and manner: by her dreamy, far-away look, and rather shy, detached way of talking. Such a person presented a challenge. It would be an achievement, Lorry felt, to get through to Mavis and rouse her attention and interest. But she realized it would be unwise to try to rush things.

To start with, she made little headway. Throughout Mavis's first day in the garden, Lorry observed her surreptitiously from a distance. Gradually she made up her mind that she would be worth cultivating. At the end of the day, as Miss Foster was taking them back to their wings, she deliberately dropped back a step or two to keep pace with Mavis walking just behind.

'Like working in the garden then, Mavis?' she said smiling encouragingly. But Mavis merely answered:

'Yes, thank you,' looking at Lorry so vaguely that Lorry wondered if she had even heard the question.

'It's not such a bad old job once you get used to it,' she tried again. This time, Mavis only said:

'Oh.' Then they reached her wing.

Nor did Lorry manage to make much progress during the following few days. Mavis and she had jobs in different parts of the garden, so her only chance of getting into conversation with her was the few moments before they started work, and when Miss Foster was taking them back to their wings at dinner and tea time. For three or four days, Mavis made only vague or monosyllabic responses to Lorry's efforts to talk. But Lorry's mounting frustration merely increased her determination to get through to Mavis somehow.

If only Miss Foster did not always give them jobs in different parts of the garden. It was not fair, for she usually had the Finns working jointly on some job. Lorry decided to do something about the matter.

'Those beds need weeding badly, don't they, Miss Foster?' she said hopefully one morning, as Miss Foster was leading them off to the tool-shed after breakfast. 'Shall Mavis and me have a go at them before they get any worse?' But Miss Foster had different plans: Mavis was to snip off dead roses; Lorry to get on with mowing.

'Oh, OK then, if you want weeds growing all over the flower beds and choking all the flowers . . .' Lorry replied crossly. Miss Foster ignored her. She was not bothered by back-chat and surliness from prisoners.

It was always the same, Lorry reflected bitterly—they were full of how you were sent to prison in order to be cured and turned into responsible citizens; then, as soon as you began to act responsibly—get some idea or show a little initiative—you were quelled and ordered about. She glowered at Miss Foster and muttered:

'Fucking old cow!' Miss Foster heard, but did not care. She just said brightly:

'Now see if you can get both lawns done by dinner time, Lorry,' then hurried off indoors for a cup of tea.

Lorry felt thoroughly cross for the rest of the morning. She not merely mowed the grass; she attacked it with jabbing thrusts of her machine.

'Shit!' she hissed, whenever a nail or stone got caught between the blades and brought them to an abrupt halt. Her responses to the usual witticisms and jovial remarks from passing prisoners were brief and sulky, her expression grim.

Perhaps the most annoying thing was that Miss Foster was not being deliberately malicious. She was not, Lorry was sure, separating them out of spite or for some ulterior reason. It was just bad luck that she always seemed to give them different jobs. This in itself was infuriating. Miss Foster, or any of the officers, could be as capricious or unreasonable as they chose, and she, Lorry, could do nothing about it. There was no good reason why Mavis and she should not be working together on the weed-choked flower-beds—the job was urgent. But it was always the same in Collingwood: you were perpetually at the mercy of other people's whims and moods. Lorry felt so cross that even an unexpected gift of chocolate from Mary in the kitchen did not cheer her up.

Then, that same afternoon, everything improved. Mavis actually approached Lorry. Lorry was absorbed in her mowing, jerking the machine viciously to and fro, positively punching the grass with it. Glancing up, she was pleasantly surprised to see Mavis wandering across the grass towards her. She immediately erased her sulky frown, and was on the point of greeting Mavis brightly, when, astonishingly,

Mavis herself spoke first. She waved her secateurs vaguely at Lorry and said:

'I've finished doing all those roses like she said, but I can't find her anywhere. What do you think I ought to do now?'

Lorry was delighted. She felt manly and important at being asked for advice and instructions. In a definite, capable tone, she replied:

'Well, if I was you I'd look round for any other dead flowers and snip them off too—any geraniums or anything that's over. They all have to come off.'

Too late, she realized what a silly thing she had said. Why hadn't she suggested some job close at hand?—weeding the path round the lawn for instance. As it was, she had merely done what she had been cursing Miss Foster all day for doing.

However, Mavis still stood there. To Lorry's amazement, she seemed inclined to linger for a chat. By now, she felt somewhat liberated: less shy and detached than at first; better able to take in what was going on around her and notice her workmates.

'Not bad is it?—working in the garden I mean on a day like this,' she remarked. Lorry was so pleased that she replied with positive enthusiasm:

'Way out—crazy job it is—best in this grotty old dump any road.' Then she was silent, suddenly unaccountably shy herself.

'You've got a lovely sun tan. You been working out here long?' Mavis asked, looking admiringly at Lorry's deep brown arms, muscular from much mowing; and Lorry, to her horror, felt herself suddenly blush like a girl. Gruff with delighted embarrassment, she responded:

'Oh well, not very long. I've not been in long—just a couple of weeks. But I got brown before.'

'Oh, you've only been in a little while too,' Mavis said. 'I thought you'd been here ages,'—and Lorry took this as a compliment. 'I've only been here three weeks. I've got three years.'

'Yes, I know,' Lorry replied. 'You were telling me the other day.'

'Oh, was I?' said Mavis hazily. But then, just as at last they had started to have a proper conversation, Miss Foster, perversely for once cutting short her tea-break, reappeared and swept Mavis off to do some weeding at the other end of the garden. However, as she was conducting them back to their wings at tea time, she said:

'I think, Lorry, if you can get the rest of your grass cut tomorrow morning, we'd better make a start on the long bank in the afternoon. You and Mavis can get going on that.'

So next morning Lorry worked happily and hard, determined to get all her mowing done by dinner time. She whistled and thought about the afternoon ahead. How should she make the best use of it? She tried to plan in advance what she would say to Mavis as they worked side by side; in particular, what picture of herself she should paint. Should she be one of those aggrieved prisoners who had 'never done it'—who had been put upon or framed? Or should she, on the contrary, have done it with a vengeance? And if she had, what sort of crime should it have been? Certainly not the rather trifling, unsuccessful housebreaking she had actually undertaken. Something altogether more swashbuckling would surely be better; holding up a bank for instance, and still having the loot stashed away somewhere awaiting her release. Or should she have been a stowaway? In any case, she decided, whatever she had done, it must have been done with aplomb and have been successful, even though (through no fault of her own of course) she had eventually been caught.

Then there was the question of her background. The truth—that before her imprisonment she had been a mere petrol pump hand in a slick filling station on the North Circular—was surely not impressive. It would be better to present herself as a long-distance lorry driver— the only woman on the road ever to get away with it and hoodwink all the other drivers and transport cafe owners into believing she was a fellow. And she wouldn't mind claiming she had once been in the army, or at sea—but perhaps that would be too much for Mavis to believe. It never struck her that Mavis might not be very interested in her anyway, but might prefer to talk about herself.

The afternoon came, and Lorry tried to carry out her plan, but in the end each woman talked almost exclusively about herself, paying scant attention to what the other was saying.

Sitting next to Mavis, leaning down the bank to clip the grass between her vee-spread legs, Lorry was saying:

'It's a real free open life you see, the open road. Can't beat it. It makes in here feel like you're locked away in a cage or something.'

It was a hot, sunny afternoon, and Lorry could feel the sweat gradually saturating the cloth in her armpits. Mavis was sitting so close to her that probably she could smell the sweat. Lorry hoped she thought it a tough, manly smell and did not find it distasteful. Mavis's attention was arrested by what Lorry said, not the part about being a lorry driver, but Lorry's sense of being caged—just as she herself was suffering from this intolerable, shut-in feeling.

'I've been feeling so like I was in a cage they put me to work out here,' Mavis responded. 'They thought the open air would do me good.' But Lorry, who did not really suffer from claustrophobia at all, reverted to her lorry driving.

'Miles and miles you can drive on the open road and never see a soul,' she lied, '—only the trees and forests and mountains.' (She had just finished reading an American paperback about hitch-hikers and hoboes.) 'Been a cabin-boy too,' she added, 'in the Queen Mary. Right across the Pacific.'

'My uncle's a driver,' said Mavis. 'And my Aunty, who he's married to, she's a Spiritualist. She's been in touch with people On the Other Side. Have you ever been?'

Lorry had no idea what she was talking about. She would like to have continued romanticizing about long-distance lorry driving, but could not very well ignore a direct question from Mavis.

'Been in touch?' she echoed, mystified. 'Turned on, do you mean?'

'No, in touch. You ever been in touch with Those on the Other Side?' repeated Mavis excitedly. 'Dead people, I mean, or even people who are alive but far away. I'm in touch with my children; with Doreen, my little girl. That's why they moved me into the garden, so's I can keep in touch with her.'

Was Mavis herself slightly touched, Lorry wondered. She looked at her closely for a second or two. Then, deciding she was not mad but just someone with some funny ideas, she asked abruptly:

'You ever been blocked—been on the weed?—or taken pills?'Without waiting for Mavis to reply, she went on. 'I get quite a buzz from pills, but pot—that's the real stuff. Makes you feel like you can be anywhere you want at the same time. Oh man, it sure gives you a groovy feeling—way out! It's like you kind of see everything, even tiny little things, clear and big like through a magnifying glass. And you hear everything different too. Real cool it makes you feel.'

But Mavis cut short her rhapsody.

'You got any children?' she said. Lorry stared at her indignantly.

'What, me got kids!' she expostulated. But Mavis, ignoring her, rambled on:

'I've got four. There's the boys. One of them's still only a baby really. Then there's my Doreen . . .'

Lorry soon stopped listening, and instead tried to work out how to re-introduce the subject of lorry driving. Or should she, she debated, embark on a lengthy, dramatic account of the impressive crime she had decided she had committed.

She snipped lethargically at the grass between her straddled legs, slowly working her way forward down the bank. She was sticky and prickling with sweat by now, and strained from bending forward for so long. All at once she felt rather bored and irritated. Why was she bothering to try to impress this woman who just yatted on and on about her kids?

Suddenly Jan appeared, walking down the path accompanied by a Red Band and called out a cheery greeting. Lorry was pleased, and shouted back jovially:

'Hi there, Kinky! Watcher doing?—absconding?'

Mavis detected Lorry's loss of interest, so she stopped prattling about her children. For a while, both women worked side by side in silence.

Lorry's thoughts slid away from Mavis to Jan. What did she think of her? Jan was being cautious, but Lorry knew quite well that she was after her. She had heard all about Jan's past reputation. And Jan kept dropping in to her cell for a chat. True, she usually talked about travelling; her conversation was not personal; but there was something about the occasional quizzical or slightly appraising glance she gave her . . . Lorry was, as usual, flattered. What else did she feel?—Jan was not young and pretty.

Desultorily she clipped the grass below her, now and again relieving her aching back by twisting round to attack the grass at her side. By all rights and reason she should feel quite indifferent to Jan. She, Lorry, was a boy—or near enough—therefore what she wanted and needed was what all boys (and butches) needed: a fluffy little doll to admire and adore her; someone who would allow herself to be dominated—an attractive young girl who would lie down under her and permit herself

68

to be penetrated: permit Lorry, her penetrator, to believe for a few moments that she really was a boy with a boy's equipment.

Someone like Mavis could fulfil this purpose, she thought, glancing briefly up at her, admiring her neat, sun illuminated profile and wavy hair glinting with metal-bright highlights. Jan, with her ageing, slightly dissipated features, would not do at all. So why was she half looking forward to the moment when Jan declared herself? It was all rather confusing and worrying. A slight frown creased Lorry's forehead, and she appeared so lost in thought that Mavis did not try to re-open the conversation.

9

JAN DID HER WORK WITH CARE AND PRECISION. SHE HAD a steady wrist and eye, so found her job of repainting empty cells reasonably enjoyable. But much of it was silly. Why, for example, paint a thin green line right round the cell half-way up the wall, and another exactly four inches above the floor? What was the point of embellishing the yellow walls with painted-on mock wainscoting? And surely it was a piece of hypocrisy to do the massive, formidable door in gleaming white?

'Whited sepulchre,' she once caught herself muttering as she covered the door with long, even strokes. Then, when all this elaborate painting was finally done, the walls and ceiling were not sleek, but ominously bumped and grooved all over with the contours of the brickwork beneath.

Before any painting could even begin, the battered, defaced walls had to be thoroughly scraped—a laborious business—and patched up here and there with dabs of plaster. All this meant that it took a week, sometimes longer, to re-decorate one cell; yet this was supposed to be a crash programme, as the Governor was badgering to get a new wing ready for the Remands.

It was typical of Collingwood, Jan thought wryly, to announce a crash programme, then complicate and prolong it by insisting that each cell be painted an elaborate pattern of strips and stripes. But she did not care. She was more amused than shocked. She had spent too many years of her life in Collingwood to be particularly aggravated by any of the anomalies or absurdities of the prison system. She had learnt to take life as it came and get the most out of it that she could.

Some of the painters worked in pairs; some on their own. Jan preferred to work by herself unless there were some particularly attractive woman on the party to have as partner. At the moment, there was not. Jan did not mind; she was glad to get away from everyone for a bit. Her own thoughts were a great deal more entertaining than the tedious babble of most of her fellow prisoners.

As she deftly inserted a knife-load of damp plaster into a particularly gaping crevasse, Jan wondered idly whether it was the result of frenzied bashing long ago by some furious or frantic woman. Or perhaps some illiterate prisoner, bored to distraction, had started to excavate the wall in order to while away the time. If so, what had she used?—the rusty, broken-nibbed pen they were all supplied with, or a knitting needle, or the broad blunt bit of tin that acted as knife for those who had their meals in solitary? Jan speculated constantly about the women who had once occupied the cells she was decorating. For some reason, they seemed more fascinating than the commonplace women she met all the time.

The graffiti she had to scrape off the walls intrigued her. Some were funny, some moving, almost all fired her imagination. There had been the rhyme about Lucy, the notorious prostitute who had practically brought the government down a couple of years ago:

> *Lushus blue eyed kinky Lucy*
> *Was General Thompson's faverit floosy.*
> *One nite in bed together for a stunt*
> *He stuffed his hole leg up her cunt*
> *Now at last he's booted out*
> *The bleeding silly soding lout.*

Jan regretted having to erase this. What kind of woman would have written it, she wondered—surely someone with a degree of wit and originality and a certain facility for putting words together. Very likely

70

she had been amusing, less boring and wrapped up in herself than most Collingwood inmates. What crime had she committed? Had she been young, attractive? . . .

> *I love my Johnny and will always stay true to him whatever they do to me*, was touching, but less interesting than:
> *Patsy I'll never forget you darling as long as I live. I'm going out tomorrow but I'll love you for ever darling and always stay true.*

What kind of woman had written this, butch or fem? And had she really been feeling utterly miserable over parting from her lover, or excited because she was going out? The arrow-pierced hearts linking pairs of names might represent prisoners and their husbands or lesbian couples; often it was hard to tell which.

When she discovered a 'Ban the Bomb' sign and slogan, Jan scraped it off quickly and gladly. It reminded her of Paula, the Peace Prisoner, who had briefly worked in the Laundry with her two sentences ago. Paula's conversation had been too interesting, and she had put her in the shade. Once or twice, she had shown her up in a political discussion; for Jan's politics consisted merely of a few stock opinions and nominal, unthinking support for the Conservatives.

> *I want to get OUT OUT OUT. This place is driving me MAD* had very likely been the product of an insane mind, or anyway of someone temporarily unhinged. The 'mad' interested Jan in an academic way. She would try to imagine what being mad felt like—was it rather like being drunk or very high? Not that she sympathized with those who became frantic and deranged as a result of their imprisonment. If she had been able to adjust and make the best of the many years she had spent inside, why couldn't everyone else? She had more sympathy for the author of *Fucking shit cows the lot of them.*

As she was carefully plastering and cogitating, Jan was disturbed by someone abruptly bursting in through the cell door behind her. A disagreeably familiar voice shouted gaily:

'It's me, Janny darling. Guess what?—I've won. They've moved me at last from that cess pool of a hospital, and here I am!'

It was Rose. Jan turned and looked at her in startled horror for a few seconds before responding lamely:

'They've moved you to painting have they?'

'Yes, marvellous isn't it, Janny?' Rose replied excitedly. 'I never thought they would. Do you know how many times now I've had to book for the Governor, or the Chief or the M.O. or someone before they'd do anything?—six times!'

'Very clever of you,' Jan said morosely.

For some while past, Rose had been disgusting everyone at meal times with nauseating accounts of her job as a Hospital cleaner. The Hospital was badly run, Jan knew, but she was sure Rose exaggerated about the dirt and the callousness and cruelty of the nurses. Everyone in Collingwood endlessly exaggerated, complained and looked for scapegoats—everyone, that is, except she herself. They did it, she realized, to boost themselves; to unload their guilt and frustration on to other people. But she did not need to do this. She was not ashamed of her crimes, nor did she regret having committed them—they brought her in large dividends, enabling her to live it up between sentences. Neither did she consider her punishment unjust; it was simply the price she had to pay for getting caught. Anyway, life in Collingwood had its compensations; her most profound and satisfying love affairs had all occurred in prison.

'I'd actually started work,' Rose was explaining, 'I was sluicing down that filthy recess—smothered with shit it was, and someone must have peed all over the floor—the stink!—Anyway, where was I?—Oh yes, well so Sister Barnes came along and said the Chief wanted me and ...' She went on to give an excited, verbose account of just what the Chief had said to her and she to the Chief.

Jan stared at her gloomily. Rose had been repeatedly announcing her intention of getting shifted from the Hospital, but Jan had hardly taken in what she was saying. These days, she found Rose so tedious and intolerable that, as soon as Rose started to speak, she automatically stopped listening and switched her attention elsewhere.

An engrained sense of courtesy gradually forced a feeble smile on to Jan's face. It was promptly replaced by a momentary look of consternation as Rose stated proudly:

'And you know what else I've wangled, Janny?—the best bit of all— I've got Miss Thomas to say I can work with you.'

'Have you?' said Jan, appalled.

Was there any way of getting rid of Rose?—Jan could not immediately think of any. It might be wise, she reflected, to take her more seriously from now on—be cautious, careful not to alienate her. Rose could probably be a nuisance if seriously upset. Obviously, she was determined and persistent to the point of obstinacy; subtle too—positively devious—for she had been careful never to mention that she was trying to get transferred on to the painting party (perhaps because she meant to spring it on her as a nice surprise). Jan would certainly have heard Rose if she had said anything about this.

'Come on Janny, aren't you going to show me what to do?' Rose said merrily. 'My, this looks a smashing job—all this clay and stuff. What do I do?'

'Well,' responded Jan wearily, 'what I'm doing is filling in these cracks. You mix up some plaster like this . . .' and she explained the job to Rose, ending up, 'By the way, are you *quite* sure you're actually supposed to be working with me and not getting on with the next cell? It's next on the list, and we don't all work in pairs you know.' But her faint hopes were dashed as Rose replied gaily:

'Not to worry, darling. It's OK. Miss Thomas actually told me to come and help you.' Jan was sure Rose must have put the idea into her head.

Rose set about mixing the plaster and slapping it carelessly into the cracks. She worked vigorously, and annoyed Jan still more by spattering blobs of plaster all over the surrounding wall and floor. Rose always seemed to be filled with irrelevant or misdirected energy— which was another reason why Jan disliked her. Every now and then, she thoughtlessly brushed straggling strands of hair out of her eyes with her dirty hand. Soon her face was grotesquely blotched and streaked. She looked, Jan thought, like an unprepossessing clown.

As she worked, Rose babbled on interminably about nothing in particular; and Jan found that after all she was able to shut out most of it, provided she made suitable assenting responses from time to time. Then abruptly her attention was aroused.

'Don't get to see much of you these days, do I, Janny?' Rose was saying. Jan winced, then was instantly apprehensive as Rose continued, 'Always with that Lorry nowadays, aren't you? She's a queer one. Don't know what you see in her.' Rose paused, as though expecting an answer. As Jan did not oblige, she went on, 'They say she's having a ball out there in the garden with some blonde bird. Lucky, aren't they?—all those bushes around, and everything, and sheds. . . .' But Jan refused to let herself be drawn.

'Oh gardening's all right,' she replied vaguely, 'except when it rains, which it almost always does in this goddam country. Give me painting any day.'

Rose looked at her briefly. But Jan had no particular expression on her face, so Rose decided to drop the subject of Lorry for the time being and revert to her previous chatter.

Rose was a dispersed kind of person, her behaviour governed by few rational or clearly-defined motives. Like many other prisoners, she had, in effect, graduated into Collingwood via approved school and Borstal. She had taken for granted that she would end up in prison, so was not particularly ashamed when she did. As soon as she arrived in Collingwood, she saw some familiar faces—people she had known at approved school and Borstal. She was dismayed. She had been thoroughly disliked at both places. For she had been a favour-currier and a grass.

As a very little girl, Rose had been sent away to a children's home. Ever since, she had been insecure, only able to feel safe if she won the grown-ups' approval; and the only way she knew how to do this was by telling tales. As she grew older, she became a gossip too. She loved to pass on things people had told her in confidence; then, when they found out and stopped confiding, she started to invent and circulate stories (mostly uncomplimentary) about them. And she would generate false rumours. All this gave her an agreeable creative feeling (it was surely a little like writing a book—she had always wanted to write a book), also a sense of power, which hid her insecurity and made up for her unpopularity. In time, she had branched out into blackmail, libel, and anonymous letter-writing—hence her two prison sentences. So far, during this one, she had been fairly restrained and indulged only in a little mild scandal-mongering. She started doing this now.

'Take Rob, you see,' she prattled. 'One bird after another she's had, and all in one sentence. First Vi, then Chris, then Jeanie, then Marie, and now Bett. And they do say she's two-timing her. Someone on F Wing told me only the other day that one of the girls on our wing—can't very well tell you who—had actually caught her in the middle of a scene with Ann Rogers—Ann Rogers, mind, who's got

74

a husband and five kids who're for ever visiting her.' She paused briefly in her spate of words, then, as Jan made no comment, continued: 'It's amazing, don't you think, Janny, how some of them carry on? Just act like they don't know what they want, don't they?—all mixed up and not kind of knowing who or what they are. What do you think about it, Janny?'

'About what?' Jan asked, reluctantly dragged out of her reverie about sailing to a Pacific Island with Lorry.

'About all this, you know, going on all the time,' Rose replied '—everyone having it away with everyone—sex, I mean. What do you think about it?' Jan retorted:

'Sex is to be had, not thought about.' This silenced Rose for a few moments. She ruminated vaguely about sex.

Although she had been sounding Jan out on the subject because she thought she would like to have an affair with her, Rose, in fact, had very little sexual feeling. The only orgasm she had ever experienced had been self-induced. Gossip had replaced sex for her: successfully sparking off rumours and suspicions gave her much the same satisfaction as igniting a blaze gives an arson addict.

She was intrigued by Jan's reputation and impressed by her upper-class background and accent. Also, Jan, so detached and composed, so different from herself, was surely someone she could lean on? Backed by Jan, might she not herself feel stronger, weightier, more clearly defined, less like an amoeba undulating at random in a goldfish bowl?

'You heard, Janny, about the new woman over on F Wing?' she resumed. 'Works in the Jam Factory, and Scotty was telling me she'd nearly died giving herself a fix in the bath—it was in the papers the other day. . . .' And so she was off again. Now and then, she paused and turned to glance at Jan, trying unsuccessfully to gauge what impression she was making on her.

Rose had for some time refused to believe that anything was brewing between Jan and Lorry, even though everyone else on G Wing knew there was. But eventually she had not been able to hoodwink herself any longer. She had not considered the situation irreversible, however—after all, Jan was her property: she had been on the wing with Jan before Lorry had ever arrived. She had engineered her transfer from the Hospital to the painting party (through making false

75

allegations about one of the nurses and two of her fellow cleaners) as a ploy to cut Lorry out. For surely, if she were working side by side with Jan all day, then she, not Lorry, would be Jan's special friend? Also, it should be possible from time to time to drop some subtly poisonous remarks about Lorry into the conversation.

Scandal-monger though Rose was, Jan knew there was sometimes a grain of truth in what she said. So, as Rose went on and on gossiping about this person and that, Jan found herself weighing up what she had just said about Lorry. It was possible, she reluctantly admitted to herself, that Lorry really was flirting with her fellow-gardener. Lorry never talked much about her; but this itself was probably a bad sign. Coming and going across the garden, Jan had noticed Mavis; and she could see that she was moderately attractive in a certain flimsy way. She was not the type that appealed to her, but she might very well be attractive to Lorry.

Jan was conscious of the difficulties ahead of her in her pursuit of Lorry. She knew Lorry thought of herself as a boy. And while this was largely why she appealed to her, still, it was bound to lead to difficulties. She would want a young, pretty girl friend—and Jan knew she was not young and pretty. However, she had not lived for forty-one years, become a wife and mother and had numerous lesbian affairs for nothing: she had learnt how confused and inconsistent most people were; so, in time, with any luck, she would get what she wanted with Lorry. Lorry, she could tell, was drawn to her. But this, she realized, might not prevent Lorry from being interested in some-one else at the same time, and so fulfilling another side of herself that she, Jan, could never wholly gratify.

'Hey, penny for them, Janny,' Rose suddenly demanded. 'You're miles away. You look quite miserable. What's wrong?'

'Nothing,' Jan replied shortly, 'I was just thinking.'

'Oh,' responded Rose, wishing Jan were more communicative. But she had succeeded more than she had hoped. For the rest of that afternoon, as she talked on incessantly about nothing in particular, Jan thought rather sadly about Lorry. Was there anything, she wondered, that she could do to preserve her for herself and discourage her from wanting anyone else?

IO

'I WAS JUST MAKING A CUPPA,' MISS HEWSON SAID STIFFLY to Miss Whittaker, 'care to join me?' It was half-past nine one night: too late to start doing anything in particular, but too early for bed. The other officers in the Annexe often dropped in on each other last thing for a hot drink and a chat. Miss Hewson would have liked to join them, but did not feel she could just walk into someone else's room, unasked; and so far no one had invited her. The next best thing would surely be to ask one of them in to visit her.

'Oh dear, I'm just whacked, love,' Miss Whittaker disappointingly replied. 'I think I'd better get an early night for once. Thanks all the same. Another night perhaps.'

Later on, as Miss Whittaker was lying in bed, it struck her that Miss Hewson always seemed dreary, never somehow able to smile and relax. So she decided to invite her out on a double date the following Saturday with herself and two male officers. Miss Hewson was delighted, but the evening was not a success: while the others joked and flirted and obviously enjoyed themselves, she remained as shy and gauche as ever.

In the middle of one afternoon, when the wing was empty but for a couple of cleaners, Mac emerged from her office and stalked majestically (she was a heavy woman and always stalked) into the centre of the wing.

'Miss Hewson,' she boomed, 'have you a few moments please!'

It was a command, not a question. Miss Hewson, reacting like a timid prisoner, clattered hastily down the spiral staircase, almost tripping as she went. When she reached the bottom, she modified her pace to a semi-trot, remembering that prison officers were supposed always to appear dignified and never run, except in an emergency.

As soon as she was in Mac's office, Mac said with disconcerting bluntness:

'Miss Hewson, there's some bloody silly things you do sometimes—pardon my language, but I believe in calling a spade a spade. First that business with Beryl Hunt over the paper—not letting her hang on to the Express all day when she always does.' She paused.

'But I thought they were all supposed to share out the wing newspapers and not monopolize them all day,' Miss Hewson protested feebly. She felt indignant and alarmed all at the same time—Mac was so daunting. Mac disliked being answered back by her subordinates, even though she did not mind it from prisoners.

'Miss Hewson, I recommend you listen carefully and take advice from your senior officers,' she went on. 'You've a lot, a very great deal, to learn. You want to watch how you go with Beryl Hunt. She can be exceedingly awkward and violent when she feels like it—you know she's in for chopping off her husband's balls? Anyway, we rely quite a bit on our Red Bands, as you should know by now. We can't afford to go upsetting them.' Again she paused. Miss Hewson felt too cowed to respond this time. 'Then what's all this,' Mac resumed, 'about letting Dawley, Harrison and Carruthers get away with it the other night?—all sitting squashed together on the same bed with the door shut. Right old carry on. You know this isn't allowed.'

Miss Hewson was surprised that Mac knew about this (she had picked up some gossip circulated by Rose); she was baffled too. First Mac blamed her for trying to keep the rules, then blamed her for letting them get broken.

'Well I—' she began haltingly, but Mac broke in:

'And while I'm about it, what about that business a week or so ago with Harrison and Carruthers? I've deliberately never brought it up before. Thought I'd better give you a chance to get your feet first.' Miss Hewson looked uncomprehending, so she went on, 'That time you had that daft barney after dinner with Harrison and Carruthers. That was bloody silly, to say the least.' She stopped expectantly.

'The women wouldn't go off to work at the proper time,' Miss Hewson responded hesitantly, 'and Harrison was very insolent when I told her to. . . .' She petered out lamely, unable to think of any excuse or explanation.

Mac glared at her for a few seconds, then said sternly and emphatically:

'Miss Hewson, you are a very new, young and inexperienced officer here, and, if I may say so, very tactless at times too. I hope, incidentally, you realize it's an offence for an officer to strike a prisoner?—and that's pretty much what you seemed to be doing that time.' Miss Hewson looked at the floor and fingered her belt. She did not answer, so Mac continued, 'It's my job to keep an eye on the officers under me, and several times I've very nearly come and told you to let it go.' The severity of her voice turned to pensiveness as she went on, 'When you've been in the Service as long as I have, you'll find it's wisest, nine times out of ten, to let it go. Let those three little words be your motto. You'll get on much better that way.' She stopped and looked enquiringly at Miss Hewson. Some response was called for, but all Miss Hewson could manage was:

'Yes, I see, Miss Macpherson.' As she obviously did not, Mac, glaring again, said fiercely:

'You do understand what I'm talking about, Miss Hewson, don't you?' Not waiting for her to reply, she went on: 'You'll find life impossible in a place like this—you'll do nothing and get nowhere, if you go round looking for trouble and picking on the least little thing. Remember, Miss Hewson, you are dealing with a pack of women in here —and when I say pack, I mean pack. Wicked as sin, most of 'em, and unhappy as Hell. Bloody fools or scoundrels, the lot of them. So you've got to make allowances. Let it go, Miss Hewson, let it go. Just remember that all the time you're here and you'll do all right. And now about weekend duty. Miss Whittaker would like. . . .'

Afterwards, Miss Hewson was sorry she had not brought herself to ask Mac a few questions about discipline: when should one be firm about prison regulations and when lax? For it was all very puzzling— the women were in Collingwood for committing crimes, so how could an officer begin to transform them into law-abiding citizens if she kept closing her eyes to disobedience and unruliness in the prison? Then Mac's personal attitude was baffling too. There was not an iota of social worker about her. She was very derogatory about the women and often shouted at them, yet she was popular; and, in her own way, she seemed actually to like them.

A day or two later, Mrs Herbert, the Wing Governor, sent for her. She smiled encouragingly at her.

'Sit down, Miss Hewson,' she said amiably. 'We've never really had a proper chat before, have we, thanks to my silly back? You were moved over here from Admissions Wing while I was still on sick leave, weren't you?'

'Yes, Mrs Herbert,' Miss Hewson replied politely with a thin, wary smile. She sat stiffly on the edge of her chair, expecting the worst. Down on her lap, her right hand grasped hold of each taut finger of her left hand in turn. Then she raised it for a second to scratch the nervous tingle on the side of her neck. Mac must have complained to Mrs Herbert about all the misdeeds she had committed in her absence. No doubt she was here to be severely reprimanded, perhaps even advised to resign.

'I like to get to know all my new officers,' Mrs Herbert went on. 'It's most important, I think, that we should all understand each other and work together as a team—don't you agree?'

Miss Hewson bowed her head and stared at her hands, now strained to bloodless whiteness. They seemed to be manipulating each other of their own accord.

'Yes, Mrs Herbert,' she replied meekly. If only Mrs Herbert would get on with it, and not keep her in suspense.

Mrs Herbert was a trifle disappointed by this enigmatic, faintly subservient response. She expected great things of Miss Hewson. There was always much more to be hoped for from these new officers than from old hands like Miss Macpherson, who thought they knew it all and were set in their ways. Looking searchingly at Miss Hewson, she astounded her by saying:

'I liked some of the things you wrote on your application form about your reasons for wanting to enter the Prison Service.' Miss Hewson was nonplussed.

'Thank you, Mrs Herbert,' was all she managed to answer. Mrs Herbert wished she were easier to draw out.

She had approved of Miss Hewson's application form because her motives for wanting to join the Prison Service resembled her own: a desire to help and advise unfortunate, emotionally disabled women. She had just re-read and been favourably impressed by Miss Hewson's brief essay on 'Why I want to be a Prison Officer'.

They badly needed someone like Miss Hewson on G Wing. True,

young Miss Rigg had the right attitudes; but only one suitable junior officer on a wing was not enough. Miss Whittaker was good humoured and popular, but never attempted to form therapeutic relationships with individual women. She preferred to relate to them *en masse*, to befriend them all. She did not believe in "making favourites"—'You never know where it might lead,' she had expostulated when Mrs Herbert had once suggested that she attempt casework with one or two specific women. Anyway, jolly and cheerful though Miss Whittaker was, she was actually as conservative as Mac herself—full of orthodox views on crime, deterrence, punishment and so on.

Speaking more briskly, and looking hopefully at Miss Hewson (she could not see her strained fingers intertwining down in her lap), Mrs Herbert continued:

'Yes, I am always delighted when a new officer on my wing turns out to be someone who shares my approach to the job. Unfortunately not all officers do, especially some of the senior ones—officers of the old school, so to speak. You will find, for instance, that Miss Macpherson and I do not invariably see eye to eye about everything. . . .' She tailed off, for it did not do to complain too bitterly about a senior officer to a junior one.

Mrs Herbert wanted some officer on her wing (preferably several) to offset Mac. She was a comparative newcomer to Collingwood, having become Governor of G Wing only a year ago, after a varied previous career as a history student, WREN, wife and mother (she was now a widow), and probation officer. From the start, there had been ill-concealed war between her and Mac. Mac despised her "new fangled ideas"—the Group Counselling, Vocational Guidance, Outside Friends Scheme and other things she had instituted. Furthermore, Mac was jealous and resented the fact that someone who might be college trained and highly experienced, but nevertheless had not been through the mill of the prison service, should just walk in and be put in authority over her. Mrs Herbert had not had to endure years of drudgery, working her way up from the bottom, as she had.

Mac knew all about the running of the wing, as, for about a year before Mrs Herbert arrived, there had been no Wing Governor. Mac had been virtually in sole charge. Mrs Herbert had found that over some matters she had to defer to Mac, who knew so much more than she did about the prison system, and day to day business of supervising the wing. This was rather humiliating for Mrs Herbert, and increased her dislike of Mac. If only Mac were not so popular with the women—she had no right to be, holding such old-fashioned, punitive ideas. She wished Mac did not form personal relationships with the prisoners. It was poaching on her preserves. The sort of simple, practical advice Mac gave the women was bound to be the direct opposite to hers, therefore likely to vitiate it. So when, as soon as Mrs Herbert returned from sick leave, Mac had reeled off a list of complaints about Miss Hewson, Mrs Herbert had at once felt on Miss Hewson's side.

Miss Hewson was amazed and relieved that Mrs Herbert was not blaming but praising her. Her father would be delighted when she told him about this. Mrs Herbert proceeded to expound her theories on delinquency, then described the various schemes she had launched on G Wing, most of which had fallen into abeyance while she was away on sick leave.

'You see, Miss Hewson,' she explained, 'I don't myself regard prison sentences in terms of punishment. Punishment is an outmoded idea. The only purpose served by shutting these unfortunate women away in here is simply to train them, while here, to deal more effectively with their lives once they get out.'

'Yes I suppose so. Our purpose, why we're here, is more to help cure them so to speak than, well, deter them,' Miss Hewson echoed, for once nearly sounding enthusiastic. Encouraged, Mrs Herbert went on:

'That's quite true, and indeed it's the essence, one might say, of our Group Counselling. We believe, you see, that if the women can discuss and work through their problems together, they will often find they have much in common and may be able to help each other. In any case, just talking about their problems may help them to find the solutions for themselves.' (It seldom turned out this way, but, for the moment, Mrs Herbert chose to forget this.)

'Yes, I've read and heard a bit about Group Counselling. It sounds most interesting and beneficial,' Miss Hewson responded pedantically. Mrs Herbert looked appreciative and nodded.

'Well now,' she concluded, 'what I want you to do is to work with me by taking on, so to speak, one or two individual women and

82

concentrating all your energy on helping them as much as you can. Miss Rigg has agreed to this approach, and I've discussed it with Miss Whittaker.' (Miss Hewson wondered if she had also discussed it with Mac, but did not like to ask.) 'Perhaps, as you're still new here, you should start off by concentrating on just one woman and see how you get on. You can of course consult me at any time—indeed, I hope you do. This is what I'm here for. I suggest that at first you see what you can do to help Rose Dawley.' Miss Hewson obediently assented, but without displaying quite as much enthusiasm as Mrs Herbert hoped she would.

Afterwards, Miss Hewson realized what a difficult task she had been given. There was much she should have asked Mrs Herbert: about Rose's background; how best to approach her; her crime . . . but it was too late now. She could hardly go straight back to Mrs Herbert with a string of questions she should have asked during the interview. She would just have to do her best.

II

MRS HERBERT UNLOCKED A STEEL CUPBOARD AND TOOK out Lorry Harrison's file. She studied it for some time, debating how best to deal with Lorry, who was one of the prisoners she had allocated to herself for particular attention. She had adopted Lorry because she considered her one of the more difficult cases on the wing. At the same time, Lorry seemed interesting and challenging; not, surely, a hopeless case, but someone with potentialities, who might be amenable to the right sort of treatment.

Mrs Herbert was apt to become interested in particular sorts of prisoners. For instance, she tended to concentrate on lesbians—on butch lesbians, that is—especially younger ones like Lorry. Lorry personified a kaleidoscope of dimly-recalled images from her past.

A long time ago, Mrs Herbert's younger brother, who had died of diphtheria, had looked a little like Lorry. Then there had been a girl at school; later, someone in the WRENS. More poignantly, and nearer the surface of Mrs Herbert's mind, was her own eldest son, killed in an air crash. He had been snub-nosed and freckled—the kind of boy Lorry tried to resemble.

Reading Lorry's file, Mrs Herbert was aware how little she actually knew about her. The 'social history' contained all the hard facts that were known about her past, but the most important information, why and when she became homosexual, was not there. The facts were roughly these:

Lorry was a country girl, daughter of a farm labourer. There was nothing particularly untoward about her childhood. She had never got into trouble: never been in a children's home or to an approved school. Her parents, both still living, were described as 'respectable and hard working though poor'. Lorry had two brothers and one younger sister. The only disquieting item about her childhood was some never wholly-verified evidence that she had been interfered with when she was six years old by an adolescent farmer's boy. Even if she had been, the experience had not at the time had any obvious disastrous effect on her. But it could, Mrs Herbert reflected, have had a hidden effect. Possibly it had sown the seeds of a profound hatred or jealousy of men. This could be the origin of Lorry's lesbianism.

At fifteen, she had, for no stated reason, left home and gone to a nearby city. Her previously stable life had at once become erratic. She had moved from job to job and from town to town. She had worked in a sweet shop, in a cannery, as a cinema usherette, in a laundry. Sometimes, she seemed to have lived in women's hostels; at other times to have shared rooms or flats with girls. Presently, she had gravitated to London; and there, almost at once, was put on probation for shoplifting from a West End store. Not long after that, she had served the first of her three prison sentences so far. What she did and where she lived between sentences was not clear, although, apparently, her last job before coming into Collingwood this time had been in a filling station.

Mrs Herbert was pleased that Lorry's case history was blurred and sketchy. There would be plenty of detective work for her to do: plenty of material to form the basis of a series of conversations with Lorry. Then, when she knew her better, she could help and advise her.

For a few moments, Mrs Herbert sat and cogitated about the reports she had just read. Very likely, she concluded, Lorry's transformation into a lesbian had coincided with the onset of her delinquency. Probably she was normal until she moved to London. Once in London, she may have got in with a tough set and started going to clubs. Could there be a direct connection between Lorry's delinquency and her sexual behaviour?

After dinner, she sent for Lorry.

'Ah, Harrison, sit down will you. We've not yet had the chance for a proper chat, have we? You came on the wing while I was on sick leave. I always like to get to know the people who come on my wing.'

Lorry stared at her unabashed; she did not consider an answer necessary. There was a slight pause as Mrs Herbert thought out what to say next.

Lorry was examining Mrs Herbert closely, trying to make up her mind whether or not she approved of her. She decided she did. Mrs Herbert was tall and august looking, with an air of authority. She looked rather manly, Lorry thought, with aquiline features, smoothly drawn back silver hair, erect carriage, and the suspicion of a moustache on her upper lip. Very likely she was a bit butch herself. Lorry felt respect and a mild sense of comradeship. It did not, however, mean that she was instantly prepared to divulge accurate information about herself to Mrs Herbert.

The more Lorry liked and respected people, the more she was inclined to fabricate a web of falsehood about herself; falsehoods designed to increase her attractiveness and arouse the admiration of her listener.

'How do you find it here in Collingwood?' Mrs Herbert said at last. 'This will be your third time in now, won't it?—you must have some views about the place I should think?'

'Could be worse, I s'pose,' Lorry replied gruffly. It surely made no difference what she thought.

'Yes, well we do try to move with the times a bit,' Mrs Herbert went on in a man-to-man tone, '—quite a few things have changed, I should think, since your first sentence?'

'Yeah, I guess,' Lorry replied in a tough, defensive tone.

'What's the most striking change in your opinion?' Mrs Herbert pursued; but Lorry merely answered:

'Oh, I dunno. Quite a few things have changed.'

Mrs Herbert decided she would have to abandon these indirect efforts to draw Lorry out, and ask her a few personal questions.

'Yes, I suppose quite a lot must have altered during the past six or seven years,' she said, then abruptly changed the subject. 'Tell me, what was your job before you came in? I always like to know where people's interests lie.'

Lorry looked hard at her. Was she genuinely interested, or just being a screw poking her nose into other people's business?

'Done a whole lot of different things,' she answered.

'Yes, I see,' Mrs Herbert responded. She smiled encouragingly and waited for Lorry to go on. The silence forced Lorry to continue:

'Had a job in a fair once. Last summer that was. In charge of the shooting—you know, shooting down those wooden duck things with an air gun.' Mrs Herbert nodded and said:

'That was last summer was it?'

'Yeah, and then after that I got this job as a stable boy,' Lorry continued, gathering confidence. 'Lord Duncan's place up at Newmarket. Used to stand in like for his jockey when he was off sick.' Mrs Herbert nodded. The bit about working in the fair just may have been true, but by now, obviously, Lorry was getting swept away into a fantasy.

Mrs Herbert was not surprised or shocked. She was used to prisoners lying about their lives outside. This boosted their morale; and, at a first interview, it was better not to humiliate them by forcing them to admit they were lying. Her job was to win her women's respect and confidence so that they no longer needed to tell her fibs. She just nodded, smiled, and inserted a few polite comments as Lorry rambled on:

'Then I went and broke my arm once falling off a horse. Dashing White Sergeant he was called—the horse. Then after that, I was on the road—on lorries, I mean—for a couple of months. I was driving stuff right up to Scotland, Stornaway, and back down to Lands End. And once . . .'

After a while Mrs Herbert broke in:

'I wonder what your family make of all this? I mean, you've had some very remarkable jobs, haven't you? What do they think of it all?'

Lorry at once looked woebegone. Speaking tragically now, she replied:

'My folks are dead. My Dad was killed in a pub down in Stepney where we was living. This Dago, he pulled one of them flick knives on him. He used to beat me and my Mum up something terrible. It's that what killed her off. Died of a broken heart, she did, and my Dad. . . .'

Mrs Herbert half listened, but, knowing most of it was lies, let her mind wander. Getting the truth out of Lorry, she could tell, was going to be a long, hard job needing a series of lengthy, intimate conversations. Yet she must be wary of appearing to single Lorry out too much; for even Wing Governors were not immune from slander in a gossip-ridden place like Collingwood.

'That was the time I was working in this betting shop, see?' Lorry was saying. Suddenly, Mrs Herbert had an idea. She did not know what working in a betting shop involved, but the job sounded vaguely secretarial. Perhaps Lorry really had been doing something of the sort and knew a bit about office work? Why not get her elected as the new secretary of the Inside Out Committee? The former secretary had been released while Mrs Herbert was away on sick leave, and the committee allowed to lapse. It should not be difficult to arrange for Lorry to replace her. If Lorry were secretary of the Inside Out Committee, she could legitimately summon her for frequent discussions, ostensibly about Committee business. So, when there was a suitable pause in Lorry's monologue, she said:

'I wonder, by the way, how much you know about the Inside Out Committee? I don't believe much has been happening while I've been away on sick leave. But we must get it going again. It's entirely voluntary you know. You don't have to belong.' Lorry's interest was slightly aroused. She approved of things that were voluntary.

'What's it do? What's the point of it?' she enquired.

'Well, we do different things.' Mrs Herbert paused. She did not want to risk putting Lorry off by saying the true purpose of the Committee was therapeutic—a way of helping the women to help themselves. 'For instance,' she went on, 'we often get outside speakers, chosen and

87

invited by you women on the Committee. So far we've had—let me see—a hospital sister, a Parliamentary candidate, a painter . . . then once Mr Ramsay came—you know, Mrs Ramsay on F Wing's husband. He's a prison officer too. Then there was the Rent Officer, and someone from Marriage Guidance.' She left out the unfortunate occasion when Committee members had asked for a notorious heroin-prescribing doctor to expound on the dangers of 'main-lining'. This proposal had been firmly vetoed, with much ill feeling all round.

'And so you see,' she ended up, 'we've had quite a few interesting people in. All the invitations are sent by the Committee secretary, not by me. And we had a sale of work and small concert last Christmas. And the secretary before last ran a kind of monthly magazine for a while. There were three issues altogether, as far as I can remember.' She looked hopefully at Lorry. 'How does all that sound to you?' she said. 'Do you think you would like to join the Committee?'

'Yeah, I guess,' Lorry replied. She had looked quite animated while talking about herself. Now her face was expressionless again. Mrs Herbert gave a faint sigh.

'Well, we'll be having our next meeting after tea on Tuesday,' she said. 'I hope you'll come along.'

The interview was over.

12

MAVIS NOW REGULARLY JOINED THE GOSSIPING GROUP that gathered in Olive's cell. She opened out, and was able by this time to chatter cheerfully to almost anyone. Even the subject of Doreen was no longer sacrosanct.

One day, when Mavis was not present, Linda remarked to Olive:

'You'd never guess Mavis was the same person as come in a few weeks back, would you?'

'Yes, she's changed so much you'd never know her,' Olive replied.

'Like she'd suddenly gone and fallen in love,' Linda added with a giggle. Sheila said:

'That's just how my Elsie was when she first fell in love. Quiet as a mouse she'd always been, then along comes this Harry—'

'Yes, and my Jane . . .' The conversation soon veered off Mavis, but Olive continued to speculate about her.

Could Mavis have fallen in love? She had certainly changed a lot lately—changed for the better. But, if she was in love, surely she would have confided in her? It couldn't be anyone on Star Wing; so perhaps it was someone she worked with—that butch-looking type from G Wing, for instance, who was out in the garden too. But Olive could scarcely believe that Mavis, seemingly so normal, always going on about her children, could really have fallen for a woman. Affairs were relatively rare on Star Wing; and Olive, being a First Offender, found the whole idea of lesbianism strange.

However, Mavis was gradually, almost imperceptibly, growing fond of Lorry. As she did not think and worry so much about her children these days, nor allow her mind to dwell on Tom, a slight vacuum developed in it. More and more it became filled with thoughts about her fellow prisoners, especially Lorry.

At first, Mavis had been puzzled by Lorry. She had never before, not even at approved school, met anyone quite so like a man—or rather, a boy. After a while, she began to be intrigued. She would study Lorry and cogitate about her: how and why had she become like this? Then, as it gradually grew apparent that Lorry approved of her, she started to respond.

For Lorry, despite being so masculine, was quite unlike Tom or any of Mavis's previous men friends. She was more considerate. Tom and the others had always just taken her for granted, often treated her brusquely, and obviously considered her, as a woman, grossly inferior to themselves. Tom hardly ever talked to her. Whenever any of his friends were with him, they talked exclusively about male subjects like boxing and cars. They ignored her and never deigned to draw her into the conversation. Tom was for ever going off on benders with his mates, leaving her alone to mind the children.

Any love-making Mavis had experienced had always smacked of

rape—snatched kisses and forced necking in doorways from the various boy friends she went out with before she 'went steady' with Tom; then with Tom, sexual encounters had been, at first, ugly and painful, and later merely tedious and distasteful. Tom always made her feel like a urinal: she was just the receptacle he used for relieving his physical needs. He did not seem interested in her body at all—although, ironically, she was practically sure he sometimes visited Soho strip joints.

Before they were married, he had caressed her clumsily through her clothes; but as soon as they were married, he did not seem to care any more about her body, or indeed any part of her. Evidently the pre-marital caresses had merely been to stimulate her, and not because he himself really cared about her. All he wanted was to plunge into her; and the moment he was legitimately entitled to, he did.

Mavis did not often allow herself to think about their first night together—it was too painfully disappointing to remember. There had been no preliminaries whatever. Tom had not even bothered to undress himself, much less arouse her with initial caresses. Once they were in the bedroom, he had undone his fly, pushed her back on the bed, wrenched down her knickers, and simply shoved his cock into her. It had been much the same ever since. Whenever he was in the mood, Tom simply took her, roughly and abruptly, as though she were just a bit of property. He had never once seen her naked; and she had never, since their marriage, experienced the flicker of an orgasm with him.

Lorry, on the other hand, was gallant. She appeared to value Mavis, not disdain her, for being a woman.

'Here, Mavey, give me that,' she said one day as they were setting off to do some hoeing. She took Mavis's hoe and propped it on her shoulder as well as her own. 'Can't have a little wisp of a thing like you carting great heavy tools around, can we?' she added. 'You'll do yourself an injury!'

'Oh, how you go on!' Mavis responded, embarrassed but gratified. After that, Lorry nearly always carried her tools or pushed her wheel-barrow for her.

Another day, when Miss Foster was not about, Lorry crossed the garden to where Mavis was working.

'Madame,' she said with a sweeping bow, 'allow me to present you with this fabulous bouquet.'

'Oh, you're a one, Lorry!' Mavis said with a pleased giggle as she accepted a small, stolen bunch of marigolds.

Lorry gave her cigarettes too, and once a packet of shampoo, bought out of her meagre weekly earnings. Unlike Tom, she seemed to want to make conversation; and, in time, she stopped talking exclusively about herself. She talked about Mavis too.

'What's it like then, Mavey, having a whole bunch of kids?' she asked. 'Must get you awful tired. No wonder you're such a thin little bit of a thing.' This encouraged Mavis to start on quite a lengthy account of her children and her day's work with them. Lorry interrupted her:

'Yes, but your old man—don't hear much about him. Don't he never give you a hand?'

'Oh Tom, him, he does his share,' Mavis replied. She was reluctant to tell Lorry about Tom, and said nothing more for the moment about her family.

Mavis began to speculate about Lorry as a lover. How did she make love? Would it be a kind of attack, as it was with Tom? Or did Lorry set about it in a kinder, gentler way? And what did she, or any lesbian, actually do? Perhaps, whatever they did, it was less painful and more satisfying than what men did—anyway, it could hardly be worse.

They were returning to their wings after work one day when suddenly Lorry flung her arm casually around Mavis's shoulders. It was a comforting gesture, and at once Mavis felt warmer and safer. Being in prison gave her a faintly unreal feeling, as though she were a bit of fluff floating about at random in a vast vault. Lorry's interest and approval acted as a kind of ballast: made her more substantial; no longer a nobody lost among a host of other nobodies. Lorry's arm laid across her shoulders helped her regain a sense of personal identity. A warm needle of pleasure ran through her loins. She recognized it as the same feeling that Tom, long ago, had sometimes induced in her with his gauche, pre-marital caresses.

Later, one Sunday morning, Mavis suffered a sharp twinge of jealousy. Star Wing were out on exercise and happened to pass by the G Wing women ambling round their stretch of lawn. Lorry was strolling along with her arm round the shoulders of another woman, talking to her so animatedly that she never noticed Mavis. Perhaps,

Mavis thought sadly, this was a habitual, impersonal gesture of Lorry's. Or was she taken with someone else? For the first time, Mavis fully confessed to herself that she was attracted to Lorry and hoped the attraction was mutual.

In fact, Lorry was deliberately being cautious with Mavis; not rushing things for fear she frightened her off. For, after all, Mavis was obviously a normal wife and mother. Before long, with any luck, she would 'turn', just as many of the others did in Collingwood, whatever their lives were like outside. Mavis might even, like some of the rest, start chasing her, bribing her with sweets and cigarettes. Not that Lorry wanted this. She didn't mind being kept in fags by someone like Mary in the kitchen who didn't interest her; but it was different if she felt at all deeply involved. Then, she preferred to be the giver and do the wooing. It made her feel more potent.

And she was, she knew, getting involved with Mavis, even though at times she found her a trifle irritating and boring. Just what Mavis thought of her she could not tell. Mavis had opened out lately—was sometimes a positive chatterbox. Still, there was a certain fascinating reticence about her. She seemed to be full of closed doors. This was intriguing; it was challenging. Lorry was determined to win her. It should not be too difficult, provided she played it cool. There was plenty of time ahead. Lorry enjoyed keeping her girl friends in a state of uncertainty and suspense. It boosted her sense of manliness: increased her effectiveness and sharpened her pleasure when eventually the affair was consummated.

The hot, dry summer passed with little bad weather to prevent Lorry and Mavis working outdoors. But one day, all the heat curdled into dense, slate-grey clouds, which presently streamed down in a summer torrent. At the first intermittent drops, Lorry hurriedly shoved her mowing machine into an outside lavatory. She herself took shelter in a small greenhouse.

Silver rivers poured down the sloping glass panes above her. Outside, the world appeared to be made of metal: everything was dull steel, like a pallid television film. The rain strands, silhouetted against the prison masonry, were fine wire, projected down from the sky to stab the recumbent earth like surgeons' needles penetrating awaiting flesh.

Battering the glass above Lorry, the rain drops sounded like a hail of bullets. She felt sure the glass would soon be shattered to small, glittering splinters, sharp and lethal as the rain wires outside. She felt practically defenceless; preserved from the fury of the rain merely by the brittle transparency surrounding her. She was sitting in the centre of a bubble, which any minute would be pierced and burst, leaving her to the mercy of terrifying outside forces.

In some way, this was like her own life, Lorry thought vaguely, as she looked out over the garden. She seemed to be perpetually threatened by menacing powers, for ever in danger of being destroyed, shielded only by some thin, barely-existent screen, fragile and invisible as glass.

Then she stopped staring away into the rain-chilled distance and studied her immediate surroundings. Although the glass walls were invisible except for their criss-crossing lines of white woodwork, she got a sense of protection from the rampart of shelves, boxes, flower-pots and gardening bric-à-brac which rose waist-high up the sides of the greenhouse. Within her glass retreat, she felt safe for the moment. Inside, all was rich and humid, lit by the flame of geranium petals, and warmed by the cosy glow of stacked flower pots. The air was heavy with the sultry spice of tomatoes glimmering orange and green, like tinted electric bulbs, amid their tangle of foliage. The warm, damp earth and the heap of crumbled soil beneath the staging seemed pulsating and alive compared with the flat, steel world outside.

A rubber hose pipe, which coiled and stretched along the beaten mud floor, then writhed away into the shadows under the staging, became, in Lorry's mind, a snake in the jungle—a dense, dank jungle. She forgot about being in a bubble and started to imagine she was in a womb, all red, moist and safe. From here, her mind followed a connecting line of thought straight on to the subject of Mavis—Mavis as a person, and Mavis as a body.

She was embarking on a sexual reverie about her, when Mavis herself suddenly appeared running through the rain towards the greenhouse.

Seen in the middle distance, her buttonless, black mackintosh fluttering open like wings, its crinkles polished by the rain to darting silver highlights, Mavis looked wraithlike—a fitting character for the monochrome film Lorry felt she had been watching as she stared at the garden. And, as she approached, Mavis certainly appeared to have been severely attacked by the rain. She was shrunk into the voluminous mackintosh, huddled down as far as she could go behind the stiff, turned-up collar. Her head was bent, as though struck down by the rain; her usually fluffy hair soaked to dark, damp strings; her clenched, bleached hands straining to hold the mackintosh together in front of her and prevent it flying wide open as she ran.

Watching her, Lorry felt passionately protective. She badly wanted to hold her in her arms; dry her; stroke her; soothe her with a warm, close embrace; defend her for ever from the hostile elements outside— outside the greenhouse and outside in the world. She felt as she had a week ago when they found an injured pigeon cringing in a fluster of bedraggled feathers on one of the window ledges. They had tried in vain to calm it and gently coax it back to health.

And so, as Mavis hurried into the greenhouse, she instantly noticed that Lorry was looking at her in an unusual way. From the wooden box on which she was seated, leaning forward a little, her hands clasped between her knees, Lorry stared up at her, her eyes slightly glittering with the moist intensity of her look. She did not immediately utter her customary, boisterous greeting, but just continued for a moment to study Mavis in silence.

Her expression was searching, almost pleading. It was also, unmistakably, a trifle sensual. Mavis knew at once that Lorry cared for her, possibly even loved her. Somehow she could tell too that Lorry had just been thinking about her body, undressing her perhaps in her mind. The needle of pleasure ran through her loins again. Knowing now that Lorry desired her, she glanced away out through the glass for a second, too shy to continue gazing at Lorry in the prolonged silence.

Then, as pleasure overcame her embarrassment, she allowed herself to look back at Lorry, this time with a slight smile. And Lorry, in her turn, had never before seen just this expression on Mavis's face, not even when she was rhapsodizing about Doreen. You did not very often see this sort of smile in Collingwood, where much of the joking, grinning and giggling was forced or hysterical. But Mavis's shy smile now, tilting up the corners of her lips engagingly and tracing lines of humour beneath her eyes, was genuine. The glint in her eyes as she smiled was the reflection of some lamp shining warmly within her. After a moment, Lorry responded with her broad, boyish grin.

'Right old down-pour, isn't it?' she said cheerfully. 'You look drenched, kid. Come and sit down over here till it's eased off a bit.' She pulled another box next to hers, and Mavis sat down on it beside her, still huddling into her mackintosh.

'You're shivering, honey,' Lorry said. She inspected Mavis with concern, then, quite naturally, put her arm round her and drew her closer.

Mavis could not remember having ever before felt so warmed and comforted, and at the same time so loved and physically aroused. Glancing round the greenhouse, she felt as if she were away in another world—at the bottom of the sea, surrounded by shimmering water and lush submarine plants. Or perhaps she was safe and sheltered in a warm, glass fish tank full of elegantly waving water-weed. She had always associated dryness with pain and moisture with pleasure—it was why she licked her lips so hard at moments of stress.

'This reminds me of a time when I was a kid down on the farm,' Lorry said pensively. 'There was pouring rain just like this—unexpected, you know, right in the middle of summer, in the middle of a heat wave. There was hail too. And we was all out helping with the hay-making, and had to run into the barn to take shelter. All crowded together among the straw, we was, and Dad told us ghost stories. Ever so creepy it was, and there was thunder too, and lightning. I'll never forget it. . . .' Her voice tailed off dreamily.

For once it had not been a tall story. In this moment of protective security with Mavis, she forgot all about the need to create a dramatic impression. She forgot that, according to earlier accounts of her childhood she had given Mavis, she had been orphaned and misunderstood; a tough East End kid, who had passed as a boy and roamed the streets with a gang of other boys, breaking into shops and warehouses, sleeping in a leaky, abandoned barge on the Thames.

However, Mavis did not notice the discrepancy. She was luxuriating too much in her own sense of being warmed and loved to pay close attention to what Lorry was actually saying.

'Your hair's soaked,' Lorry remarked 'It's gone all dark and exotic, like you'd given it a rinse.' Her voice sounded lower and huskier than usual. Presently, she stroked her fingers through Mavis's wet hair strands.

The needle pierced through Mavis's loins again, almost painfully this time. No one had stroked her hair lovingly and gently like this

95

since she was a little girl; and when, a moment or two later, Lorry buried her face in the top of her hair and moved it slowly to and fro, the needle became a crowbar working and jolting inside Mavis till she reached a peak of excitement.

She put her arm round Lorry's waist and squeezed her, quite involuntarily. Lorry at once lifted her head. She put her hand under Mavis's chin, raised her face, and looked at her wonderingly. She had not realized Mavis felt like this. She had never given any sign of it before; yet now, Lorry could tell, she was, with next to no preliminaries, ready for her.

It was, after all, going to be much easier than she had anticipated; and, for a second, Lorry felt a flicker of disappointment. The longer the wooing, the more difficult the conquering, the greater the triumph when the battle was finally won. But her faint disappointment was soon dispelled by the knowledge that came to her as she looked at Mavis, that here, at last, was a woman that really loved her for herself; who genuinely liked her, Lorry. Mavis was not just a married woman hunting for a makeshift cock, doing the best she could until the moment of her release, when she would joyfully rejoin her man. She was in love with her, Lorry.

It was a moment of swift intuition. Lorry could not have said how it was that she could instantly assess Mavis's feelings so acutely. Possibly it was Mavis's sudden tight grip round her waist that told her; or else the expression of combined tension and relaxation that she discerned as she studied Mavis's face.

For Mavis's eyes were now closed by the intensity of her feelings, which demanded that the outside world be screened off. Her very slightly parted lips looked taut, yet expectant and potentially yielding. They were full, yet delicate, like the rest of her features; and just now as invitingly pink and moist as other parts of her should be at such a moment.

Experimentally, saying to herself that these lips were set elsewhere in Mavis's body, Lorry put her forefinger between them. To Mavis, this was a surprising, not particularly stimulating gesture. She opened her eyes. Seeing her puzzled expression, Lorry smiled and did what was expected of her: placed her mouth on Mavis's, slowly obtruding the tip of her tongue, then working it right into her mouth.

Mavis relaxed in Lorry's arms, relishing the kiss. It was much more satisfying to her than any man's kiss had ever been—less rough, abrupt and brutal. Lorry's kiss began lightly and gently, gradually working up to a crescendo of lip pressure and tongue movement. It was lingering, with a rounded off completeness that Mavis had never experienced with a man. And the skin round Lorry's mouth was smooth and creamy, matching her caress—much kinder than the bristly harshness of a man's face.

After a moment or two, Lorry raised her head. She looked down at Mavis staring intently back at her.

'I really go for you, baby,' she said in a low voice, 'you really send me—those crazy lips of yours, and your eyes. You're way out, kid. . . .' She paused. Her words seemed inadequate. Then she said simply, 'I love you, Mavey, really I do.' And it was the first time she had ever meant the statement so sincerely.

She became aware of the slight, steadily accelerating vibrations in Mavis's body; the involuntary movement of her expectant limbs. She rested her hand on Mavis's breast for a moment or two, kneading the flesh slightly, then lowered it to start the search for those other lips.

The moment she began, however, the sun, that had been fighting off the clouds for the past few minutes, suddenly won through. A wan shaft of light pierced the glass and played over Mavis's pale face, carving it here and there in polished ivory.

Reluctantly, Lorry sat up. A greenhouse was not after all the ideal place for having a scene. They had the whole garden at their disposal, full of bushes and sheds. The greenhouse may have been all right so long as it was pouring with rain and everyone taking shelter; but now the sun was out again, a prisoner or officer might suddenly appear and catch them at it. Further intimacy with Mavis would have to wait. Lorry sighed and drew away from her. Mavis opened her eyes and looked at her with baffled disappointment.

'It'll have to wait, baby,' Lorry explained. 'See, the rain's stopped, and Foster or some other screw could come along any minute.' She saw with pleasure and pride how frustrated Mavis was, and added consolingly: 'There'll be plenty more times and places, you'll see. We'll figure a way. Trust me.'

As soon as she had spoken, they both saw Miss Foster approaching across the lawn.

'You may as well go back to your wings now,' she said, 'it's almost dinner time. And this afternoon I want to explain to you, Lorry, what I want you both to do when I go on leave next week. You two will be in charge till I get back—I've arranged it with the Chief. I'll only be gone a couple of weeks, so not much can go wrong in that time.'

Ignoring the implied insult, Lorry replied jovially:

'You'll find we make it into the Garden of Eden while you're away!' She turned to Mavis and grinned happily.

13

SO LORRY AND MAVIS BECAME LOVERS. THEY KEPT THE garden tidy enough to satisfy any officers who might be interested. The rest of the time, they lay together; sometimes, when they felt carefree, in a dense shrubbery tucked away in a remote corner of the garden; at other times, when they were feeling more cautious, or it was raining, in a small potting shed. As a precaution, they would wedge the door from inside, and set an old bench against it as a barricade. There was just enough space for them to lie side by side on the ground on some sacking at the foot of a garden roller and a collection of extinct mowing machines.

The half light, let in through the one minute, grimy, window-pane, revealed Mavis's face again as an ivory carving. Lorry would lie studying it, delicately tracing its outlines, looking down at Mavis, full of wonder because she had never felt so intensely about anyone before. Then she would give Mavis prolonged, probing kisses. And Mavis, in her turn, would be full of wonder because she had never before so enjoyed being kissed.

Lorry's love making, like her kissing, was gentle and gradual, as Tom's had never been. There was nothing rough or abrupt about it.

Lorry did not force her way into Mavis, but put her hand on her and caressed her for minutes on end until she was fully aroused and ready for her. Sometimes, she put her face right down on her, offering a degree of personal intamacy that Mavis had never imagined before. When, finally, Lorry went into her, she was not tight and dry, needing to be prized apart, as she always was with Tom, but wide open, wet and waiting. And the acuteness of her final excitement made her welcome, rather than resent, the vigour, now verging on roughness, that Lorry ultimately worked up to. For, to achieve satisfaction herself, to feel for a moment wholly masculine, Lorry had to press down on Mavis with all her might, and work to and fro with a force that would have been painful to Mavis were it not the peak of a gradually achieved crescendo.

During those two weeks, when they were working unsupervised and alone together (the Finns had been deported), Lorry and Mavis got to know each other well. They became friends as well as lovers. Lorry, by degrees, stopped pretending and telling lies; she found she no longer needed to act a part all the time.

'Why are you, you know—like you are?' Mavis asked Lorry one day, as they were sitting smoking together among the bushes.

'Why am I bent, you mean?' Lorry responded. She drew deeply on her roll-up and stared unperceivingly ahead of her. She did not know the answer, or thought she did not. Then, as she continued to stare ahead, the scene before her began to impress itself upon her consciousness.

The silver glitter of breeze-stirred sunlight on the evergreen shrubbery almost reminded her of something. So did the glimpse of prison wall and turret, seen through a gap in the bushes. Jaggedly framed by the silhouette of sparkling foliage, hazed mauve and made distant by the summer afternoon light, the prison looked, at that moment, mysterious and romantic, like a childhood castle.

That was it—something far off and long ago; to do with her childhood; to do with the shiny balls on the Christmas tree she had always craved but never been given; and something remote too, exciting and majestic, seen only vaguely in the distance, and surrounded by an aura of light, yet always unattainable.

The answer to Mavis's question was contained somewhere in this. But it was only a feeling, not an explanation—nothing she could put into words or offer to Mavis as a rational reply to her question. So, after silently drawing on her roll-up for a minute or two, she merely said stallingly:

'Why's anyone anything? You trying to tell me it's queer to be bent?' She was momentarily annoyed with herself for being unable to answer Mavis, consequently annoyed with Mavis for asking the question.

'Well, I mean not everyone is,' Mavis replied hesitantly.

'Damn near everyone is,' Lorry said harshly, resenting the suggestion that she was abnormal. 'Just look around you. Use your eyes. *You* are—' and Mavis was taken by surprise, as it had not struck her that by letting Lorry make love to her she had become queer. 'And Mac is. Half the screws are, and nearly all of us cons. People outside—nine out of ten of them are too.' Then, carried away by her own exaggeration, and, in her moment of indignation, reverting to her former habit of lying, she stated. 'As for our precious Wing Governor—she's so fucking bent she's just about bent in half. She really fancies me, you know. You should just see the way she looks at me sometimes. Always sending for me for cosy little chats, isn't she? You think it's all about the Inside Out Committee, but it's not. Talks about us meeting after I get out.' Swept away on a tidal wave of mendacity, Lorry continued '—like Miss Francis did after I went out last time. Chased me for weeks. I met her once, and that was enough. But the letters I got from her, the messages from people coming out! Even came up the West End looking for me one night. Went through all the clubs, they told me, till she met Dolly, who gave her a right earful. That finished her.'

Lorry tailed off. She had a dreamy distant expression, as though she had been talking to herself rather than to Mavis; trying to impress herself this time, even more than her audience, with grandiose fables.

For this was one of her persistent fantasies, repeated so often in her mind that by now she herself half believed it. To be pursued and desired by any woman was gratifying, but if a prison officer, a figure of authority, wanted her, that would be doubly gratifying. There was a tasty spice of irony about the imagined situation—she, Lorry, the reprobate, yearned for by someone who epitomized all the proper, accepted, lawful attitudes that she had rebelled against for years. Then, when in her mind she rejected all the overtures of the craving officer, she would be giving the world a good kick in the balls; getting her own back for all the kicks she had suffered in her time. For while, of course, she was glad and proud to be a lesbian, yet at the back of her mind she was also ashamed. And it was somebody's or something's fault that she was one, for queers as a whole were despised by most people in the outside world.

Mavis felt, for the first time, slightly indignant with Lorry. She was ruffled over being called a lesbian herself; also Lorry might at least have tried to answer her question. If she was not prepared to tell her the vitally important thing about herself—why she became a lesbian— then they could not, after all, be as close to each other as she had supposed. And why must Lorry start telling her tall stories all over again?

Mavis had not minded when, to begin with, Lorry was obviously often lying. She herself was apt to exaggerate and put up a bit of a front with strangers and casual acquaintances. But she had taken it as a compliment when, soon after they became lovers, Lorry's accounts of herself and her doings became less colourful and more credible. So now she felt affronted. Surely Lorry did not expect her to believe this unlikely tale about an officer chasing her through the West End? She deserved better than this from Lorry by now. Mavis had told her deeply personal things about her own life that she had never before confessed to anyone: about her unsatisfactory marriage with Tom, her own father's brutality to her mother; about her sense of guilt over preferring Doreen to her other children; about her terror and misery when she was taken away from her mother and sent to a children's home. In return, Lorry had certainly, as time went on, told her many things about her own family and childhood in the country, and her various jobs in different towns. She had even told her about her previous girl friends. But she had never yet told her the most important thing of all about herself; and now that Mavis had asked her to, she had simply stalled, then told her this silly story about herself and an officer.

They were both silent for a few moments. Then, once Lorry had finished savouring her account of the yearning officer, and allowed her attention to return to her immediate surroundings, she noticed Mavis looking at her in a peculiar way. Mavis, as a rule gentle, loving and out

to please, was glaring at her. Her usually reticent expression was tight-
ened into indignation; her eyes were wide open with crossness. Lorry
was puzzled.

'Have a fag,' she said. Ignoring the offer, Mavis said abruptly:

'Why don't you tell me the truth? Don't you trust me? Why do you
keep telling me all those stupid stories? As if a screw would do that!
Do you do it for kicks or what? I've told you all about me and Tom,
but you don't tell me nothing about yourself, Lorry, nothing that really
matters.'

For a second Lorry felt deeply insulted. Why should Mavis have dis-
believed her story? She was about to retort angrily when she saw the
shiny crossness in Mavis's eyes turn liquid and start to well out and
slide down her face. Instantly, Lorry's whole body was soaked with
tenderness. It was the first time she had seen Mavis cry, and it made
her feel protective and loving as never before.

She put her arm round Mavis and consoled her for a few moments till
she stopped crying; then she said thoughtfully:

'Honestly, I don't know why I'm bent, Mavey, honest to God I don't.
That's God's own truth.' But no sooner had she said it than she began
to latch on to snatches of her past that might be relevant. 'There was
the farm, you see,' she said ruminatively. 'Farming's man's work.
I guess I always wanted to be able to do all the heavy stuff like my
brothers and the men, and I always tried to, like. Strained my back once
loading hay. And I hated my sister. She was Dad's favourite. . . . And
I always wanted to go to sea. Crazy about the sea, I was. Nearly got
drowned once, Bank Holiday on the beach at Skeg. Only I couldn't
go to sea, could I?—not properly as a sailor I mean because I wasn't
a boy.'

'But what about, you know, sex?' Mavis persisted. Lorry looked at
her helplessly.

'I don't know,' she replied. 'I always liked girls—big girls—more
than boys—I mean I liked boys my own age more than girls because girls
like my sister were daft. Then there was this big bloke when I wasn't
much more than a baby. Made like he was going to pee into me in the
hay loft—any road that's what I thought he was after. I hated him.'

She stopped, and Mavis nodded. She could tell that Lorry had at
last done her best to answer her question.

'Yes, I see. But please don't go telling me stories any more, Lorry,' she said. Her look was so pleading that Lorry drew close to her again and put her arm around her. Soon they were making love.

So Lorry stopped telling lies when she talked to Mavis. She was frank with her as she had never been with anyone before. The search for truth about herself, and telling it to Mavis, who in her turn confided more and more intimate things to Lorry, deepened the feelings the two women had for each other. It was the first time either of them had really been in love.

14

MISS HEWSON WAS STANDING ALONE ON THE TOP LANDING, gazing dismally around her. The lofty bleakness of the wing, the metal bars, stone floors and dull yellow paintwork, epitomized the dreariness of most of the inmates' lives; also of her own as their wardress. Her job appeared to be purely custodial: standing guard over the women and bossing them about. And when she was not giving orders, she was herself receiving them from Mac or some other senior officer. The whole job was wearying and futile—not at all what she had expected.

From somewhere down the wing, came a burst of raucous laughter. She could hear the group of women seated in the circle of chairs down on the flat chattering and joking. They all seemed surprisingly cheerful, Miss Hewson thought resentfully. Really, as prisoners, they had no right to be.

It was a Saturday evening, and, before long, a number of women assembled round the record player to dance. Miss Hewson watched disapprovingly as the all-female gathering, grotesque in drab, ill-fitting dresses, relaxed and danced, singly or in pairs, on the ground floor of the gloomy wing. Her envy was disguised as disgust—disgust over the incongruity of the scene. For the crowd of women, swaying and posturing to the beat of current pop hits in this ill-lit, now shadowy, rather sinister-looking setting, appeared like some macabre arabesque of lost souls in the halls of the dead.

She focused her attention first on the strained, split skirt of old Maggy, who was grossly over-weight, and should surely just be sitting quietly in the Television Room. Then she noticed Dora's burst-open, button-missing bodice, and Beryl Hunt's absurdly brief, thigh-revealing skirt. She wondered that Beryl, who was in her late forties, dared to go flaunting her varicose-knotted legs like that. And there was Lorry, with her tattooed arms and knee-length stockings, making a pathetic effort to look masculine as she flung herself energetically about.

For some while, Miss Hewson stood watching them all, growing steadily more and more jealous and depressed. At seven-thirty sharp, she went to the Television Room and switched off the set.

'Right, show's over, girls,' she said unusually briskly. There was an immediate chorus of protest:

'But it's the middle of the film!'

'Can't we have an extension?'

'It's Saturday. Miss Whittaker always lets us stay up late Saturdays.'

'Blood cloth woman!'

'I said, show's over. Time you all went and got your water,' said Miss Hewson with surprising firmness; and, for once, was fairly promptly obeyed.

Then she went down to the flat and, without saying a word, switched off the record player. It was gratifying to end the dance simply and abruptly like this. If she could not bring herself to relax, join in the dance and enjoy herself (as Miss Whittaker sometimes did) then surely no one else had the right to either.

Back in her own room later on, Miss Hewson felt a little uneasy. For she was here to reform the women, not punish them, so oughtn't she to want them to be happy and enjoy themselves as much as possible?

To make amends, she resolved next day to carry out Mrs Herbert's instructions and tackle Rose. She had been pleased and flattered when Mrs Herbert enrolled her in her unofficial therapeutic team; nevertheless, she had been putting off her initial encounter with Rose. It seemed such a difficult undertaking, and she felt nervous and uncertain about how to start. Besides, Rose herself was so nasty—if only Mrs Herbert had asked her to take on somebody else.

She need not have worried. It was not difficult to draw out Rose, who was even more ready to disgorge a spate of information about herself to an officer than to her fellow prisoners.

Miss Hewson had decided to make her first approach to Rose after dinner. Rose had just been brushed off by a group of women whose conversation she had interrupted. Their snub had been so blatant that even Rose, usually obtuse and impervious to insults, could not ignore it. Now she was sitting by herself at one of the small dinner tables, doing a crossword.

She was bored and disconsolate, not fully concentrating on the crossword; so she was pleasantly surprised when Miss Hewson, having approached her cautiously from behind, suddenly laid her hand on the back of her chair and said:

'You like doing crosswords then, Dawley?' Her voice was staccato with forced brightness.

'Oh, you gave me quite a shock, Miss Hewson!' Rose responded with a startled giggle. Sensing that Miss Hewson was out to be friendly and make conversation, she immediately seized her opportunity and started to pour out a great gush of words.

Rose's need to talk was like a reversed voracity: she was perpetually famished to gabble words out. Lately, her appetite had not been sufficiently appeased by Jan and her other fellow prisoners; so now, almost as soon as Miss Hewson had spoken, the momentary startled look on Rose's face was replaced by a ravenous, greedy, even slightly obsequious, expression.

'Oh yes, Miss Hewson,' she replied in a spluttering rush, 'I'm just crazy about crosswords.' (Although she was not.) 'Do you like doing them too?' Not waiting for an answer, she continued at full speed, 'I've always done them ever since I was a little girl, and do you know —I won prizes for them at school. And for drawing. My teacher always used to say, "Rose is my little artist". Art was my best subject—except for English and geography. I always came top in those. I got lots of prizes. Did you like school, Miss Hewson?—I hated it to begin with, then I got to love it. I made so many friends, you see, and joined Guides and was a prefect. Then there was games—they elected me netball captain and I won the swimming cup and. . . .'

She went on like this for some minutes, until Miss Hewson began to feel it was proving almost too easy: no skill at all was required to get Rose talking. She did not stop to wonder whether or not Rose was telling the truth. Indeed, these days, Rose's whole pattern of thought and conversation had become such an intricate web of fact and fiction that she herself often hardly knew when exaggeration turned into fabrication.

After this first, apparently successful talk with Rose, Miss Hewson embarked on a series of conversations with her—or rather, listening sessions, for Rose seldom gave her much opportunity to speak. As a result, Miss Hewson gained a sense of purpose and became happier and more relaxed. But although the prisoners now treated her with somewhat greater respect, they disliked her still more. It would have been different if she had singled out some less unpopular woman. But Rose was so hated, also feared because of the trouble she stirred up, that some of these feelings now rubbed off on to Miss Hewson. There was no knowing what tales Rose might not be telling her during the long periods when she was on evening duty and Rose slouched in the office doorway talking incessantly with an avid expression on her face.

'Get this scene,' Lorry said bitterly to a cluster of women in the Television Room one evening. She spoke in the tough, contemporary tone she always used when holding forth to a group. 'Just get this. There's this cunt, this fucking grass, Dawley, or whatever her fucking name is. And there she is propping up the fucking office door like a bleeding cow's arse. And I come up to ask Hewson to turn the box on, don't I? And I overhear this cunt say some name—won't mention who's —but I hear her say it. So I turn round and cut in real quick, "I don't dig that, baby, I don't dig that at all. Don't you go mixing it on this wing. We don't dig fucking grasses here—nor fucking screws neither who carry on like fucking spies"—and by Jesus, they both shut up quick and turned red as fucking sausage meat.'

She paused and someone else took up the narrative, describing a similar incident.

'We ought to say something to Mac,' Beryl Hunt suggested.

'Don't be daft,' Rob rejoined. 'Do you want to go and be a grass too?'

'Any road, Mac don't dig grasses,' Lorry said. 'What I think is, we ought to fix the cow ourselves.'

So two nights running Rose found, on retiring to her cell, that every-thing was topsy turvy: the bedding chucked about; the pictures ripped off the walls and replaced with lewd, threatening messages; the chair and table knocked over; books and paper torn and scattered; the jug of water spilled all over the floor. She complained, of course, to the officer on duty, who reported the matter to Mac. At tea-time the second day, Mac made one of her rare formal speeches to the wing.

'Now listen here, all of you,' she boomed. 'Someone, some of you've gone and messed up Dawley's cell. Doesn't matter a tinker's curse to me who's cell you turn over—could be the Queen's for all I care—but I'm not having this sort of carry on on my wing. You're on G Wing, remember—supposed to know how to behave yourselves. And don't think I don't know who's done it . . .' (they didn't) 'so if anything like it happens again you'll all, the whole lot of you, miss your associa-tion at the weekend.' They knew she meant it, so they did not wreck Rose's cell again.

'I guess there's nothing much else we can do,' Lorry said gloomily after tea, 'and I don't see as we can do much about Hewson either. I'm not one for this complaining about screws jazz. Too much fucking trouble, and they always beat you at it in the end. We've tried fixing Dawley, haven't we? Smashed up her cell an' all, and what have we got out of it? Bugger all—fucking confined to fucking cell all fucking weekend if we aren't careful.'

'We might try something at Group Counselling,' Bett suggested. 'That's the time to stir it a bit ourselves and fix that pair of gits. Shouldn't wonder if they wasn't knocking on themselves, the way they carry on together.'

Everyone laughed; but in the end no one did raise the matter at Group Counselling. They did not, after all, know for certain what Rose said to Miss Hewson, and it was not easy actually to prove that anyone was a grass or that an officer made favourites.

Miss Hewson herself was growing more and more weary of Rose's outpourings. At first, Rose went into interminable, repetitious detail about her appeal.

'You see, it's like this, Miss Hewson,' she would say. 'If I get leave to appeal but lose, then I've still got a very good chance, haven't I, to take it on to the Three Judges. Mr Penfold says I've got a cast iron case—I'm bound to win. But, if I don't, I can go to the High Court, or even the House of Lords, and then. . . .'

Miss Hewson just said yes and no as she strove not to let her thoughts wander. Presently, Rose branched out from the day-to-day details of her appeal to broader aspects of her case. She was innocent. She had been framed.

'The point is, Miss Hewson,' she said, 'seeing those letters were all planted and I couldn't possibly have known. . . .'

But all this diverged so much from the information in Rose's case paper that Miss Hewson was forced to the conclusion that she was a liar. Reluctantly, she admitted that she had got nowhere with her. If Rose could be so consistently dishonest with her, it showed that so far no bond of confidence whatever had been forged between them. She made one or two futile efforts to get Rose on to more interesting and useful topics.

'Did you have a lot of friends—a best friend—at school?' she ventured on one occasion. 'I mean, you say people have, all your life, planted things on you—like those letters in your case this time. But did this happen at school too, or were people friendly there?' Rose was seldom caught off her guard. She had no intention of telling Miss Hewson just how hateful her school days had been—besides, earlier on, she had said just the opposite. She staved off the question by reverting to her case.

'It wasn't that they actually precisely planted the letters, you see,' she said hurriedly, 'it was this incriminating powder they put down—a kind of bait like, or trap . . .' and off she went again. This time, Miss Hewson, like Jan, simply switched off and stopped listening.

Then at last Rose herself seemed to get tired of her case. She began to talk about other people. Miss Hewson tried repeatedly to get her back to more personal matters, even at the risk of further monologues about her appeal—but in vain. Rose seemed to have surrounded herself with an unscalable brick wall. Perhaps she did not want to submit to the humiliation of being rehabilitated. Whatever the reason, she now embarked on a course of verbal cookery.

Standing in the office doorway one evening, she said in a hushed, hurried voice.

'You know, Miss Hewson, you want to watch Dora Brown. She's always in and out of the girls' rooms. And you know how they're all going on these days about their fags getting pinched. Well, only yesterday I saw Dora with my own eyes coming out of Bett's room with a whole packet of Senior Service. And you know she doesn't usually go visiting Bett, and anyway Bett was in the Television Room, and Bett says her fags have been pinched.'

Sneaking had been deplored at Miss Hewson's school.

'Yes well, Rose,' she said, 'I can't really do anything about this I'm afraid. After all, it's what most of you are in here for anyway, isn't it?—stealing of some sort or another.'

'Not *all* of us,' Rose replied righteously. 'I just thought you might like to know. I mean, you do need to know what goes on on the wing, don't you?'

'I daresay,' Miss Hewson answered tartly, 'but I'm perfectly capable of seeing what goes on for myself, thank you, Rose.'

'Oh well, I was only trying to help,' Rose muttered, then changed the subject.

Miss Hewson was no longer merely bored by Rose's dissertations; she positively dreaded them. She tried to avoid Rose, but Rose was determined and not easily kept at bay. By now, she needed Miss Hewson's interest and attention far too badly to be able to see how much Miss Hewson disliked her. She would plant herself firmly in the office doorway whenever Miss Hewson was in there alone. Miss Hewson was trapped.

The trouble was, Miss Hewson did not know what to believe or what not to. This did not greatly matter so long as Rose talked exclusively about herself, but once her stories began to be about other people in Collingwood, Miss Hewson was in a perpetual dilemma. If what Rose told her was true, ought she to act on the information? Should she, for instance, tell Mac what Rose had said about Dora stealing Bett's cigarettes? She did not want to. She was alarmed of Mac and these days kept away from her as much as possible. Ought she to tell Mrs Herbert? But if she did this, she would be in trouble with Mac for 'going over her head'—one of the most serious misdeeds a junior officer could commit. Anyway, she did not want to offer Mrs Herbert a collection of insalubrious facts divulged to her by Rose about other people; she wanted to report good progress in her therapeutic efforts with Rose.

So, for some time, Miss Hewson did her best to ignore and forget the unwelcome information Rose continued to force on her. After all, what did it really matter if Rob managed to pinch a bit of cheese from the kitchen now and again, or if Dora, cleaning the Chapel, took an occasional swig of communion wine? If only Mrs Herbert would send for her herself for a discussion about her work with Rose, then she could legitimately tell her all these things. But Mrs Herbert had decided to let a week or two pass before having a 'case conference' with her and Miss Rigg.

Unfortunately, Rose's allegations began to grow more serious.

'Did you know, Miss Hewson,' she said one day, 'that those women over in the Phone Shop really know their stuff? Gail Carter used to work at English Electric or somewhere before she bashed up that woman—that's how she knows all about waves and electronics and things.'

'Oh yes,' responded Miss Hewson in a bored discouraging tone. She did not look up from the report she was writing.

'So, well, the other day, someone on Star Wing was telling me, Martha Fry it was—Gail's on Star Wing,'—Rose rambled on that 'they'd actually gone and managed to fix up some sort of radio set or something out of old bits of telephone they pull to pieces. And they're using it to talk to the 'Ville men working down in the yard. Might even be able to use it to help escape over the wall mightn't they?'

'I very much doubt it,' Miss Hewson replied shortly. She did not believe this tale. Rose was momentarily disconcerted by Miss Hewson's cold response. For once, even she could detect her displeasure. However she soon started off again.

'Carol Simon, you know, Big Carol on F Wing,' she said, dropping her voice conspiratorially, '—works over in the Hospital. Took over from me when they moved me on to painting. Well she does out the Clinic. And do you know what? Sister Barnes doesn't even keep the medicine cupboard locked. So Big Carol, gets all these pills and stuff: phenobarb, soneryl, largactyl—the lot. That's why she's always got a buzz and acts queer like. She and some of the others had a real freak out last Sunday, Nelly Smith was telling me.' She paused and looked expectantly at Miss Hewson.

'Mmm,' she stalled. In an even more conspiratorial tone, Rose added:

'And they do say Sister Barnes actually gives them to her—gives them mind—in return for you know what.'

Miss Hewson raised her head. She looked hard at Rose for a few seconds. Then, deliberately adopting a quizzical tone, answered:

'My, you're a great story teller aren't you Rose! What got you this way, I wonder?'

'It's not a story. It's God's own truth,' Rose expostulated. 'If you don't want to believe me you needn't—but I'm telling you, it's true.'

'I daresay,' Miss Hewson rejoined sarcastically. She could not think what else to say. Perhaps the story was true; perhaps both were. If so, she debated later, shouldn't she report them? But then, if they were false, how silly she would look. What would Mrs Herbert, Mac and the others think of her? She would be a laughing stock. Still, as neither story was about anyone on her wing, perhaps she need not bother about them. She was a G Wing officer. What happened elsewhere was none of her business. So she persuaded herself not to pass on what Rose had told her.

But she was so torn and guilty about the matter that her health and behaviour were affected. She became even more tense and withdrawn, lost her appetite and could not sleep at nights.

Her colleagues, including Mac, began to notice her perpetually strained look and the insomnia shadows under her eyes.

'Won't last long, that one, you mark my words. She'll pack it in any day now,' Mac said to Miss Whittaker one morning as they both sat observing Miss Hewson from the glass office. She was trying ineffectively to hustle a group off to the kitchen to fetch the dinner. 'I've seen that sort before,' Mac went on,—'brittle as twigs. No give in 'em. They snap sooner or later. Usually sooner.'

Miss Hewson did continually wonder whether she ought to hand in her notice, but somehow could not bring herself to do this either.

15

JAN DID NOT BECOME ACCLIMATIZED TO ROSE AS A WORK-
mate; she found her increasingly insufferable. Her words penetrated
all the barriers Jan tried to put up. They chased her attention down the
by-roads along which it tried to escape, caught up with it, collared it,
and pulled in forcibly back to where she wanted it. And the place where
Rose wanted Jan's attention was nearly always somewhere unpleasant.

Endless prattle about other people was bad enough (Jan despised and
was bored by gossip), but it was still worse when Rose went on about
herself. Jan could tell she was perpetually out to impress her, and that
she was expected to respond. When Rose paused in the middle of some
extravaganza about herself, Jan always wanted to come out with a
crushing rejoinder. So far she had not done so. She could not afford to
risk seriously alienating Rose.

There was one thing to be said for Rose, however; she had recently
been wise enough to keep off the subject of Lorry. Even Rose could see
that maligning Lorry would be the surest way of spoiling whatever
friendship she had with Jan.

As time went on, Rose grew more daring. Her sessions with Miss
Hewson had increased her self-confidence. If she could win Miss
Hewson, then surely she could also win Jan? And it was important to
her to have Jan because she needed to reassure herself that she was not
doomed to be inevitably and universally disliked. So she stopped gossiping about others so much and talked about herself—or rather, herself
in relation to Jan.

One morning, she said ingratiatingly:

'You and me've got an awful lot in common, haven't we, Janny?'
Jan gave a grunt. She was smacking great brush-loads of paint as hard
as she could against the brickwork, hoping she spattered Rose in the
process. She worked savagely and haphazardly, not caring whether
the paint trickled down over the mock wainscoting.

Rose continued in a hushed, confidential tone, 'Smashing, working together like this, isn't it?—I mean it makes all the difference, working together with someone you feel, you know, about, doesn't it?' Jan drew her lips into a firm line and decided not even to grunt a response this time. But Rose was not put off. 'They call this job the honeymoon sometimes, don't they?' she persisted, 'because, you know, all the opportunities like it gives for painters working in pairs like this in separate cells all day. And someone told me that they specially went and put Miss Thomas in charge of this job because she turns a blind eye—doesn't keep coming poking around and checking up on you.'

'Don't be ridiculous,' Jan replied curtly, 'it's against the rules. Anyway, the Governor wouldn't encourage an officer to encourage anything like that'—although in fact she thought Rose was possibly half right: lesbianism was condoned by a good many officers, including Mac, who seldom barged into anyone's cell without first giving a warning knock.

'Oh I don't know . . .' Rose answered, tailing off vaguely. An argument was the last thing she wanted just then, so for a while she was actually quiet as she tried to think out something to say next.

Jan continued to slap angrily away at the wall. Rose was going too far. Her determination to have an actual affair with her was by now unmistakable. She would have to do something about it, even at the risk of gravely upsetting her.

She was right: Rose had decided the time had come to have a scene with Jan. It would really link them together and suppress the faint nagging doubt in Rose's mind about whether Jan actually did consider her a friend. Besides, it was high time she had an affair with someone, man or woman, it did not matter which. Rose was ashamed of herself for still being a virgin at twenty-seven.

So she did not allow herself to see how unresponsive and sullen Jan had become. Presently, she resumed chattering about other people, trying, as she talked, to work out the best method of approaching Jan and putting the question. All at once, she turned from the wall she was painting, stuck her brush back in the pot, and crossed over to the wall where Jan was working. Standing a little behind Jan, she put her arm around her neck and tried to twist her towards her.

'Oh Janny,' she said effusively, 'couldn't we, you know? We could right here. No one would ever catch us.'

Although Jan had been expecting a proposition from Rose sooner or later, she was caught off her guard at that moment. She was not prepared for a sudden physical gesture from Rose. She would have expected her to say something, then she could have staved her off with reasoning and argument.

The unexpected contact of Rose's bare, faintly pimpled arm with the flesh of Jan's neck acted like an electric shock. Instantly and automatically, Jan cringed down and away from her; and, as Rose tried to tug her round to face her, she resisted. But Rose was determined, and Jan so taken by surprise that she did not immediately muster all her strength to resist. Soon Rose had managed to swivel her round. In a hushed, sibilant voice, she said:

'Oh Janny, me and you. Let's have a scene. Let's do it.'

A waft of pungent, sour breath struck Jan; so did a speck or two of spittle, as Rose's mouth was just then over-salivated with emotion. During the horrifying moment in which Rose's slightly cross-eyed face was turned to hers and began lo toom ever closer, Jan noticed the cluster of blackheads at the corner of her thickish lips, now pouched and parted with unmistakable, revolting intent. She saw the thicket where her unplucked eyebrows converged above the bumped bridge of her pore-pocked, spongy nose; the wisps at each corner of her mouth; the collection of spiders' legs sprouting beneath the base of her practically chin-less head. She studied these details so intently, and saw them, during that brief moment, so clearly, that she missed Rose's over-all expression of determination and stubbornness, oddly mixed with uncertainty and desperation.

Had Jan seen this look, she just might have pitied Rose and realized that she was pathetic rather than hateful. As it was, just before Rose's mouth reached hers, she wrenched herself free, and, her voice rasping with rage and disgust, she exclaimed:

'You filthy slag! Filthy, phoney pussy-plater! Get away from me. Don't you dare ever to come anywhere near me again!' She stood stock still, staring at Rose from a few feet away, holding her paint-brush limply at her side, careless whether it stained her trouser leg. Jan was so shocked and revolted that, for a moment, she felt sick. She stood there rigid, as anger and nausea seethed within her.

Rose slumped back against the wall, stunned by the violence of Jan's response. Jan's eyes were transmuted by fury and hatred into small, sightless glass discs, flashing like torches with rage from within. For a second, Rose thought Jan had turned into some terrifying science fiction figure.

Then Jan regained self-control and suppressed both her anger and the upsurging vomit. Her eyes came back to life, and she focused them on Rose so keenly that Rose felt she was being painfully X-rayed. She cringed and shifted a step or two further away. Then, in a low, even tone, Jan said:

'You know you're the most odious, despicable person I have ever had the misfortune to encounter. Everyone loathes you, including your precious Miss Hewson—only you're too vain and blind to see it.' Then, her words falling like steady, well aimed blows on Rose's mind, she went on, dropping her voice still lower, 'Do you know what you are? You're a bore, a cow, a liar, a gossip, a grass and a creep.'

Rose, too cowed to look at Jan, bent her head and, because Jan's words were too painful to listen to, tried to shut them out by counting and comparing the different coloured paint blobs that had dripped on to the canvas-spread floor.

'Well, I've had just about enough of you,' Jan stated after a moment or two's silence. She stooped down and gathered her painting materials together, then walked purposefully out of the cell. She clattered off down the iron staircase to the first landing, where Miss Thomas was having a leisurely tea break.

'Take me back to G Wing, Miss Thomas,' Jan said peremptorily. Miss Thomas looked up in displeased surprise from the magazine she was reading. More humbly, Jan added: 'I can't cope with this job any more, Miss Thomas, really I can't. It's too much altogether. I'll just have to get a transfer.' Miss Thomas was taken aback.

'Don't be absurd, Carruthers,' she replied. 'I can't just single you out and let you stop work early for no good reason. I'd have to let everyone else who felt like it do the same whenever they fancied, wouldn't I?'

The words came out like a gramophone record. Then Miss Thomas scrutinized Jan. She looked slightly hysterical. Probably she was not malingering and something really was wrong. She looked as though she might explode at any minute. It might be as well to get her back to

G Wing before she ran amuck and poured buckets of whitewash all over the freshly painted cells, or worse.

'Well, all right, Carruthers,' she said dubiously. 'I'll take you back this once then. I must say, you don't look too well. I'll tell Miss Macpherson you came over queer suddenly. But I expect,' she added with a trace of malice, 'you'll be locked up for the rest of the day.'

'I don't mind. I'd be delighted if I were,' Jan replied with relief. Miss Thomas took her back to her wing.

16

MAVIS HAD NOT NEEDED TO LICK HER LIPS FOR SOME time. Her love affair with Lorry was making her happy and secure. The days passed now, not as drudgery, but as an agreeably ordered routine, spiced with the pleasure and excitement of Lorry's company at work.

Lorry remained gentle and loving; and, as they were left relatively unsupervised in the garden, even after Miss Foster returned from leave, there were still frequent opportunities for love-making. They did not have to suffer the frustrations of many other Collingwood couples who did not live on the same wing as each other, hence could only snatch kisses or clinch in clumsily abrupt embraces for a few moments at a time in lavatories or semi-private corners of the Laundry, Work Room or Jam Factory. Mavis and Lorry were lucky. There was nothing squalid about love-making in the garden; on the contrary, this setting made their affair seem romantic, fresh and innocent.

But one afternoon, as Mavis sat in the visiting room awaiting the arrival of Tom, her lips were so dry that they felt almost fluffy. She licked them repeatedly until they began to feel flaky and sore. Miss Whittaker, supervising someone else's visit across the room, noticed her. She mistook Mavis's lip-licking for sensual anticipation of the one permitted kiss from visiting husband or boy friend, and she was wryly amused. She could not tell from Mavis's expressionless face that a flood of dread was rising and surging inside her—so furiously that she badly needed, all at once, to go to the toilet. It was too late for that however. In a few seconds, Tom would be sitting before her.

A few weeks ago Mavis had, mechanically and without much reflection, addressed her first Visiting Order to Tom. A husband was the obvious person to invite—in her case he was about the only one to invite. Anyway, at the time she sent out the order, she had not yet become so deeply involved with Lorry. Nor had she seriously expected Tom to come. He had not troubled to answer either of the letters she had written to him, and the period for which the Visiting Order was valid had by now nearly expired. So Mavis got a shock when, as she was hoeing a flower bed on her own that afternoon, a Red Band arrived with the message that she had a visitor.

Without thinking much about the matter lately, she had assumed Tom would not accept her invitation. Surely he didn't want to see her again. No doubt he was glad to be rid of her. Probably the woman over the road was helping to look after him—she had always fancied him and aggravatingly sung his praises to Mavis. Very likely he almost lived in the boozer these days and had taken up with a score of other women.

Since the start of her sentence, Mavis had not permitted her mind to drift on to the subject of life after her release. She could not imagine what it would be like, and, at the back of her mind, had felt fairly certain that Tom would not be waiting for her: her whole life would be disrupted.

In time, as her affair with Lorry progressed, Mavis had stopped thinking about Tom at all—or about any of her friends and relations outside, including, eventually, Doreen. She talked freely and frequently about them to Lorry, and this seemed to exorcize her need to think or worry about them any more.

Her bond of communication with her children had melted so gradually, however, that she had not even noticed its disappearance. It was only now, as she sat at the small wooden table in the bare visiting room, waiting for Tom to take his seat opposite her, that she suddenly realized with shame how remote the outside world had become; how little thought she had given to it lately. Collingwood had become her world—chiefly because of Lorry, who was the dominating, only really important person in it. It was largely on account of Lorry, however, that now, sitting waiting for her husband, Mavis felt so guilty and uneasy. What if he somehow detected what she was doing? He would be disgusted and contemptuous. She felt she could not bear to face him.

She had to wait about ten minutes before Tom was finally conducted in. It seemed much longer to Mavis, sitting poised on the edge of her straight, wooden chair, muscles taut as though she were about to take flight. Her anxiety accelerated into nervous dread. Her tongue rubbed her lips faster and harder. Her heart throbbed like a motor, her finger tips drumming the table top in time with it. Inside her shirt, a trickle of sweat slid insidiously down her left armpit. She could feel blood and enzymes coursing through the tubes of her body like petrol in a revved-up engine. The momentum of her dread increased to the point where it was about to become terror—terror so acute that she would feel compelled either to spring up and try to rush out of the room, or give up and collapse on to the floor.

Just before she reached this pitch of terror, however, Tom entered the room, accompanied by Miss Hewson, who was to supervise the visit. Mavis more or less reverted to normal. Her extreme fear subsided into agitated nervousness at the sight of Tom, so familiar, yet after this interval in which so much had happened to her, curiously strange.

Tom himself seemed cowed rather than brash. He walked into the room with his head slightly bent and avoided looking at Mavis. All his usual bluster had evaporated. He appeared as nervous as Mavis, and this somewhat reassured her. Miss Hewson indicated the chair on which he was to sit across the table from Mavis; and he thanked her with extravagant, almost servile gratitude.

'Well duck, how's things?' he eventually forced out with artificial brightness, making himself at last look at her. His look was wavering however, and he kept glancing away, as if his real interest were focused on another visit being conducted on the opposite side of the room.

'Oh, all right, I suppose,' Mavis replied vaguely. 'How's things with you?'

Her mind now felt a blank. There were many questions to ask Tom: questions about the children; about how he himself was managing; about the court case for not having a TV licence; about the insurance for the damaged car (the subject most likely to engage Tom's interest); about the leaky roof and the re-housing. But now, suddenly, she could think of nothing whatever, either to ask him, or tell him.

Tom evidently felt the same way; for he chucked his head abruptly back, and brushed away the hair overhanging his forehead (a habitual nervous gesture). He glanced repeatedly across the room, as though to dissociate himself from Mavis and shrug off her predicament.

If only, Mavis thought, they were in private, and not in a room full of other people, either having distracting conversations of their own, or, worse, perhaps eavesdropping on hers while they waited for their visitors to arrive. And if only that stiff looking, expressionless young officer were not sitting opposite her too, a little back from Tom. Were she and Tom alone together, it might not be quite so hard to think of something to say. But how could a husband and wife, who had been separated for weeks on end, be expected to hold a natural conversation when a kind of spy was sitting practically on top of them, listening to everything they said. It was like this telephone tapping business you heard about, only worse, as now you could actually see the eavesdropper. It was impossible to forget her presence when she was sitting so close, watching your every move in case you tried to smuggle in fags or hash.

'Kids miss you—specially Doreen,' Tom volunteered after a moment or two's silence.

'Oh, how are they?' Mavis asked automatically, still not feeling sufficiently at ease to be interested in anyone or properly take in anything Tom said.

'She's at her Gran's, Doreen,' he answered, 'and the boys have gone to Bob's for a couple of weeks.'

'Oh,' was all Mavis could manage in reply.

They had a perfunctory conversation about the children for a few minutes. Then Tom, by now more relaxed, sounding warmer and less stilted, said:

'Well, so what's it like in this bleeding old dump then?—pardon me,' he added, turning to Miss Hewson with a sweeping gesture, 'What's it like in here? As bad as they say? What they give you to eat? What time do you get up? You sewing mail bags? Tell me all the dope—what you do all day like.'

Mavis was glad to be offered a specific topic. She started to answer his questions, and had just embarked on an account of a typical Collingwood day, when the stiff officer interrupted primly:

'McCann, it's not permitted, I'm afraid, to discuss details of prison life with your visitors.'

Tom turned on Miss Hewson and, with his familiar bluster, exploded:

'Oh, so it's not is it? Why in fucking hell not? Why in fucking hell shouldn't she tell me? It's her life isn't it? And she's my wife. You lot stuck her in here. She'll talk about what she sodding wants to.'

Miss Hewson did not reply; so he turned back to Mavis and said angrily:

'You go on, ducks. Just you tell me all the crap about this bleeding old barracks. We're tax payers aren't we? We pay their wages, so we've got a right to know. They can't stop you saying what you bleeding well like to your own husband.'

Mavis did not want to get into trouble, and would rather have obeyed Miss Hewson. But, as in the past, Tom's commanding tone and magnetically angry stare compelled her. She obeyed against her will, almost as if she were hypnotized.

'Well, like I was saying,' she said hesitantly, almost mumbling in a vain attempt to prevent Miss Hewson overhearing, 'they ring a bell about six, I think, and put your light on at about half-past. Then it's breakfast at seven. Then—'

'McCann,' Miss Hewson broke in, 'I can put you on report you know. It's against rules to discuss prison life with your visitors. If you don't stop, I shall have to terminate the interview.' She sounded infuriatingly unruffled. Tom and Mavis could not see the anxious flush spreading beneath her collar and up the back of her neck; nor did they realize that her swift glance at her wrist watch was a way of reassuring herself rather than because she wanted to tell the time.

Tom turned on her again. Mavis was sure he was going to hit her. He was, as she well knew, quite apt to let fly with his fists at anyone, man or woman, who provoked him. This knowledge suddenly galvanized her. The nervousness and embarrassment over meeting Tom again vanished and were replaced by alarm lest he explode uncontrollably. The alarm re-activated her brain. She tried rapidly to think of something that might distract Tom and get his thoughts onto another wavelength.

'Tom,' she said breathlessly, 'I've met someone in here who told me about a man she knows who gets hold of second-hand Yank cars and sells them ever so cheap. Second-hand Yank cars, Tom,' she repeated in a louder voice '—real bargains.'

She succeeded. The words operated some lever in Tom's mind. At once, his thoughts switched off Miss Hewson and her outrageous interruption of his conversation. Cars were Tom's passion—almost a mania. And the bigger, faster and noisier they were, the better. He was for ever on the look-out for huge, powerful cars at bargain prices; but the ones he saw that took his fancy were always too expensive.

He turned now to Mavis, his expression avid, and jettisoned a volley of questions at her about this dealer she had heard of and the sort of cars he sold. Mavis was relieved, and answered him as well as she could. Miss Hewson (although it was not evident from her enigmatic expression) was equally relieved.

Once they had lingered on this neutral, impersonal topic for a while, both Mavis and Tom found it possible to move on presently to more important subjects: to discuss family and personal matters without feeling as acutely embarrassed as they had been at first. Mavis no longer felt tongue-tied. She was able to start asking Tom a few of the list of questions on her mind. But she had not asked many before Miss Hewson looked at her watch again and announced abruptly:

'Visit over. Time's up I'm afraid.'

Mavis's mind had just emerged from the world of Collingwood. By the end of the interview, she had more or less re-entered her old world —yet with a difference: Tom seemed, unaccountably, more lovable. For the short while in which they had talked freely about the children, and how Tom was managing on his own, Mavis had, surprisingly, felt all at once closer to him than for a very long time. For a few moments, they had forgotten where they were, and that Miss Hewson was sitting listening. They had talked with some of the intimacy and enthusiasm of their courtship days.

Perhaps, Mavis reflected afterwards, Tom, incredible though it seemed, had actually been missing her. Could she all along have been doing him an injustice? Had he stayed faithful to her? And perhaps she in her turn had been missing him too. Whatever the reason, when the time came for them to part, Tom kissed her tenderly, and she responded with a warmth she had not displayed to him for many years. As Miss Hewson led Tom away, to her own amazement, Mavis found she was sobbing.

17

'THAT POLLY,' REMARKED THE WOMAN SITTING ON Olive's bed beside her, '—didn't ought to be on this wing at all, I tell you. Filthy bitch. First Offender, my foot! Been on the game for years, she has. She ought to be over on F Wing with the other hustlers.' There was the usual collection of gossiping women in Olive's cell, passing round a roll-up as they chattered.

'Ought to be in the Hospital, if you ask me,' said Linda. 'I'm sure as hell she's got crabs, the way she picks and pulls at herself. Always dragging up her skirt like that. Disgusting. She didn't ought to be in with us at all, a woman like that. Bloody nut case.'

'I mean to say,' agreed quiet-voiced Sheila, 'we may all be prisoners, but on this wing we're supposed to be Stars. I mean, we're First Offenders—a bit better than the rest, aren't we? And you should just hear the language they use over on that Admissions Wing—effing this and effing that. I had three days over there when I first come in, and it nearly finished me off, I can tell you.'

'You know what,' remarked Nelly, leaning against the wall by the door '—someone told me—Amy in the Work Room it was—that that Polly used to be a hostess—a hostess in one of them posh joints up the West End.'

'Do me a favour,' said Linda, '—that Polly a hostess! I've seen her with my own eyes in Praed Street—'

'Well whatever she is, she didn't ought to be in with us. First Offender!' someone else, sitting on the floor, cut in.

Olive surveyed her visitors with pride, feeling almost proprietorially about them, yet a shade anxious. Did they like her jar of sweet peas (sent in by her husband)? Did they approve of the new magazine photographs she had stuck up, and of her well boot-polished black floor? Was Mary reasonably comfortable squatting on it, or should she offer her her cape as a cushion? She felt slightly bothered about something, she was not quite sure what. Letting herself get drawn into the gossip, she said:

'Yes, but you know she's not in for soliciting. It's hoisting, or doing cheques or something.'

'Doing cheques, you're joking,' Linda countered. 'That Polly can't even sign her own name. She's a nut case, I tell you. Ought to be in a nerve hospital, not in here at all. Let's have a drag, love.'

'Well I think we all ought to book for the Governor about it, don't you?' said Sheila, passing Linda the roll-up. 'I mean it's not fair, is it? She ought to be moved over to F Wing. We are at least respectable here, aren't we? Who'll book for the Governor with me?'

'No good booking for the Governor, is it?' Olive replied. 'They don't do nothing for you, do they? Don't care if you get crabs or clap or anything, do they? When they give you the test when you first come in, well with me they just shoved it up my whatsname—'

'Oh, they don't care—take that new screw come on the wing yesterday. Why only this morning—' began someone else, and was promptly interrupted by Mary on the floor announcing:

'Dr Green says I'm to go in for a scrape in a couple of weeks.' This immediately launched an animated exchange about ill health.

Olive half listened and contributed occasionally. Her attention was not fully on the conversation this evening. Presently she realized what was bothering her. It was Mavis. Where was she? Nowadays, she always dropped into her cell on Saturday evenings. What could have happened to her? Was something wrong? At length, when there was a lull in the chatter, she said:

'Anyone seen Mavey? She watching the box tonight? I haven't seen her since dinner time.'

'She had tea in her cell. Said she wasn't feeling well or something,' Linda answered.

'Oh, I see,' replied Olive. She withdrew from the conversation, and, frowning slightly, thought anxiously about Mavis.

Olive felt motherly and a little protective towards Mavis, who slightly reminded her of one of the horde of younger sisters she had often been put in charge of as a child. Mavis seemed so frail and dependent, and she had confided in her about so many of her troubles. Olive was therefore worried by her absence this evening. Popular though she was, still she could not bear to lose a single one of her friends. If she did, it was as though she had lost part of her own body: she felt incomplete and frightened. It all had to do with the war when both parents and all seven of her sisters were killed in the blitz. Olive alone had survived; and she had, in a way, been searching for her family ever since.

As she sat silent in the centre of the chattering women, Olive badly wished Mavis would join them, or at least that the group would disperse so that she could go and seek her out. But the women remained in her cell till cocoa-time. Olive could not see Mavis queueing up mug in hand with the others. She meant to go to her cell, but was waylaid by someone and kept in conversation until it was too late.

Instead of reading that night after she had washed and got into bed, Olive lay cogitating about Mavis. Mavis had become one of her closest Collingwood friends—at any rate, the one who appeared to have confided most in and become most dependent upon her. Why then did she, these days, seem to be holding something back from her?—especially when the subject of husbands and sex came up. Once or twice she had even tried to change the subject. It was puzzling. Mavis couldn't really have fallen for someone inside surely? The idea was incredible —in any case, wouldn't she have told her if she had?

Collingwood might appear to be massively built, but sounds penetrated and reverberated through the hefty walls and floors as though they were made of plywood. Consequently, that night Olive could hear sobbing through the brickwork separating her bed from Mavis's. She knocked on the wall a few times, but, receiving no answering knock, presently gave up and lay wondering what had upset Mavis. She did not know Mavis had had a visit. Perhaps, she thought drowsily, she had had bad news about her children. Doreen might be ill. Then she decided to shelve the matter. Next day was Sunday; there would be plenty of time for talking to Mavis about it all then.

Mavis lay sobbing in bed for half-an-hour before she too eventually dozed off. She was too wretched even to hear Olive's knocking on the wall, much less answer it. As she wept, she tossed and turned so strenuously that the sheet and narrow blankets came untucked and got dragged askew. After a while, she curled up tight, pulling the bed-clothes back over her, at the same time winding them around her so that she felt like a bird in a nest. With her knees drawn firmly up towards her chest, she felt smaller, more compact, safer; and by compressing and diminishing her body in this way, she was also able to subdue her misery a little. Eventually, she dropped off to sleep.

She had been weeping on and off ever since Tom left that afternoon—having received permission to retire to her cell for the rest of the day. But she did not know precisely why she was crying. She was confused, not having expected to see Tom at all; and she was still suffering from the aftermath of the severe, mounting panic she had suffered as she sat in the visiting room waiting for him.

She felt ashamed of herself too, for some reason. Once her sobbing had abated, she tried to work out why—there was such a melée of things to make her feel guilty. Why, for instance, had she more or less wasted the visit with Tom? She had hardly got round to asking him about anything that really mattered: about Doreen and the other children. Could this mean that she no longer loved them so much? Then it dawned on her for the first time that these days she seldom thought about the children. And Tom himself—had she been unfair to him? He had seemed genuinely fond of her that afternoon: had talked to her quite warmly and gently once the barrier of mutual embarrass-ment between them had dissolved. His parting kiss had been tender. Did this mean that all their past quarrels and misunderstandings had really been her fault, not his. Then there was Lorry. Suddenly, Mavis felt guiltier about Lorry than anything else.

Tom's visit had been like a bright snapshot of life outside, taking her abruptly back into the past as well as forward into the future. So sharply focused and brilliant had the picture been that it seemed to have left an indelible imprint on Mavis's mind. This sudden clear awareness of the outside world made life inside appear unreal, even preposterous. Making love with another woman all at once struck her as absurd and disgusting. Whatever would Tom and her other friends and relations say if they knew about her affair with Lorry. They would be astounded, contemptuous, repelled. . . .

Like most of the other prisoners, Mavis had managed to construct an unstable shelter for herself inside—a shelter from the harsh realities both of life outside and of life in the prison itself. By joining in, accepting, in the end even becoming dependent upon the Collingwood routine, many women were able to insulate their emotions; in a sense protect themselves through sheer drudgery. In Mavis's case, the protective monotony of prison life had been lightened and brightened by the excitement of her affair with Lorry. Despite this, however, her emotional hide-out was no less fragile than anyone else's: a mere flimsy collection of brittle screens, liable to collapse and be smashed by the slightest draught or impact from the outside world.

So Mavis awoke next morning as miserable and confused as she had been the night before. She still did not want to talk to anyone. When Olive invited herself into her cell after breakfast, and, seating herself on the edge of the bed, said kindly:

'Well, hullo stranger. I've not seen you around since yesterday morning. Anything wrong?' Mavis, sprawled out on the bed, just looked blankly at her, unable to think of anything to say.

Her face was still red from the hours of sobbing; her eyes compressed to almonds by the puffed up flesh surrounding them. Despite still not knowing what was wrong, Olive was filled with pity. She leaned over Mavis and stroked the straying hairs back from her forehead. Speaking in a soft, maternal tone, she tried again:

'What's the matter, Mavey? Everyone's been asking about you, you know. Bad news from home or something?' Still Mavis remained silent for a moment or two, staring helplessly at Olive. At last she managed to stutter:

'It's nothing really. Just Tom came and visited me unexpectedly like yesterday. Kind of a shock,' and she started to sob again.

Olive was not surprised. Collingwood women frequently had bouts of weeping after being visited by relatives, even if they had enjoyed the visits at the time and had not received bad news. She did not press Mavis any more, but just remained sitting beside her for a while, holding her hand.

On the Monday after Tom's visit, Lorry greeted her with her usual exuberant affection.

'Hi, baby,' she said as soon as she entered the garden shed. 'Have a good weekend? Been missing me?' and she squeezed Mavis in a tight hug, kissing her firmly on the mouth. (By now Lorry did not bother whether Miss Foster saw her embracing Mavis—Miss Foster didn't either.) Mavis stood rigid with her lips compressed as Lorry tried to kiss her. Lorry drew back surprised and looked hard at her. 'You OK, honey?' she said. 'Don't look too good this morning, do you? Been living it up over the weekend? Had a freak-out over on Star Wing?' She paused, then, as Mavis avoided her eyes and did not reply, she continued, 'Not been two-timing me with some bird over on your grotty old wing, have you, darling?' She was merry rather than suspicious. Then she turned round to Miss Foster, and, concealing her concern with jocularity, squared her fists and remarked with mock ferocity, 'If ever I catch anyone messing with my girl, you know what I'll do?—I'll—'

'Yes, well,' Miss Foster cut her short, 'this morning I think we ought to do some watering, so, Lorry, if you'll. . . .'

Later, Lorry dumped her watering can and crossed the garden to where Mavis was clipping a bank. Seating herself beside her, she rolled a cigarette and said:

'Have a fag, Mavey.' Mavis did not look at her. She just shook her bent head and continued clipping. Lorry took two deep draws on her roll-up then, absent-mindedly, stubbed it out in the grass. She took the shears from Mavis, who did not resist, then grasped hold of her hand. Tilting Mavis's face up so that she was obliged to look back at her, she said rather hoarsely: 'What's wrong, baby? Really? Are you sick or something? It's not me is it—I've done nothing to upset you have I?' Mavis dropped her head again as soon as Lorry removed her hand from beneath her chin. She licked her lips ferociously and muttered:

'I'm OK.'

'But what is it? It's something—it must be,' Lorry persisted. 'You've never acted this way before with me. What is it, Mavey?' But Mavis could not have told her even if she had wanted to. 'Can't I do something? Please tell me what it is—I'll do anything,' Lorry tried once more. Then, as she tilted Mavis's face up again and approached it with her own for a testing kiss, Mavis suddenly gave her an unexpected shove.

'Go away will you. I want to be on my own,' she said abruptly. She picked up her shears and went on clipping. Lorry was dumbfounded. She gave up for the moment and returned to her watering.

In the days that followed, she made further attempts to find out what was wrong with Mavis and whether it was her fault—but all in vain. Mavis gave her the briefest of replies; would hardly even look at her when she spoke. At last one day, Lorry's hurt bewilderment turned to anger.

'You know what you can do then?' she said crossly after yet another rebuff '—you can just go and get stuffed.' She turned abruptly away from Mavis and started to banter loudly and flirtatiously with the new girl who had just joined the gardening party. After that, she more or less gave up trying to get through to Mavis. If Mavis had anything to tell her, then she could tell it—she, Lorry, wasn't going to make a fool of herself any more.

Mavis retired into herself. She no longer regularly joined the gossiping group in Olive's cell, and, when she did, remained silent. She resumed wandering about with her former vague, detached expression, suffering from an acute though blurred sense of loss. She strove to re-establish the bond with Doreen, but could not. The bond had been a kind of umbilical cord. It now seemed irreparably severed. Doreen and the boys had grown away from her and left her. They no longer needed her.

And Tom—could his gentleness at the end of the visit really have been genuine? Had his attitude to her fundamentally changed? The more Mavis thought about it, the less could she believe it. But seeing him again; being brought up short against the outside world, had changed her feelings about Lorry permanently, it seemed. She had had a violent collision with reality which had shattered all her love for Lorry at one blow. She became as insecure and unhappy as she was before ever Lorry and she met. She was in torment, because actually she needed Lorry's affection more than anything else; yet now, after Tom's visit, their affair seemed false and sordid.

One day, Mavis's flood of misery rose so high and became so turbulent that, to prevent herself getting completely swamped, she decided to pour some of it out. She just must talk to someone. Olive was the obvious person, so, one Saturday afternoon, when for once

128

Olive was alone in her cell, she hesitantly approached her. Standing awkwardly in the doorway, she said:

'You busy? Mind if I come in a moment?'

Olive looked up from the letter she was writing in pleased surprise. She immediately stuck the pen back in the ink-well, pulled her chair round so that she faced Mavis, and said welcomingly:

'Of course, duck. Haven't had a proper old gossip for a bit, have we? Have a fag.' She rolled cigarettes for Mavis and herself.

Mavis seated herself stiffly on the edge of Olive's bed. Now she was here, she felt dumb. She licked her lips between each shallow puff on the roll-up, alternately glancing down at the floor, then back up at Olive. Her eyes were dilated with nervousness and the effort she was making to communicate her distress through them and thus avoid the difficulty and embarrassment of speech.

Olive decided to help her out.

'You don't look yourself you know, Mavey,' she said. 'You haven't been at all yourself for a week or so, have you?' She paused, then continued, 'Are you poorly? Bit off colour, you know—'

'It's—I'm all mixed up like, Olive. Don't know how to begin to tell you.' Mavis at length replied jerkily, 'It's Tom . . . the children . . . things in here too.' She glanced down at the ground again, not knowing how to continue. Olive responded:

'Yes, duck, I know. Really gets on your wick sometimes, don't it? And being in here makes things ten times harder. Wondering about the kids. Wondering if he's off having a ball with someone else. And all the time you're cooped up in here.'

Her soothing tone and total misunderstanding of her main trouble suddenly galled Mavis. She looked back up at Olive and said abruptly:

'It's not a matter of being cooped up like. It's the people in here . . .' she petered out. Olive thought she was talking about the officers and replied:

'Yes, some of the screws are cows, aren't they. But some aren't so bad. We've to take the rough with the smooth in here, as they say, and try to make the best of it.' She was puzzled when Mavis responded:

'No, it's not the screws I mean, but some of the people.' Could she possibly be getting at her for some reason? Olive wondered.

Suddenly, Mavis could contain the flood of worry and wretchedness no longer.

'It's like this, Olive,' she began, 'you know how people can get in here—the way they can get with no men and that? Well, there's somebody I work in the garden with—I mean there was—and I'd been so miserable, and nothing was real like. But she kind of helped.' She stopped, at a loss for words. Olive nodded encouragingly, so she continued, 'I mean she, this friend in the garden, kind of seemed to help me to feel I was wanted like—you know, that somebody cared. Everyone wants that, don't they? They all do. It's not wrong, is it, to like having someone—anyone—wanting you?'

'Of course not. We all want that,' Olive agreed. She was far from clear what Mavis was talking about. And why should she have been feeling so forlorn and uncared for with her, Olive, as her next-door neighbour?

Mavis gave a discursive, disconnected account of her affair with Lorry, full of long-winded rationalizations. At intervals, Olive nodded sagely or made some appropriate remark; but it was some time before she finally gathered that her previous half-guess was correct: Mavis had been having it away with her fellow gardener.

'And so, there it was,' Mavis rounded off. 'It just seemed right—you know—like it had to be, not wrong at all. So she asked me, ever so nice mind, if I would, and we did, you know, have a scene like. Then on and off after that till, like I said, Tom came. It wasn't wrong, was it?' She looked at Olive so anxiously that Olive felt obliged to be reassuring. Smiling kindly, if a trifle vaguely, she said:

'Of course it wasn't, duck. Anyway, they've no right to shove a lot of women all together like this, have they? Herd of cows, that's what we are. Bound to get this sort of thing happen.' Mavis looked pleading, as though she expected something more, so she added: 'Shouldn't wonder if I don't go and get that way myself if they keep me stuck in here much longer. Only natural, really, isn't it, when you come to think of it.'

It was a lie: Olive did not consider it natural at all. She was still too much of a newcomer to Collingwood to have got used to lesbianism. Although down in Deptford all sorts of things went on, nevertheless Olive had always found homosexuality puzzling and repugnant. How could any woman prefer to go with another woman? There was nothing she herself preferred to a good long cock and a stout pair of balls.

Also, beneath her sympathetically smiling exterior, she was actually rather indignant with Mavis. Why had Mavis never told her all this before? They had been close enough, surely, for her to have confided in her? And how could someone like Mavis, whom she had thought she knew all about, go and let herself get involved with a queer? She proceeded to offer Mavis some gratuitous advice. Sounding now rather didactic she said:

'You know, Mavey duck, you need to watch your step in here. These butch types—they can act ever so funny sometimes. Get ever so jealous, then beat you up. I'd keep clear of them all if I was you. Down in Deptford once I knew a girl whose whole face was bashed to pulp. . . .' She continued to lecture Mavis until someone else entered the cell and they had to change the subject.

Mavis went away feeling relieved. She was deceived by Olive's apparent sympathy and understanding. At last she had been able to talk about her troubles to someone. But Olive did not feel the same way towards Mavis after this. Mavis would seek her out in order to pour forth once again all her confused feelings about Lorry. Olive did not actually brush her off, but generally contrived to be busy or on the point of rushing away somewhere. And when occasionally she could not avoid Mavis for a while, she would listen reluctantly, with a constrained expression on her face. In time, Mavis sensed she was no longer welcome. She gradually stopped calling on Olive and dropped joining the group that met in her cell.

At work, she continued to avoid Lorry, always asking to be given some solitary job as far away from her as possible. Her feelings about her were now so sharply conflicting that even the sight of her was becoming intolerable; but she was too emotionally spent and lethargic to ask for a job transfer. Before long, she became as isolated and solitary as she had been at the beginning of her sentence.

18

LORRY JETTED HER HOSE VICIOUSLY AT THE FLOWER BED.
With half her mind, she was machine-gunning a line of enemy troops;
with the other half, pondering morosely about Mavis.

Why did Mavis spurn her these days? Whatever could she have done
to make her scuttle off like a scared guinea pig if she so much as
approached her? Was it possible that Mavis had found out about the
intermittent correspondence she had kept up with Mary, the woman in
the kitchen who fancied her? Indeed, why had she kept on answering
Mary's persistent passionate notes even after she and Mavis had started
having an affair? Mary was not attractive—she didn't want to have
it away with her. Yet there it was, she had not wanted to give her up
either. She never wanted to give anyone up. Lorry needed to feel adored,
and had something of a collector's attitude towards her adorers.

As she fired the hose at one plant after another, glad when some frail
stem snapped under the force of the water, her thoughts veered
off Mavis for a moment. How many were there now in Collingwood
who fancied her?—seven, she reckoned, counting Jan and Mary, but
not Mavis; ten-and-a-half if you included the various women who
regularly made flattering, flirtatious remarks to her as they passed by
in the garden. Then there was Mrs Herbert, who was forever sending
for and having, or trying to have, little heart-to-heart talks, on the
pretext of discussing Inside Out Committee business. Lorry could not
quite make up her mind what Mrs Herbert thought of her, but she
rather hoped she too fancied her—that would bring her total up to
eleven-and-a-half.

The hose spray bowled over a cluster of columbine. Bedraggled yet
light and dainty, they reminded Lorry of Mavis. Her thoughts reverted to her.

Lorry was sincerely in love with Mavis; as in love as she was ever
likely to be with anyone. Mavis had made her, for the first time in

her life, unselfish. She had given Mavis endless little presents and done things for her. Once, she had even shielded her from Miss Foster's scorn and anger by pretending it was she, not Mavis, who had up-rooted a crop of marigolds by mistake, thinking they were weeds. So now that she had evidently lost Mavis, Lorry was miserable—not merely because she had lost Mavis's affection, but also because there seemed no point any more in being generous and unselfish.

Suddenly Lorry turned the nozzle of the hose round and directed it on herself. She was soon soaked, her clothes clinging darkly and damply about her.

'What on earth have you been doing, Lorry? I told you to water the plants, not take a shower,' Miss Foster said crossly when she saw her.

'Can water myself if I want to, can't I?' Lorry grumbled. 'I was hot.' It was not true. There was quite a cool breeze blowing, and now she was shivering. She did not know why she had sprayed herself.

Lorry was hurt and miserable that things had petered out between her and Mavis, however there was still Jan. Lorry began to see more of Jan, and they frequently went into each other's cells for long conversations, usually on subjects that had nothing to do with Collingwood. Lorry soon discovered that prison gossip bored and annoyed Jan.

'You see, Lorry,' Jan said to her on one occasion, 'the American desert, Nevada and Arizona, isn't all sand as you might imagine, like much of the Sahara. It's all covered with tufts of stuff called sage brush—a bit like colourless heather. It's got a gorgeous strong scent though.' Jan liked nothing better than to describe the foreign countries she had visited. It was not conceit; it was just that talking about far away places was a form of escape from the present dreari-ness; also, she liked to re-live her experiences by describing them to others.

Lorry was envious, but quite interested.

'What about the mountains?' she said. 'I mean like you see in Westerns. All funny and flat shaped on top—weird. Are they like that?'

'Yes, pretty much,' Jan replied. 'Those films are usually made on location I think. Yes, there are these isolated, flat-topped mountains, all blue and hazy against the grey desert.'

'What about the Rockies? Isn't that where Buffalo Bill was?' Lorry asked. And so this and many similar conversations continued for an hour or more at a time.

Lorry was a good listener—once she knew Jan well enough to stop putting up a facade and pretending she too had had all sorts of unlikely adventures. She would question Jan almost avidly about what she had seen and done, trying vicariously to share her experience. She acquired, in this way, a valuable store of knowledge, which, in subsequent conversations with other people, she was able to use to good advantage. She even managed to hoodwink Mrs Herbert into believing she really had once been hitch-hiking in Turkey, so accurate was the information she was able to produce about the country, which Mrs Herbert herself had visited.

Her conversations with Jan were not invariably travelogues. Sometimes they branched off into religion or philosophy. Jan was talking about the Far East one day, describing a trip to Thailand.

'It used to be called Siam,' she said.

'Oh, "Anna and the King",' Lorry responded. 'All full of temples and pagodas and things, isn't it?' Jan assented. 'They're Buddhists aren't they?—those Chinese and Eastern people?' Lorry went on, 'all lying on nails and not feeling them, and floating in the air and meditating. Smoke a lot of hash too, don't they? I've met some people up the West End were Buddhists—not Indians and that, just ordinary English people. Once began reading a book on it myself.'

'Yes, well you may have got Buddhism and Yoga a bit muddled up,' Jan replied.

'But they're all a good thing, aren't they,' Lorry pursued. 'I mean much better than this grotty old Jesus stuff we have here. I mean, they believe in peace and not killing and leaving folks alone and things, don't they? And these people, these Buddhists and Fakirs and that, they meditate and get in trances, just like they're taking a trip—you know, blocked or on LSD or something.'

Another time they got on to politics.

'I was on one of them marches, see,' Lorry said. 'I go on all of them. This was for Ban the Bomb and all that. It was a ball, I can tell you. Camping out. I got to sleep next to this crazy chick—'

'Do you believe in that then, banning the bomb?' Jan asked warily, remembering Paula, the infuriating peace prisoner of two sentences ago.

'Yeah, of course. Don't you?' Lorry replied. 'Thought everyone who wasn't mad did. And I believe in peace and freedom and the individual and letting the spades stay and socialism and all that. Of course I do—don't you? I'm a red.' She sounded very proud of the fact. Probably, Jan thought, all this was just veneer, a kind of political varnish intended to add a rabid, romantic lustre to her personality.

'I wonder,' Jan probed 'just what you mean. You can't have peace and freedom, you know, without fighting for them.'

'Course you can,' Lorry rejoined scornfully.

'And,' Jan continued, 'freedom for the individual is democracy, isn't it?—the opposite of socialism and communism. You can't have it both ways you know.' Lorry was getting out of her depth.

'You a bloody Tory then?' she responded.

'I am a Conservative, yes,' Jan replied stiffly, 'because I do believe in the individual. As for coloured people—so long as they stay here you won't get proper houses for ordinary English working people—so much for your precious socialism!'

'Sodding Tory. You must need your head looked at!' was all the answer Lorry could muster. She did not know how to cope with Jan's arguments; also, she could tell Jan had seen through her. It might perhaps be wise to stop pouring scorn on Jan's conventional political views, seeing she herself was incapable of countering them effectively. It was important to Lorry that Jan should have a high opinion of her. She did not want Jan to think her as dull, stupid and small-minded as she apparently considered most of the others on the wing. After that, by mutual, unspoken consent, both women usually avoided political debate.

So Lorry forced her thoughts to follow the same tracks as Jan's; compelled her interest and imagination into the same grooves. This required some effort at first, as any serious, semi-intellectual conversation did not come easily to her. But, by degrees, her mind seemed to stretch and expand until it could contain all kinds of new thought patterns. The early stages were almost painful: her mind felt like a strained rubber pouch. In time, however, as she came to feel more at ease with Jan, and was no longer striving to impress her, she began to take these novel conversations in her stride, even to enjoy them. She got more education during the time she knew Jan than ever she did throughout her ten years at school.

Jan herself enjoyed the conversations with Lorry, apart from considering them the necessary preliminaries to an affair. But the time came when she felt she ought to be taking the relationship further.

One evening, Jan stood in Lorry's cell doorway studying her as, with her back to her, she bent over the wooden table, scrubbing it vigorously, almost viciously. It was Cell Clean-up Night again, as it had been the first time she called on Lorry. Surely this was a good omen? Had the moment arrived for trying to carry their friendship a stage further? She swiftly scanned Lorry all over, allowing her eyes to linger admiringly on the narrow hips and well muscled legs tapering beneath the rolled up dungarees to slim ankles.

For some days, Lorry had been rather morose and withdrawn, apt to respond gruffly and laconically to any remarks or questions. She seemed unhappy about something, Jan was not sure what. Still, this might help. Bev, three sentences ago, had been wretched. Her need for sympathy, for someone to depend on and confide in, had been transmuted into desire for her, Jan. Perhaps the same thing might happen with Lorry?

'Not finished yet? Aren't we thorough!' Jan exclaimed. Lorry started and turned abruptly. Jan was smiling quizzically at her.

'Get banged up and lose my weekend association, won't I? if I don't make a proper job of it,' she responded dourly.

'Well, why not take a break and have a fag,' Jan suggested. She rolled two cigarettes and handed one to Lorry, then inspected her closely as she lounged against the wall with a vacant expression on her face, puffing away in silence, one hand stuck in her dungarees pocket. She was certainly unhappy. Why? Jan wondered. Could it be something to do with the girl she worked with in the garden?

'My, you are on the turn, aren't you?' she teased, smiling quizzically again. 'Really down on your luck.'

'Who wouldn't be in this fucking hole,' Lorry replied glumly. She had made a fool of herself that afternoon: made a further vain attempt to talk to Mavis, who had just looked at her with startled eyes, then rushed off without replying.

136

'What's up? Are you in any trouble?' Jan pursued, dropping the bantering tone. But she couldn't get anything out of Lorry, who merely replied defensively:

'No. Why should I be?'

She was going to have to work hard, Jan realized, if she were to break down Lorry's barrier of surliness and get what she wanted. She was certainly very upset about something, probably something quite serious. It must, she decided, be the girl in the garden.

All along, Jan had more or less known Lorry was carrying on with someone—Rose had seen to that—and that most likely it was with her fellow gardener—a fluffy little thing, quite likely to appeal to Lorry. It would have been strange if a person like Lorry had not been carrying on with anyone in Collingwood. It did not much bother Jan if she were, provided it was not with anyone on G Wing. In her opinion, it was perfectly normal for someone to be conducting two affairs at once: she would not unduly mind sharing Lorry for a while. Anyway, she was confident that she would win her for herself in the end. Already, even before they had once slept together, she had begun the process of dominating and absorbing Lorry: she had crumbled her initial gruff shyness; penetrated and shattered all her facades; forced her thoughts into the same channels as her own. It was high time they made love. She must cash in on Lorry's present despondency: make the most of her need for comfort and reassurance.

As she looked hard at Lorry, still propped up against the wall, smoking in silence, Jan, almost without thinking about it, formed a simple plan of action. They would sit side by side on Lorry's bed. Then, once she had thawed Lorry and succeeded in drawing her out, verbal sympathy should lead on to the placing of a consoling arm round her waist. This in turn would lead gradually to greater intimacy: the chummy comforting would slide naturally, almost imperceptibly, into physical passion. But she must start off, she decided, by talking about something impersonal rather than trying immediately to extract confidences or be comforting.

'I got a very comic letter today,' she said, 'from that Indian I met in Singapore—the one in the big import-export business I was telling you about. Don't know why they let me have it actually—Mac must have been in a good mood. Want to see it?'

'OK,' Lorry responded without enthusiasm. She took the letter from Jan, appeared to glance through it, then said dully, 'Yeah, charming.' Jan could tell she had not read it and was not interested, so she decided to drop the subject. Venturing on to more personal ground, she said cautiously:

'Do you get letters much? Hear from your family or anything? You've never told me about getting letters from anyone.'

'Yeah, sure, I hear from the folks and people,' Lorry lied, then pulled again on her cigarette. Clearly she was not going to enlarge on the subject. Jan tried once more.

'If they know you're in here, Lorry—your parents I mean—what do they think of it? Do they mind? You've never told me.'

It was the most personal question she had yet asked Lorry. The occasion seemed to warrant it. But again she had evidently made a mistake; for this time Lorry simply did not reply at all. She had not, in fact, been in touch with any of her family for over two years.

Jan watched her as she stood in silence, drawing hard yet jerkily on the cigarette. She puffed out the smoke explosively, not allowing it to filter with languid sophistication through her nostrils as she usually did. All at once, Jan realized that this strenuous, staccato smoking was an attempt by Lorry to prevent herself bursting into tears. Her face was flushed with the effort of restraint.

Jan was right: her question abruptly launched a slurry of wretchedness in Lorry's mind; unsuspected wretchedness (for Lorry always assumed she was quite cheerful and basically content with life). She was confused too, because while her wretchedness was to do with her family, and shame over having let them down, it was also mixed up with a host of other unhappy, although apparently unrelated, feelings, that were usually thoroughly suppressed—about her dull childhood in the country; her bad education and general ignorance (so appallingly revealed lately in conversation with Jan); her failure to get a worthwhile job and her haphazard life outside; her lesbianism and succession of unstable love affairs; her certainty about what and who she really wanted; and above all, somehow epitomizing everything, Mavis.

Jan, observing her, guessed more or less how she was feeling. Suddenly, she felt maternal as well as sexually aroused. She went over to Lorry and put her arm around her. As soon as she did so, Lorry gave

138

way. Tears ran down her face, and she sobbed and gasped quite violently, allowing herself to flop forward and lean against Jan. Jan stood still, holding her tightly round the waist, saying nothing. Then, still without speaking, she drew Lorry to the bed. They sat side by side on the edge of it, as Jan had planned. Still clasping Lorry round the waist, she said in a low voice:

'There, take it easy, Lorry. Don't take on so. Talk about it if you feel like it; or don't if you don't want to.'

Then Lorry, knowing she was being invited but not forced to speak, began jerkily to try to put into words the mixture of miserable feelings that had just been exposed and tipped all over her mind. They were too confused and obscure for her to be able to express them fully or coherently; however, Jan got the gist of them.

'You couldn't understand properly,' Lorry managed to get out between chokes and sobs '—it's my Dad, the folks—what they'd say . . . only I don't never see them now. They'd be ashamed like . . . I never got no proper schooling, see—though 'twasn't my fault.' She stopped, sobbing too hard to go on.

'Of course not, of course it wasn't your fault,' Jan said soothingly. What was Lorry getting at, she wondered. Encouraged, Lorry resumed:

'Then, you know, being queer and that—it's a ball in here, but outside there's this place and that you can't go or they'd beat you up. Once had to run for it from a gents. Then if you go to a ladies they tell you to get out . . .' she tailed off.

'Yes, I see,' said Jan, although she didn't.

'Well and then,' Lorry continued, 'nothing never stays, does it? People don't stick to you like—even the ones that really matter, like her.'

'Who?' asked Jan abruptly.

'Her, of course,' Lorry replied, 'Mavis McCann works in the garden with me. Her and me was having it away grand, then she just goes and stops. Won't have nothing more to do with me now. I don't know why.'

Jan was momentarily despondent. Lorry was evidently more deeply in love with someone else than she had bargained for. It might not after all be so easy to wean her away and win her for herself. But she was soon reassured. Lorry's sobbing abated, and she suddenly rested her head on Jan's shoulder—although whether through affection or plain exhaustion Jan could not immediately tell. A second or two later, however, when, testingly, she drew Lorry's arm round her own waist, Lorry did not resist or withdraw it.

Again they were silent for a few moments. Then, speaking in an undertone, so low it was not much more than a murmur, Jan ventured:

'What you need is someone to look after you, isn't it, baby? You've had it rough on the whole, haven't you? It's time someone cared for you.' She stroked her fingers through Lorry's wiry, close-cropped hair, and smiled at her. Lorry realized Jan was right: she did need someone to care for her—someone to initiate the love-making; to take her for a change; perhaps even to mother her a little.

'Why not let it be me?' Jan pursued. The rhythmic movement of her fingers on Lorry's scalp, combined with her hushed yet compelling tone, had a calming, almost hypnotic effect on Lorry. She looked back into Jan's smiling face with a bemused expression that Jan could not quite fathom.

Nothing like this had ever happened before to Lorry: she herself had always done the courting. Yet now, as she stared back at Jan, she could see that she had been wrong all these years. She was not quite as masculine as she had supposed, but was, after all, still a woman, boyish though she tried to appear. Much as she might disown them, she still had the glands and framework of a woman; still the empty tunnel in her emotions waiting to be entered, and the corresponding socket in her body needing sometimes to be filled.

She suddenly more or less understood why her most passionate love-making with other more feminine women had never been wholly satisfying. True, the excitement of arousing them, prising them open and penetrating them, either manually or with a dildo, had so boosted her own ego and sense of power that she had experienced orgasms of a sort. But she had been aware that her partner's physical excitement and gratification had always exceeded hers—not, however, that she herself had wanted in her turn to be caressed and penetrated. She had even slightly resented her partner's extreme pleasure, and would eventually press down heavily on her, then, regardless of whether or not she hurt her, work to and fro quite savagely until the friction more or less appeased her desire.

She knew now, as Jan leaned towards her, that she wanted what Jan wanted: to be taken by her. Her stare relaxed into a shy smile. Jan's mounting physical desire for Lorry was abruptly saturated with a great warm fountain of maternal feeling, spurting up from some underground spring in her mind. Her own unwanted daughter had never drawn up such a flood of motherliness. She propelled Lorry gently back on the bed and made love to her.

19

ROSE SAT AT THE WOODEN TABLE IN HER CELL; BUT instead of reading the library book lying open before her, she scratched and jabbed pointlessly at the rough table top with her rusty pen nib. She felt itchy, fidgetty and cooped up that evening; resenting the ugly, compressed window, more bars than thick, smeary glass; the hard seat of the stiff wooden chair, on which she writhed irritably from time to time; the battered walls, smudged here and there with the remnants of sellotape used by previous occupants, and stained by who knew what; the harsh, dingy strip of coconut matting, its pores blocked by clots of dust; above all, the hefty door, finally clanged to for the night by Miss Hewson about half-an-hour ago.

Usually, Rose was not bothered by prison drabness and locks and bars —she was too used to them. But tonight, for some reason, she felt shut in and fretful. She ought to be up and about, doing something—she did not know what.

She stuck the pen back in the china inkwell, and, for a moment or two, stirred the chunky ink dregs, as she allowed her mind to flit discontentedly from one unpleasant subject to another. The cocoa that evening had been horrible—more watery than ever; and she was sure she had detected bromide in it. It had not appeased the hunger she had felt ever since tea at four o'clock. And it had been one of the worst teas of the week: just a hunk of flaky cheese and a limp lettuce leaf to accompany the six, flabby slices of white packet bread she had stuffed into herself in a vain attempt to satisfy her hunger.

Eating too much starchy food was steadily thickening Rose round the waist. Her cotton dresses were getting more and more strained every day. Now, as she thought about this, she wriggled impatiently; then stretched, ripping an inch or so of seam under her arm as she did so.

Nor had she been able to get near the stove in the Wing Kitchen at tea time in order to toast her bread and cheese under the grill. Every time she had said it was her turn next, someone else had denied it and pushed ahead of her in the queue. Sensing no one was on her side, Rose had not dared do more than expostulate, although she would gladly have slapped everyone in sight. In the end, there had been no time for her to toast her bread and cheese at all. She had no food in her cell either to fill the gap; for she spent all her weekly earnings of four and three-pence halfpenny on tobacco and cigarette papers. She hadn't even a roll-up left, and had failed to ponce one off the potentially gullible new arrival on the wing at cocoa time.

Presently, she stopped twiddling the pen and stared down at her book. This evening, she found she could not concentrate on it—although, as a rule, she enjoyed reading. After being locked up for the night, she would skim through about seven novels a week. She enjoyed light novels in much the same way as she enjoyed gossip. Reading them made her feel like an agreeably omniscient spy.

But tonight, Rose could not take in anything. As she listlessly turned a page, she found she needed to re-read it. After a while, she gave up and simply sat gazing before her at the picture of a group of film stars she had stuck on the wall. However, she did not take this in either; her entire mind was shrouded in boredom and frustration. She did not even know why she was feeling like this.

In fact, ever since Jan had walked off the job and left her, Rose had felt so insulted and injured that for a while she had been silenced. Indignation had been submerged in humiliation so severe that she had been temporarily stunned. She went about her business in a kind of daze, hardly trying to make conversation with anyone, much less engage in gossip. Then, gradually, the humiliation had subsided and been replaced by extreme loneliness and boredom. Clearly it was useless to pursue Jan any more, so now Rose felt stranded and purposeless. She could no longer spread scandal and rumours among the prisoners, as no one on the wing would listen to her. Even Miss Hewson, she now at last noticed, was avoiding her.

So for an hour or more that evening, Rose sat at her table, doing nothing; thinking of nothing. She could not even be bothered to pour her jug of fast-cooling water into the tin bowl and get ready for bed.

Although nothing so coherent as thought was occurring in Rose's brain, a succession of feelings were forming and re-forming. Sometimes one took precedence, sometimes another; until suddenly a new shape, indignation, clicked abruptly into the kaleidoscope. And, as her feelings continued to revolve and re-set themselves, this new element in the pattern steadily enlarged till presently it predominated. Her growing resentment increased Rose's sense of impotence and frustration. She bent and stretched her forearms till the elbows cracked. Her skull felt itchy all over, so she scratched it savagely till the scalp was sore.

After a time, she heard Miss Hewson's footsteps echoing along the stone-flagged landings as she made her final round before going off duty. Immediately, all Rose's feelings, seemingly of their own accord, wrapped themselves swiftly into a tight little ball of determination. She rose from the table and stood over by the spy-hole in the door. As soon as she heard Miss Hewson stop outside her cell and call mechanically:

'Are you all right? Goodnight,' she thumped on the door and shouted back:

'Miss Hewson, can you open up a minute please?'

Miss Hewson reluctantly unlocked the door.

'Well, what is it, Dawley?' she said dubiously as she hovered uncertainly in the doorway.

'I've had something on my mind for quite some time, Miss Hewson,' Rose found herself saying, 'which I thought I ought to tell someone about—tell you about. I think you ought to know—though it isn't very nice.' She paused.

'Well, what is it?' Miss Hewson repeated brusquely. Rose, with her sycophantic manner, was a welcome scapegoat for her own frustration —a target for her pent-up aggression. 'I'm in a hurry. I haven't got all night,' she added impatiently, and turned as though about to go without listening to Rose. Then Rose said hurriedly:

143

'It's about Miss Macpherson—Miss Macpherson and Carruthers.' Miss Hewson halted and turned back.

Speaking more slowly now she knew she had Miss Hewson's attention, Rose continued:

'I think you ought to know, Miss Hewson, that Miss Macpherson visits Carruthers' cell almost every night when she's on duty. And she stays there a long time—I know, because Jan's cell's just opposite mine, and I can see the door through my spy-hole.'

It just seemed to come out spontaneously. Miss Hewson was surely bound to take this story seriously. It was Rose's way of getting her own back both on Jan and on Mac, who was for ever picking on her and making sarcastic remarks at her expense (Mac too despised grasses). She did not dare tell Miss Hewson the truth—that Lorry was carrying on with Jan—for fear Lorry took her in the recess and beat her up. Besides, it was more fun, more creative, to invent a scandal than merely report what was actually happening.

Miss Hewson listened carefully while Rose elaborated for some minutes about Mac and Jan. Then, glancing at her watch, she said non-committally:

'Yes, well thank you for telling me all this, Dawley. It's important to know about this sort of thing. Goodnight.' She clashed the door to, and clattered off down the corridor. Rose felt much better. She was almost exhilarated as she got ready for bed.

Miss Hewson had become so guilty about not passing on what Rose had previously told her about Sister Barnes and the pills and the Phone Shop women and their radio communication with the 'Ville men that eventually she had compromised: she had not told Mac, but had one day let the information slip casually into a conversation with Miss Whittaker. Miss Whittaker had quickly passed it on to Mac, who in turn had told the Chief, who told the Governor. The stories were promptly investigated and found to be true—or partially so: Sister Barnes had been guilty of negligence over locking the medicine cupboard; the Phone Shop women had contrived some sort of shaky communication system with the 'Ville men.

If these stories were, after all, true, Miss Hewson reflected uneasily, then perhaps everything else Rose had told her was true. She had therefore been very remiss not to have reported all Rose's stories to Mac.

Never again would she be so irresponsible. So, after hearing this latest tale of Rose's about Mac and Jan, she had no hesitation in reporting the matter straight away to Mrs Herbert. Indeed, she quite relished the prospect of doing so. She had a few scores to settle with Mac, who had heaped incessant rebukes, insults and sarcasm on her from the day she first came on the wing. She hoped Mac would be disgraced and sacked. And there was a chance she might be—this story of Rose's could well be true. Everyone knew Mac was queer (she lived with one of the prison hospital sisters), and she and Jan always seemed to hit it off surprisingly well.

Next day, Miss Hewson knocked quite firmly on Mrs Herbert's office door.

'There's something I think perhaps you ought to know, Mrs Herbert,' she said, speaking more clearly and deliberately than usual. 'It's not very pleasant though, I'm afraid.'

'Yes, what is it, Miss Hewson?' Mrs Herbert replied with an encouraging smile. She was always eager to receive confidences, whether from officers or prisoners. Ever since Noel, her eldest son, was killed, and her other children had grown up, she had badly needed people to pour out their troubles to her.

'Well, it's something Dawley—Rose Dawley you asked me to work with—told me last night,' Miss Hewson went on. 'Her cell, you know, is right opposite Carruthers'. I don't like gossip and that sort of thing, but, well, I thought perhaps I ought to tell you this.' She paused, suddenly finding it difficult to come to the point.

'Yes?' repeated Mrs Herbert.

'I don't like telling tales myself or complaining about my superiors and that sort of thing,' Miss Hewson continued, 'I was always brought up not to. Still, I think you ought to know this. I gather from Dawley that Miss Macpherson is in the habit of, well, going to visit Carruthers in her cell at night after they're locked up. Dawley says she's seen this through her spy-hole. It apparently happens quite frequently.' She stopped. Mrs Herbert looked at her keenly. Miss Hewson could not tell whether she had done the right thing or not. At length, Mrs Herbert said:

'I see. Thank you for letting me know, Miss Hewson. It's a very serious allegation. I shall have to think over what you've just told me.'

Mrs Herbert was careful not to let Miss Hewson see how agreeably surprised she was by this news—even slightly excited. At last she had the chance of putting Mac in her place, perhaps even of getting rid of her. But later on, as she weighed the matter up, her excitement diminished. For how could she use or even verify this information? She could hardly question Mac, and it would be a difficult, tortuous process to have her watched. Nor was it likely she would get much out of Jan, who was not the kind of prisoner Mrs Herbert knew how to help or even talk to. Jan seemed to be covered all over with a protective, impenetrable layer of polish. It was impossible to adopt a motherly or counselling tone with someone who was socially her equal, if not superior. Indeed, now she came to think of it, it was surprising, perhaps even a trifle unlikely, that such a well bred woman should be having an affair with anyone as common, vulgar and boorish as Mac.

All she could do, Mrs Herbert decided, was send for Rose herself and get her to repeat her story. If it contained any discrepancies and inconsistencies, this would indicate whether or not she should take it seriously.

Rose guessed the reason for her summons to Mrs Herbert's office, and was gratified. It was much more exciting, and made her feel important, to narrate her story to the Wing Governor rather than to a mere junior officer who never seemed to take her stories seriously anyway.

'I have just heard something rather disturbing from Miss Hewson, which apparently you told her last night,' Mrs Herbert began as soon as Rose was standing before her. 'Perhaps you would be good enough to repeat to me just what you told her.'

Mrs Herbert sat very upright at her desk and spoke primly. This interview with Rose would have to be strictly businesslike. In any case, she too disliked Rose. She disapproved of grasses, and realized with disquiet that, by getting Rose to tell tales now, she, the Wing Governor, was actually fostering a bad trait in Rose's character—the very trait that had got her into prison in the first place.

'Well, it's like this you see, Mrs Herbert,' Rose said, creasing her features into the ingratiating smile she always wore for officers. 'My cell's right opposite Carruthers', and I've seen—I've just not been able to help noticing—that quite often, when Miss Macpherson's on duty, she comes to Carruthers' room after we're locked up for the night.

Sometimes she even stays as long as three-quarters-of-an-hour there. She stopped. Mrs Herbert made no response, so she added lamely, 'I mean, I know it may just be nothing like, but I mean, you know. . . .' She tailed off.

'How do you know this, Dawley?' Mrs Herbert asked sharply. Flushing slightly, Rose answered:

'Well I've, you know, seen through my peep-hole.'

'I see,' Mrs Herbert replied with heavy sarcasm. 'So you've stood by your door have you, Dawley, for as long as three-quarters-of-an-hour on end simply in order to watch what other people outside were doing?'

'Yes, well, no—I mean, yes, but I never really—' Rose began, but Mrs Herbert cut her short:

'So you say you can see Miss Macpherson visiting Carruthers' room through the hole in your own door?' Looking hard at Rose, she noticed a split-second tightening then loosening of her expression, a glazing and clearing of her eyes. It was over in a minute however, and Rose, her tone as favour-currying as ever, answered:

'Why yes, Mrs Herbert. My cell's right opposite Jan's, you see.'

But Mrs Herbert had received her sign.

'I think, Dawley,' she said purposefully, 'that I'd better come up to your room and just see for myself. You have made such a serious allegation about Miss Macpherson that all the evidence must be carefully examined before any action, if any, is taken.'

'Yes of course, Mrs Herbert,' Rose replied flatly. She had not bargained for this, and was dismayed. She had no idea whether or not in fact it was possible to see Jan's cell door through her spy-hole.

During previous sentences, Rose had made a point of pushing back her spy-hole shutter on the outside of the door before being locked up for the night. She liked to be able to peep out on to the landing from time to time in case something was going on. This time she was unlucky. The shutter was loose and perversely flopped back into position whenever her door was slammed. Rose had never discovered precisely what was to be seen through the hole once her door was closed. Jan's cell certainly was more or less opposite hers; but the area to be scanned through the minute spy-hole was so circumscribed that, for all she knew, Jan's door was not visible through it at all.

Her anxiety mounted to dread as she ascended the metal staircase, ahead of Mrs Herbert, to the third landing. As soon as they reached her cell, Mrs Herbert told her to stand outside and hold back the shutter while she looked through the spy-hole herself.

'I suppose, Dawley,' she remarked, 'you wedge the shutter back somehow before you are locked in?' Why had she never thought of doing this? Rose wondered regretfully. 'That's against the rules,' Mrs Herbert added.

After she had peered through the hole, Mrs Herbert straightened up. She glared contemptuously at Rose, and invited her to look through the hole herself. All Rose could see was a blank stretch of wall. She raised her face, and, blushing deeply, started to gabble:

'Yes but, honest to god, even so, I could see her, Miss Macpherson, going by along the landing towards Carruthers' room, night after night. Honest to god I could, and I could hear them—'

'Lies from beginning to end, Dawley,' Mrs Herbert cut in, scathingly. 'I don't know why some of you women insist on making life even more unpleasant for yourselves than it need be by spreading scandal and making trouble for yourselves. You're beneath contempt, Dawley. It's lucky for you this business has gone no further, otherwise you'd have been in real trouble. As it is, it's not even worth punishing you for something so mean and despicable.'

With that, Mrs Herbert turned and swept off down the corridor to her own office, leaving Rose more crushed and wilted than ever before in her life.

20

LORRY FELT UNCOMFORTABLY PULLED OUT OF SHAPE: AS if she were being dragged in two or more opposite directions at once. She was made of rubber, and was being stretched so taut that surely she would soon snap. Meanwhile, she could hardly recognize herself any more. All the stretching and pulling seemed to have elongated or expanded some parts of her, while other parts were shrinking alarmingly. She tried to cover up her anxiety by periodic bursts of artificial gaiety and hilarity. At other times, she was withdrawn, morose and silent, trying to sort out her feelings and come to terms with them.

Her affair with Jan was progressing according to plan—Jan's plan. Being next-door neighbours, they had plenty of opportunities for love-making in the evenings, and at week-ends. Sex with Jan was more physically gratifying to Lorry than any of her previous affairs had been. Very occasionally, Jan got her to take the initiative; more often, it was she who lay back passively and was caressed and penetrated by Jan. But novel and physically satisfying though the experience was, it upset Lorry's image of herself. She felt abnormal: no longer thoroughly butch.

One evening, as they were lying side by side on Jan's bed, Jan said:

'Do you have to keep those dinky little tits all squashed in like that, darling? It must be terribly bad for you. It might even give you cancer.'

She began to pull the restraining girdle up off Lorry's chest; but Lorry abruptly pushed her hand away. 'What's wrong baby? Can't I see them? They must be sweet. I've seen the rest of you, haven't I?' Jan said. She had a teasing smile. She rather enjoyed humiliating Lorry.

'I wish you wouldn't,' Lorry remonstrated gruffly.

'But why, baby? After all you're a grown girl you know—and ever such a cute one. You're not a fellow. I wouldn't like you if you were,' Jan responded. Her eyes glittered with affectionate amusement as she went on: 'I like my baby as she is.' Part of Lorry writhed; part wriggled with suppressed excitement. 'Have you always had them like this?—your breasts, I mean?' Jan added, lightly marching her finger tips along the mesh of the girdle.

'Yeah,' Lorry replied, 'any road, for a few years. Keep 'em strapped back with plaster when I'm out. Looks better under a suit.' All at once she felt ridiculous and ashamed of herself.

'Oh, honey, how terrible! You shouldn't do that,' Jan expostulated. She replaced her hand on the girdle and gently but firmly rolled it back. To her delight, Lorry blushed deeply. The girdle was right up in a sort of ruff round her throat. She was exposed and naked. Lying before Jan like this, she felt blatantly and absurdly female. And her breasts, she knew, were not pretty at all; they had become limp and flaccid through years of being strapped back. Still, Jan did not seem surprised or put off by this. She placed her head between the breasts and murmured: 'Sweet, sweet. What a little silly you are. Why ever do you want to hide them.' She rubbed her face to and fro for a moment, then touched each nipple in turn with the tip of her tongue. 'You know you don't have to pretend with me, baby,' she said.

Before long, Lorry, almost against her will, was thoroughly aroused, and they were making love. She lay back with mingled shame, rage and excitement as Jan stroked and plated her. Then, when eventually she went into her, she was swept over the brink as never before.

Jan could gauge how Lorry felt. She sensed her resistance and had mixed feelings about it. While it was fun to conquer a butch, interesting and challenging to have to win Lorry anew after every bout, yet it was also rather wearying. And why couldn't Lorry, unprompted, ever take the initiative with her? After all, she herself was basically fem surely, and Lorry butch. With Bev, she had had a more balanced, satisfying affair. They had both been versatile.

These days, she and Lorry no longer seemed able to have the impersonal conversations about everything under the sun that they used to. They both missed this. There was always a subtle undercurrent of flirtation and courtship in almost everything they said to each other: wooing and resistance; seduction and repulsion. And all this was complicated by the fact that they would both simultaneously be employing similar tactics, frequently affecting an artificial, blasé, I-don't-care-if-you-want-me-any-more-or-not manner.

'How's the world then, darling?' Lorry would say, as she stood preening herself in Jan's doorway.

'No better for not having seen you since dinner time,' Jan would reply with a coy smile. 'Got a moment to spare for your poor, lonely girl friend?' And Lorry would go into Jan's cell, and fling herself down full length on the bed, announcing:

'Got to rest me aching limbs after all that hard graft with the pitch fork all morning, haven't I?'

'Oh my, great strong man, aren't we?—real big lover boy! I can't wait,' Jan would respond, half humorously, half sarcastically, knowing quite well Lorry had not lain down on the bed exhausted by her labour in the garden, but merely as an indirect invitation to her to iie alongside and start petting her. Lorry, aware of this, would feel ashamed and resentful. She would sit bolt upright on the bed and expostulate:

'Well I bloody well am tired—whacked. I've been working bloody hard all day, digging, mowing, clipping—see, just feel my arms. All muscle.' Jan would come over and squeeze her biceps.

'Lovely, darling,' she would murmur, 'super, tough.' Then she would add teasingly: 'And didn't I see you with your wee little hose-pipe too, peeing away with it, fancying you had a wee cock?'

Realizing how true this was, Lorry would angrily exclaim:

'Who's talking about cock?—I'll give you cock!'

'Pity you can't, darling,' Jan would mock her; then, with Lorry apparently about to hit her, would add soothingly: 'There, there, baby, don't take on so. You're really a cute little laddy and I'm crazy about you.' Lorry would still feel infuriated and degraded; all the same, before long, they would both be down on the bed together. There would be no talk of foreign travel or exotic religions, merely a bit more quarrelsome bantering, then Jan would take Lorry's hand. Soon, they would be in a close embrace; then Jan's hand would reach for Lorry's buttons.

However exciting the encounter was to Lorry while it lasted, after-wards she always felt flat and sulky, full of distaste for Jan and disgust with herself. Jan, on the other hand, found the affair reasonably satisfy-ing, for she had grown genuinely fond of Lorry. It was physically gratifying and gave her an interest in life. In any case, she was by now too cynical and worldly wise to expect perfection. These days, she seldom suffered anything worse than boredom, tepid bitterness, mild self-dislike and an occasional, unacknowledged sense of loneliness. Con-tradictory or ambivalent feelings would never stretch her to the limit in opposite directions as they could Lorry.

Lorry, in addition to being so confused about Jan, still badly needed Mavis. She might like, respect, even admire Jan, but she loved Mavis. Jan was so different from her, so superior; Mavis, despite her remote, elusive, almost mystical quality, felt much closer. But by now it was quite impossible to get through to her. Nothing Lorry said or did made any apparent impression on her. Mavis did not respond on the rare occasions when she tried to open a normal conversation with her;

barely even thanked her if she carried her tools for her; showed no resentment when, in desperation, Lorry tried to arouse her jealousy.

'Hiya, baby, hoochy coochy—roll on tonight, darling!' Lorry would shout with forced gusto whenever they passed by the window of the wing kitchen, where Jan was now working. She would exchange winks, knowing grins and loud flirtatious remarks with anyone they happened to encounter in the garden who had ever shown the slightest interest in her—but all in vain: Mavis never seemed to hear or notice, much less mind.

If only, Lorry thought, she did not still want Mavis, then perhaps she could let go more with Jan and make the most of what she had to offer. As it was, she felt perpetually abnormal and, in a way, a hypocrite. She needed to confide in someone about her problems. As time passed, the need mounted almost to desperation. But who was there to talk to about anything so intimate and hard to put into words? One day she attempted to express her feelings at Group Counselling.

It was a normal enough Group Counselling session. There the ten of them were, sitting in a circle with Miss Whittaker, the officer attached to Lorry's group. Mrs Herbert and the Chaplain (who circulated round the four different groups on the wing) were also present that morning. Lorry herself sat silent, slumped despondently in her chair. The usual pointless chatter was going on. For a long while, she hardly took any of it in.

'So like I was saying,' Spook grumbled excitedly, 'like I was saying to this new prat—"Do me a favour," I says, "just don't go sticking your stinking bum all over the table we're all going to eat our dinner off of. We don't all come from the slums and live in toilets." And do you know what,' she went on, her tone becoming shrill with rising indignation, 'You know what, Mrs Herbert?—she turns round and says, "An' we don't all come from the fucking jungle neither—that's where they ought to send all you fucking spades—back to the fucking jungle where you fucking belong." '

'Yes, yes, I know,' Mrs Herbert responded rather wearily. 'Very provoking, and she had no right to say something like that to you, Chris.'

She had heard this story from Spook (Chris, a Jamaican, in the third time for hoisting) so often that she knew it almost by heart. It cropped

152

up at Group Counselling at least every three weeks. The ensuing argument was apt to last so long that there was little time left for the rest of the group to pour out their deeper feelings—not that they often did anyway, but they were supposed to.

Continuing to address Mrs Herbert exclusively, although she was meant to be speaking to the whole group, Spook went on:

'Disgusting, isn't it, Mrs Herbert? No decent people would do it, would they?—go and sit on the dinner table. So I turns round and I says, "Belt up you dirty cunt. Don't you go speaking to me like that." And you know what she says to me, rars cloth woman?—she says, "You go and get stuffed, you fucking nigger,"—yeah, fucking nigger! And she lets fly at me with her fists, so all I can do is defend myself, isn't it? . . .'

It had all happened weeks ago. As far as the authorities were concerned, the whole matter was over and done with. But unfortunately, it was against the rules to stop any member of the group disgorging what was on her mind. Mrs Herbert was therefore reluctantly obliged to let Spook continue until her record expired. Meanwhile, she allowed her attention to wander.

She glanced across the circle of women at Lorry, who was unusually quiet today. As a rule, she had plenty to say at Group Counselling, even if half of it was not the kind of thing they were supposed to be talking about. Lorry looked morose. She had now drawn her skirt up slightly and was scratching some design with a pin just above the knee. Mrs Herbert was tempted to tell her to stop, but managed to refrain. For all she knew, Lorry might, at that moment, have a deep inner need to punish herself with a pin. If so, it was not her business to stop her, irritating and distracting though the sight was.

'What I think is, we should have those long tables,' another woman volunteered, '—long ones, like they have for school dinners. It would be friendlier like. What I mean is, we wouldn't always have to be sitting with the same people like we do at these little tables we've got here. Could pick and choose more, couldn't we?'

'You're joking, Maisy,' Rob rejoined. 'See us carting great twenty-foot long tables about after every meal. Charming! It's bad enough having to shove the small ones all over the shop.'

'I don't think we should have to push tables about at all,' Bett remarked. 'They're too heavy. Could do you an injury. They should send in some blokes from the Scrubs to do it.'

'Do me a favour, Bett, whoever's seen you ever helping to shove the tables?' Beryl Hunt derided. 'Anyroad, what d'you want fellows in from the Scrubs for?—thought you was happily fixed already.'

And so they continued to banter and swap superficial insults. Mrs Herbert sat in silence, wondering gloomily whether there was really much point in Group Counselling after all, even though she herself had been its chief advocate in Collingwood. The women themselves obviously did not think much of it—if what they said was anything to go by. She had overheard some of their contemptuous remarks about it; and once, when she had deliberately launched a formal discussion on the subject, Rob's immediate blunt comment had been, 'Bloody shit.' Everyone seemed to have shared her opinion, even if in different words. The women scarcely ever produced personal problems for mutual inspection and debate as they were supposed to. Mrs Herbert was not sure why—perhaps it was because none of the staff had had enough training in how to promote and lead a useful discussion. It was a pity Miss Canister hardly ever seemed to have time to attend the sessions.

She looked across at Lorry again. She had stopped scratching her leg, and was now leaning forward, staring straight ahead of her with a vacant expression, her hands dangling between her knees. All at once, the side of her face twitched twice in swift succession. Mrs Herbert was surprised; she had never noticed before that Lorry had a nervous tic. But perhaps in fact she had not. She may have recently developed one as a result of some emotional strain. Whatever could be wrong with her, Mrs Herbert wondered. Then suddenly she realized guiltily that she had not been listening to a word anyone had said for some while. She forced her attention back to the current speaker. If only it was not always so tedious. Dora, in her usual, stony voice was grumbling:

'So then she goes and takes me off piece-work, don't she?—the old cow—an' she puts me on these bleeding mail bags again. An' then she goes an' times me, don't she?—times me to see like I get enough done in an hour—same number as the others as 'ave been doing them all the time. Then when she finds like I'm two bags behind—only two mind—she goes an' puts me on report, don't she?—me as got all me fingers all pricked and bleeding from pushing that damned needle in an' out o' the cloth so's to get 'em done in time—an' what cloth!—tough as a bleeding tent. We're not in here to bloody graft. They've no right to go treating you like that, have they?' She glared across at the Chaplain, who promptly nodded his head hard and switched his features into an appropriately sympathetic expression.

Dora's contribution was also out of order, Mrs Herbert thought ruefully. She was not airing a deep personal problem—at least she didn't think she was—but merely being peevish about some trivial incident in the Work Room. Too often, she thought wearily, the women abused Group Counselling: they would make trifling complaints about some item of prison discipline—matters they should really book to see the Governor about. If only they would attack one of the prison officials actually present in the group, this might lead to useful, therapeutic discussion. Unfortunately they seldom did.

Once again, her thoughts had wandered. She must rouse herself, and, say something. The officers were supposed to take a back seat at Group Counselling and let the women talk about what they wanted. All the same, at this stage, Mrs Herbert decided, it was her duty to try to stimulate more meaningful discussion. Now she came to think of it, Dora's statement may have been the symptom of a profound mood. Trivial complaints uttered in a despondent tone served, she realized, as a sort of container for Dora's basic depression: a tightly-lidded can full of concentrated gloom. If she could once get the lid prized off, then Dora's depression would be revealed and could be extracted into the daylight, examined and dealt with.

'I wonder, Dora,' she said, looking searchingly at her, 'why it mattered so much to you that Miss Richards timed you as you worked? Did it, perhaps, make you feel at all nervous, being, so to speak, watched like that?' But Dora just looked at her as though she was a simpleton, and said pityingly:

'Well, I knew I couldn't do the bags that quick, didn't I? I'd only just started the job, hadn't I? And I knew she'd go an' put me on report if I did 'em slow.' Mrs Herbert felt rebuked. She nodded in assent, and decided to stay silent for a moment while she thought out some more sensible remark or question.

She lost her chance however. The other women quickly took their cue from Dora, and soon the session deteriorated into an endless succession of petty complaints. Mrs Herbert and the Chaplain sat back looking resigned. They made no attempt to quell the grumbling. Every now and then, the Chaplain switched on his synthetic smile. Miss Whittaker was unable to restrain herself from occasional expostulation in defence of some fellow officer under attack.

At last the women ran out of complaints and turned to gossip.

'There's this new butch type just come in,' Bett said excitedly. 'She's fab. Did her last sentence in Cranham. Works over in the Laundry. Alice was telling me all about her. Real smasher, she is. Got ever such a kinky hair do, Alice says. Bright red—bright as you ever saw—and all in crazy little curls all over her head. Alice says she keeps wanting to run her fingers through them.' She giggled, and Rob, glowering at her, said ferociously:

'She's no butch, that one. And just you mind what you do. Never mind any new fancy pants over in the Laundry, my girl. Anyway, Linda, over in Receptions, told me all about that one. She come in in a silk evening dress, what she was picked up in. And was telling some other tart, just come in too, as how she was going to turn while she was in because it pays off to be bent in here. Linda heard her say it. Butch type nothing. Tell it to the birds.'

'Anyroad, she's having it off with Daisy. Seen them walking round hand in hand together,' Beryl Hunt remarked. And so the gossip continued for a while.

Mrs Herbert marvelled at how uninhibited the women were over discussing the lesbian affairs that went on in the prison. True, everything they said at Group Counselling was supposed to be treated confidentially by the officers present. Still, homosexual behaviour was against the rules. Was it even a trifle disrespectful of them to talk about it all quite so openly when she and the Chaplain were present? Besides, they were never useful discussions: no one ever seemed to display the least shame or disquiet about what went on—going with a butch on another wing or landing was considered no more abnormal than, say, dating the boy next door. If only someone would sometime bring up lesbianism as a personal problem instead of just a piece of gossip.

At today's session, however, someone did for once express anxiety over complicated personal feelings. Lorry was, by now, staring down

156

at the pattern scratched on her leg. It was the skeleton of a Union Jack. The red and white stripes were there, more or less, but not the blue bits. She scratched away with her pin until the red crosses were properly blocked in, hardly aware of the growing rawness she was inflicting upon herself. Then she took her biro out of her pocket and inked in the appropriate triangles. Now it looked quite a neat, well finished, flag: a balanced, geometric pattern containing the right amount of each different colour. It represented all that Lorry's life was not at the moment.

The others were just then speculating about some famous butch who had recently been sent to Cranham Court. Lorry's attention was caught by what they were saying. It corresponded somewhat to how she herself was feeling just then. All at once, she wanted to join in the discussion—or rather, use it to get her own worries off her chest. After all, Group Counselling was, she knew, supposed to be the time for expressing personal feelings. And she had reached the point where she just had to unburden herself to someone, somehow, about her confusion over Jan and Mavis (Jan, luckily, was not in this group). It should be easier to hold forth to a gathering than to just one person. She would feel agreeably martyred if the group, so to speak, spat on her; while it would be merely humiliating and embarrassing to reap the scorn of an individual. It might even be rather fun to make a public confession to a whole group—a bit like acting in a play. And she quite liked her fellow group members, who did not include nasty people like Rose and Miss Hewson. Mrs Herbert was all right too, and Miss Whittaker. The Chaplain didn't count.

Abruptly, more or less irrelevantly, she broke into the gossip:

'Funny, isn't it, how you—how some people—can go with quite different sorts of people at the same time like—isn't it? I mean, like you—they—was kind of two different people at the same time themselves.'

At once Mrs Herbert was interested. Lorry was not just chattering; she was saying something about herself. Even the other prisoners were dimly aware that she had veered off idle gossip on to some more complex, personal matter. They were all silent for a moment. Then Dora said dourly:

'That's schizophrenia, what you're talking about—when people split in two like—their brains I mean.'

157

'My Gran had that,' Bett said. 'She was in the nut-house ten years with that. They tried everything on her—electric treatment, dope, the lot.' She sounded quite proud of the fact.

'So now we know why you're the way you are, love,' Hunt remarked with heavy jocularity.

Lorry was annoyed because they were all promptly sliding away from the topic she had introduced. Mrs Herbert was pleasantly surprised when Lorry forced them back to it by asking:

'Hasn't anyone here, any of you, ever felt this way at all?—kind of funny, like you was two people, wanting two quite different things at once—or people, I mean?'

As almost all of them had felt like this at some time or another, but did not care to admit it, no one answered. Again they were silent, resisting venturing out on to the quicksand of self-revelation.

But Mrs Herbert was delighted at Lorry's efforts to turn the session into real group counselling for once. She decided to help Lorry out and prevent the others from immediately changing the subject again:

'I wonder, Lorry,' she asked quite kindly, 'whether you could amplify what you've just said—explain a little more in detail what you mean?'

'Well, what I mean is,' Lorry tried, 'you might kind of have one bird like, mightn't you? and she'd be one sort of person like. Then you might kind of find you wanted someone else too—that one wasn't enough—wasn't right, like, on her own.' She halted lamely, unable, after all, to bring herself to make a clear, personal statement. Holding forth about herself to the group was not as easy as she had imagined.

'Greedy prat. Just get a load o' that!' Spook exclaimed in a mock-shocked tone. Lorry bent her head and scratched the skin on her leg a little more. She looked sullen. Mrs Herbert studied her intently. There was certainly something the matter with her. She remembered now how at Staff Meeting, Miss Rigg had remarked on how volatile she had become lately: almost hysterically noisy and vivacious at one moment; submerged in gloom the next. She would have to plumb this strange mood. If Lorry could not be persuaded to talk about herself coherently in front of the group, then she would have to have a private interview with her.

'Well, what I think is, I think it's unfair to go two-timing anyone,' Beryl Hunt stated severely.

'Yeah, isn't one bird at a time enough for you, mate?' Rob said jovially. 'It's enough for us, honey, isn't it?' and she nudged and grinned at Bett, sitting next to her.

'Though the fact is,' Mrs Herbert contributed, hoping to prevent the discussion tapering off into banter and gossip again, 'that so many people, whether in prison or not, do seem to be dissatisfied with just one partner. I wonder what it is about us humans that—'

'There's three up my street's divorced, three—' Dora cut in, while almost simultaneously Rob said:

'Yes, and did you see that in the paper yesterday about that man from Barningstoke or Barnstable or some place who's committed bigamy and . . . ?' Soon the conversation had yet again gone off at a tangent.

Lorry did not try to retrieve it this time. She just sat in silence with her head bent, looking abstractedly down at her feet, as, pointlessly, she turned her toes in and out like pieces of clockwork.

The session ended ten minutes later.

21

MRS HERBERT WAS DETERMINED TO UNEARTH LORRY'S buried problem; so, the following day, she sent for her on the pretext of drafting the agenda for the next Inside Out Committee meeting.

'I think,' she said, sounding at first quite businesslike, 'that it might be useful to have a discussion on life in the Women's Forces next time, don't you? I know someone—someone I used to be in the WRENS with —who could give an interesting talk on this. What do you think? Should we put it on the agenda for the next committee meeting?' She always appeared to give Lorry and the committee the chance of vetoing her ideas; although as a rule she voiced them so compellingly that no one dared to.

'Yeah, OK,' Lorry replied without interest. Mrs Herbert gave her a brisk, penetrating glance, as she sat beside her at her office desk, apparently poring over the sheet of paper on which they were drafting the agenda. The moment had not yet quite arrived for discarding the businesslike tone and becoming personal. She must work round to this gradually via discussion of the agenda.

'Well then,' she continued, 'we haven't had much debate lately on the problem of adjustment after release. I think—don't you?—that this should come up again now, because several people will be going out soon—Dora, Betty, Jessy.' She paused for Lorry's response, which was as bored and laconic as before; then went on, 'And poor Jessy's got gate-fever quite badly, hasn't she? You can hardly get a word out of her these days—we ought to try and think of some way of bucking her up a bit, oughtn't we?'

Again she paused. This time, she looked hard at Lorry, trying to assess whether or not the time had come to adopt a more intimate, personal tone. She could not tell what Lorry was thinking, but, as it seemed natural to slide from the subject of Jessy's gate-fever to Lorry's own present dejection, she said, speaking now a trifle more hesitantly:

'And while I think of it, Lorry, is something bothering you these days? You don't seem to be your usual self at all.'

'I'm OK. It's nothing,' Lorry mumbled. She sounded surly, but Mrs Herbert's kind tone, and her urgent need to talk about her troubles, made her suddenly want to burst into tears.

'I felt,' Mrs Herbert continued, 'that at Group Counselling yesterday, there must be something on your mind which you couldn't quite put into words. You can tell me, you know—that's what I'm here for, to try and help you. We're all here to help you, you know, not to punish you.'

As she spoke, part of her mind was remembering her son Noel. Lorry was extinguished for a moment by a picture from the past; or rather, she was transformed to fit into the picture: to become, in a sense, Noel himself on the awful occasion (awful to him rather than to Mrs Herbert) when he admitted having got some waitress into trouble, and that he was being blackmailed into marrying her. In almost the same words as she had just used to Lorry, Mrs Herbert had reminded Noel that he could tell her anything; that she was there, as his mother, to help him—that that was what being a mother meant. Saying this had so suffused her with warmth and motherly protectiveness—a kind of maternal power—that, in fact, she now recalled the occasion with pleasure rather than pain.

Lorry, at this moment, started to cry. Mrs Herbert automatically, without thinking what she was doing, ran her fingers consolingly through her hair, which, being short, coarse and sandy, was so reminiscent of Noel's that, for an instant, she forgot it was not his head she was stroking. After a few seconds, she returned to the present. Still sounding kind and sympathetic, she said:

'Well, what is it then, Lorry? Try to tell me, and see if I can't help.' Lorry did not immediately answer, so she added reassuringly, 'I can quite often be of help to you women, you know, if you'll only tell me what's wrong, what's on your mind.'

She sounded almost cajoling. Had Lorry not been feeling so dejected just then, she might have been suspicious and refused to give away anything. As it was, she felt so wretched that she would have poured out her troubles to almost anyone prepared to listen. Besides, Mrs Herbert sounded so warm and consoling, behaving rather as Jan had the time she cried just before they first made love.

Lorry's own mother had been a perpetually busy farm labourer's wife; undemonstrative and apt to be off-hand with her children. Lorry's mixed feelings later about being pursued by older women were partly due to the fact that she had never been adequately mothered as a child. Quite often, she wanted to be petted and cuddled in a motherly fashion. She felt like this now; and allowed herself to lean forward, prop her elbows on the desk, and weep freely into her cupped hands.

Mrs Herbert continued to stroke her hair for a few moments. Then, when she felt she had let her sob enough misery out of her system, she again enquired gently what was wrong. Lorry was relaxed and purged by the weeping. All her defences were down. She found herself stumblingly talking to Mrs Herbert.

'Well you know—everyone knows—I'm gay,' she began. 'Butch, you know. And I've been going with a bird, see—girl I work with out in the gardens. And it was crazy till she went and packed me up—dunno why. I mean, I was crazy about her, more than I've ever been about anyone. Really my kind of girl, she was—just the sort I go for. Delicate, you know—kind of ladylike—only not, if you see what I mean.' Mrs Herbert didn't, but she nodded wisely. 'So, well, I guess I got lonesome like after she packed me up,' Lorry went on, '—and I still want her—so but when Carruthers, Jan Carruthers—she's ladylike too, only not like Mavis——so, well, when she was like after me, I, well, kind of agreed to go with her. She's queer too—has been for years—everyone knows—but not fem exactly—at least she is and she isn't. She's a bit of a kickster really.' She stopped.

'Yes, I see,' Mrs Herbert responded sagely. Lorry could tell she had not yet really explained what was wrong. Haltingly, she resumed:

'It's OK with Jan—fine. I mean, I get real kicks from it. So does she. But we, like, do it for kicks, see, me and Jan. With Mavis, the one in the garden, it was different. Love, I guess you'd call it—though I never got quite such kicks as I do with Jan.' Again, she stopped; then at last managed to blurt out: 'It's wrong, isn't it?—me butch, and getting more kicks with Jan when I'm, like, passive?—she's older, see, and most times takes the lead. But I don't love her. She's not my sort. I love Mavis, but I get less kicks from her even though she's my type and I'm butch, not passive, with her. It all makes me feel wrong—queer.'

Despite the incoherence, Mrs Herbert gathered what Lorry was talking about. But she felt out of her depth. If Lorry had expressed guilt and anxiety over being homosexual, she would have been able to help and advise her—or so she thought. But for Lorry to be ashamed of herself for not being as masculine as she would like to be was baffling, even rather shocking.

Clearly, Lorry had no desire to reform—to become normal. On the contrary, she apparently needed, or believed she needed, to become more consistently abnormal. How could she possibly help her to accomplish this, Mrs Herbert thought a trifle resentfully. Her job was to do the opposite: to rehabilitate the women she was in charge of; try to turn them into respectable citizens. At the same time, it was, of course, up to her to get them to feel happier and more self-assured; to enable them to regain their self-respect, this being the first step towards becoming respectable. But Lorry, evidently, could feel happy and at ease with herself and the world only if she were thoroughly butch—thoroughly unrespectable. So, beneath her sympathetic exterior, Mrs Herbert was bewildered and frustrated. She had tried to solve some difficult problems in her time, but this of Lorry's was tougher than any she had so far been faced with. She did not know what to say. They both sat silent for a moment or two.

In the recesses of Mrs Herbert's mind, behind the perplexity and frustration, a secret cupboard had been opened ajar by Lorry's confession; a cupboard whose unacknowledged contents were not wholly dissimilar from Lorry's own feelings. Mrs Herbert had been impeccably feminine as a wife and mother. But there had been those days in the WRENS, when she was a tall, upstanding officer, revered and admired by many of her subordinates—even a heroic figure to one or two. How had she felt about them?—it was not something she often chose to remember nowadays. The recollection was still there, however, flimsy and blurred, stored away in the secret cupboard, very occasionally half-revealed by something someone said or did. And, when the cupboard door was opened a crack, and Mrs Herbert became dimly aware of some nuance of a forbidden thought or feeling which must at all costs be kept out of sight, she would feel tense and worried and fall silent as she strove to pull the door to again. It was so on this occasion. Only after her brief mental struggle was over, and the secret cupboard door firmly shut again, was she able to concentrate once more on Lorry's problem.

It might be best, Mrs Herbert decided, to try to get Lorry's mind off her present situation and focused on her future instead—a future which should, if possible, be conducive to normality. Perhaps if Lorry could be led into a more settled life—get a job she liked among nice, ordinary people—then she might gradually change into a normal young woman. Anyway, as Wing Governor, she ought to try to achieve this. After a moment or two, she broke the silence. In a speculative tone, she said:

'I wonder, Lorry—since we were just talking about getting the Committee to discuss adjustment after release—I wonder whether you have given any thought to your own future? What job you would like us to try and get for you?' She paused. The abrupt change of subject took Lorry by surprise, and she did not at once reply. Mrs Herbert continued, 'This may not seem to have much to do with what you've just told me, but it has really. I know you've not been in very long yet, and your release must still seem a long way off. But time goes by, and many women do, I know, find it helpful to concentrate more on the future than on the present. After all, that's why you're here, isn't it?—to prepare yourself for the future.'

Lorry looked at her crossly and still said nothing. She was in Collingwood as a punishment, and that was that as far as she was concerned. What she did in the future was her business. What right had Mrs Herbert to try to reform her?—for that was obviously what she was after. It was an insult, she did not want to be reformed. She was in prison simply as a punishment for carelessness and clumsiness over the house-breaking. She was not in the least ashamed of herself for being a thief. The people they had tried to burgle were obviously well off, while she was poor. Wasn't it right for the rich to share their wealth with the poor?—after all, that was socialism, and she was a socialist. It was also more or less what for years she had been taught at church and Sunday school. And there was nothing disgraceful about being in prison. True, she would not care for her family to know where she was—they were such good, respectable country people that they would be bound to be deeply shocked if they knew, and, for some reason, she did not want to be utterly despised by them. But her immediate circle of friends and acquaintances outside would not be shocked or surprised at all. Many of them had done time themselves.

'So what do you feel as though you might like to do for a living, Lorry, when you get out?' Mrs Herbert pursued. She sounded so genuinely interested, her expression was so sympathetic and concerned, that Lorry's momentary indignation evaporated and was replaced by her customary liking and respect for Mrs Herbert.

'I'd like something to do with the sea,' she replied, for once telling the truth. 'Always wanted to go to sea. Could I get a job as a cabin boy do you think?'

Mrs Herbert smiled at the ingenuous question, and replied indulgently:

'Well, Lorry, I wish for your sake you could, if that's what you really want to do. But I, as an Assistant Governor in a women's prison, could hardly help you get a man's job, could I?'

'But couldn't I pass?—I mean, people often take me for a bloke,' Lorry persisted.

She was presumably pleading for reassurance again about being boyish. Mrs Herbert decided to be firm and not pander to her. Lorry might well manage to look like a nice, jolly, cabin boy; still, it was up to her to try to make her face reality: accept the fact that she was a woman and behave like one. Straightening up her face, looking now stern rather than quizzical, she said:

'No, Lorry, of course you couldn't be a sailor. You may look a little more masculine than some women—but remember, sailors all share cabins.' She let the point sink in, then resumed, speaking now very deliberately, even coldly: 'We all have to face up to unpleasant truths about ourselves now and again. And what you have just got to realize, Lorry, is that, whether you like it or not, you are a woman, and no amount of disguises and acting a part can change that.' She stopped and looked hard at Lorry, who replied peevishly:

'Well I can change, can't I?—have one of those operations. I've read about them and heard about them on telly.'

Mrs Herbert decided to treat this remark as irrelevant.

'What I can and will do for you, if you like,' she went on, sounding slightly kinder again, 'is see if we can't get you a woman's job on a liner or ship of some sort. Ships have to have stewardesses, nannies, cleaners, cooks and so on. It just might be possible to find you something along these lines. How about that?'

'I don't mind,' Lorry replied listlessly. She felt cheated. Mrs Herbert had got her to pour out all her troubles to her—tell her about her deepest private feelings; yet now she had rejected her; told her to get rid of an essential bit of her character. It was like ordering a tortoise to crawl away from under its shell. She had always thought that she and Mrs Herbert had something in common, that Mrs Herbert was a bit butch herself; so she had counted on her sympathy and understanding when she made her confession.

'Well, I'll make some enquiries for you, and we'll see what we can turn up,' Mrs Herbert said brightly. 'Perhaps, if you could get a job that you really liked, all the other things would sort themselves out happily too.'

She looked hopefully at Lorry, who responded with a non-committal snort. Mrs Herbert was saying, in effect, that she ought to marry and settle down and be happy ever after. Never again would she confide in her. She didn't care one way or the other now if she tried to get a job for her on a ship or anywhere else. Let her waste her time. She wouldn't take the job when the time came, whatever it was.

The interview was over.

'So when I've got any news for you,' Mrs Herbert concluded, glancing at her watch and rising from her chair, 'I'll send for you and let you know. Meanwhile, do try and think ahead to the future and not let yourself get too downcast about life at the moment. After all,' she ended in a final, desperate attempt at cheeriness, 'life's what you make it, isn't it?'

Lorry snorted again, this time with obvious contempt. She rose from her chair too, knowing she was dismissed, and left the room.

After she had gone, Mrs Herbert sat down again and flopped gloomily forward on to the desk. She had failed. She had lost Lorry's confidence, perhaps irretrievably. She did not know why. How else could she have acted? What else could she have done? And she would have particularly liked to succeed with an intriguing, complicated prisoner like Lorry. Victory with her would have been worth half-a-dozen with the dull, flat prisoners who were far less challenging and required relatively little insight and skill on her part.

She dragged herself up from the desk, and set off drearily to hear Mac's daily report on the state of the wing.

22

ROSE FELT CRUSHED AND DEEPLY DISGRACED BY THE failure of her ploy to get Jan and Mac into trouble. However, this did not lead her to mend her ways. On the contrary, in order to allay her shame, she needed to stir up trouble more than ever. She still needed to get even with Jan for spurning her. Also, she would be only too glad to upset Lorry. It might therefore be a good plan, she decided, to try telling Lorry that Jan and Mac were having it off. If she could get Lorry to believe her, then Lorry might chuck Jan in disgust—might even beat her up. The only difficulty was, how to get hold of Lorry on her own.

Her opportunity came one evening when Jan was closeted away in her cell with a headache. Most of the others were either in the Television Room or the Wing Kitchen making toffee. Lorry was lounging back in one of the tough armchairs by the record player, scanning the paper. The only other people in sight were a couple playing a noisy game of table tennis in the centre of the flat. She must talk fast, Rose realized, otherwise someone else might come over and occupy one of the empty chairs near Lorry.

She stood hovering in front of Lorry.

'Busy?' she asked tentatively. Without bothering to look up from the paper, Lorry replied curtly:

'What's it look like?' But Rose, frightened though she was of Lorry, was not to be put off. In a rushed, breathy voice, she tried again:

'There's something I think you ought to know, Lorry—I don't quite like to tell you. It's about Jan. The fact is, Lorry, that Jan and Mac—'

'Look, do me a favour, will you,' Lorry cut in. 'Can't you see I'm reading—or trying to.'

'Yes but,' Rose persisted, 'you see, I must tell you because I'm sure you'd want to know this. Jan and Mac are having—' But she did not get a chance to finish this time either.

'Shut your bleeding mouth,' Lorry cut in again. 'I don't want to hear any shit from you. We're on to you, Dawley, you cunt. Mixing it all the time.' She glared ferociously at Rose. Abruptly, her own present dejection and confused frustration were transmuted into a great jet of rage. Rose was a welcome target. 'You know what you are?' she said in a loud, menacing voice, that would have brought the officer on duty running had it not been drowned by the shouts of the ping pong players. 'You're a fucking grass—that's what you are. And you know what happens to fucking grasses?—they get smashed. And you know what's going to happen to you now?—' She got up from her chair, her fists clenched. But Rose was too quick for her: she was on her feet and half-way over to the ping pong table before Lorry had quite finished speaking.

Once Rose was out of reach, Lorry's fury abated into muddy sullenness. These days, any fountain of hilarity, anger or excitement was swiftly quenched, smothered by a great sludge of moroseness. Staring after Rose, she just thought dully: Why bother? What was the point of attacking someone as insignificant as Rose? What was the point of it all anyway? So she just slumped back in the chair, and tried to concentrate on the paper again.

167

But Rose was not defeated. She felt even more determined to stir up trouble, preferably at Lorry's expense. She would stick to the truth next time. She would get her own back on Lorry and Jan simultaneously by reporting that they were carrying on with each other. The only snag was, almost certainly everyone on the wing, including the officers, already knew this. Still, it was one thing for an officer to know in theory about some lesbian affair going on under her nose, quite another for her to catch a couple at it. So long as she had never actually witnessed an affair in process, she could pretend she knew nothing about it— which was what most of the older, wiser officers did. But if a prisoner could firmly prove that an officer knew all about some illicit affair, then she could no longer afford to overlook it; for this would amount to condoning the breaking of prison rules, and might hinder her promotion or even cost her her job. Rose knew all this.

So, the following evening, when Miss Hewson was on duty, Rose observed Lorry's and Jan's movements closely. It was Sunday, a Free Association day. After tea, they both watched one show on television. Then Lorry and Rob played table tennis. Rose saw Jan go up to her cell. Before long, Lorry finished her game and followed her up. She pulled the cell door to behind her.

Rose drifted about for a while on the flat, to allow them time to get properly started. She did not want to risk getting Miss Hewson up to catch them in the act only to discover them having a friendly chat. She could not face another humiliating fiasco.

After a while, she decided to venture up on to the third landing and find out if she could overhear anything incriminating, or even contrive to look through the spy-hole and verify that they really were having a scene. She scampered up the metal staircase as quickly and unobtrusively as she could; then tiptoed along the landing to Jan's cell, where she paused, wondering whether she dared to peep through the spy-hole. She would never hear the end of it if one of the others caught her doing so. As various women were wandering about the wing just then, someone was quite likely to do so. So she decided to be cautious, and just stood, not quite outside Jan's cell, leaning nonchalantly over the landing rail, straining to hear what was going on behind the door. She lit a cigarette, and gazed out across the wing with a far-away expression, trying to appear as casual and detached as possible.

Jan's door was ajar. Indeterminate, muffled, occasionally sibilant sounds came through the crack. They could mean anything: either that the women were in the throes of a passionate clinch, or that they were merely having a quiet conversation. The latter was quite possible, Rose realized. She continued to stand leaning over the rail smoking for a few minutes, trying to make up her mind what to do. Did she dare risk getting Miss Hewson up here on a wild goose chase? Then suddenly she heard what was surely a vague moan. That decided her. A moan could mean only one thing.

She hurried downstairs and burst into the office, where Miss Hewson was sitting busy writing. Rose knew she must not waste time. There was no knowing how long Jan and Lorry's scene would last. It might already be nearly over.

'Oh Miss Hewson, come quickly!' she said. Miss Hewson looked up reluctantly from the evening report she was writing.

'What is it?' she said peevishly.

'Come upstairs to the third landing, quick—it's urgent,' Rose replied.

Her sense of urgency communicated itself to Miss Hewson. A prison officer must always be on guard, ready to cope with any crisis that might suddenly occur. She followed Rose upstairs to the third landing. Rose halted outside Jan's cell, and, waving at the door, said peremptorily:

'In there—quick.' Still swept along by Rose's urgency, Miss Hewson automatically obeyed her and flung open the door. Rose giggled with relief. She had not misjudged or mistimed it. There they were, coupled on Jan's bed. Lorry's bare buttocks faced them, cupped at that moment by Jan's hand.

'How disgusting!' Miss Hewson exclaimed. She really was aghast, never having had an affair with anyone herself. To have witnessed love-making between a man and a woman would have been shocking enough; but to see two women fondling each other was quite revolting. Acute embarrassment combined with horror, and made her involuntarily clash the door to. Then, a second or two later, once she had got over the shock, she realized she must do something. So she unlocked the door and gingerly pushed it open again.

By now, she wanted to look more closely at what was going on, while delivering a suitable reprimand. But during the moment or two while the door was shut again, Jan and Lorry had abruptly separated and

169

quickly covered themselves. They were both seated sheepishly side by side on the edge of the bed by the time Miss Hewson had opened the door a second time. She was unaccountably disappointed.

'Anything so disgusting! I just can't think what to begin to say!' she exclaimed. 'Go to your room immediately, Harrison. I'll have to put you both on report for this.'

Lorry was too dazed to attempt to defy her. She got up from Jan's bed and retired obediently to her own cell. As she passed Rose, standing smiling on the threshold, she looked straight at her, almost through her, so expressionlessly that Rose was at once filled with fear. Perhaps she had made a grave mistake. Supposing Lorry punished her in some horrible way. She would have expected an instant blaze of rage and flailing fists; this bleak, stony look was much more frightening.

Miss Hewson did not hesitate to report what she had just seen to Mrs Herbert. Indeed, she was glad to—and not solely because she welcomed the chance of getting Jan and Lorry into trouble. By now, she knew that most of her fellow officers took lesbianism in Collingwood for granted. She herself did not, and was baffled and shocked by the official attitude to lesbian revelations at Group Counselling: by the fact that no one ever acted on the information gathered on these occasions.

'But, Miss Hewson,' Mrs Herbert had said sententiously when she had once raised the matter with her, 'surely you realize by now that Group Counselling is confidential or it is nothing. We must not on any account abuse the women's frankness, must we? Otherwise we would invalidate the whole procedure.'

However, the more her colleagues appeared to condone these abnormal love affairs, the more strongly Miss Hewson disapproved of them. Deep in her mind, she grew more and more determined to stamp out all this perversion. She developed quite a crusading spirit about it. After all, she had always been taught to consider homosexuality dirty and sinful; and here they were, supposed to be rehabilitating the prisoners, not permitting and encouraging unnatural vices. So far, there had been nothing tangible to crusade about: she could not report mere hearsay; she had to produce concrete, incontrovertible evidence. And now at last she could—about one affair at any rate. She was delighted.

She felt dutiful and righteous as she made her report to Mrs Herbert next day. Mrs Herbert might be surprisingly lax and tolerant about the

Group Counselling revelations; even so, surely she would be glad to learn from an officer about a specific instance of illicit lesbian behaviour? Hadn't it been commendable of her to catch two women red-handed?

'Yesterday evening at about six-thirty,' she stated formally, 'on information received from Dawley, I went up to Carruthers' room and found her and Harrison having—well—a carry on—a sexual liaison. They were right in the middle of it. There was no doubt about what they were doing. I know this is contrary to prison regulations, so I'm immediately reporting the matter to you.' She stopped, and looked at Mrs Herbert, expecting praise. She was disappointed.

'Thank you, Miss Hewson. Yes I see. I must decide what is best to be done about this,' Mrs Herbert replied. 'You're absolutely sure, are you, beyond the shadow of a doubt, that they were actually having an affair?'

'Oh yes, there was absolutely do doubt about it,' Miss Hewson answered primly.

'Yes, I see,' Mrs Herbert repeated meditatively. She needed time to think. It would not do to act precipitately or commit herself in any way until she had given hard, careful thought to this unwelcome news Miss Hewson had brought her. It would be best to change the subject. She would take the opportunity of interviewing Miss Hewson about her casework progress with the women on the wing.

'You know, Miss Hewson,' she said slowly, after a slight pause, 'we've not really had much of a conversation about what you make of it all, have we?—not since I had that first chat with you about taking on one or two particular cases. I deliberately like to give my officers a little while in which to form proper relationships with the prisoners before asking them how they think they're getting on with them.' She looked enquiringly at Miss Hewson, who replied hesitantly:

'Well, it was Dawley, Rose Dawley, you asked me to give particular attention to, Mrs Herbert.' She stopped. There seemed nothing further to say. Presumably Mrs Herbert could gauge for herself what, if any, progress she had made with Rose.

Mrs Herbert stared disconcertingly at her, evidently expecting her to say something more. Actually, it would make no difference what she said; Mrs Herbert had already made up her mind about her. She was useless: she had obviously got nowhere with Rose; she had formed no creative relationships with any of the prisoners on the wing. On the contrary, she was, Mrs Herbert knew, thoroughly unpopular. Nor had she proved to be the slightest use as an ally against Mac. Worst of all, she had got her, Mrs Herbert, into awkward, embarrassing positions by telling her things she would much rather not hear, or knew already but did not wish to do anything about—such as this latest information about Lorry and Jan. In short, Miss Hewson was a great disappointment. She might hold all the right theories, but she was about the most inept young officer Mrs Herbert had yet encountered. She would have to get rid of her, she decided, as she inspected her, looking hard at her tensely-focused eyes and rigid lips, noticing the pink tide gradually mounting up her neck above her collar.

Miss Hewson was conscious of this critical scrutiny. She tried to reassure herself by lowering her eyes and glancing surreptitiously at her wrist-watch. Then her fingers, which had been fidgeting together down in her lap, rose involuntarily and fiddled pointlessly with the knot in her tie. The side of her neck started to tingle. She scratched it.

A promising new young officer had just arrived in Collingwood. At present, her talents were being wasted among all the old hustlers on F Wing. Mrs Herbert decided to ask the Governor to swap her round with Miss Hewson. Breaking the brief silence, she remarked:

'Yes, well I know all about Dawley of course. We all know only too well about her.' She stopped, then added: 'But what about the others?— have you got anywhere with anyone else?'

'Anyone else?' Miss Hewson echoed blankly. What did Mrs Herbert mean? She had not assigned her anyone but Rose. Mrs Herbert knew this quite well, but she felt spiteful. She was deliberately embarrassing Miss Hewson as a punishment for causing her embarrassment.

'Yes, anyone else,' she repeated severely, '—the other women you have decided to concentrate on.'

'But I thought I was only to take on Dawley for the moment,' Miss Hewson replied lamely. 'You said you'd suggest some others later, after I'd worked with Dawley for a bit.'

'But, Miss Hewson,' Mrs Herbert said sternly, 'surely you would not simply wait for me to point out which women need helping and befriending? Surely you could see that for yourself, and would do something about it of your own accord? Prison officers nowadays are supposed to employ some personal initiative. We aren't in the nineteenth century any longer. I shouldn't anyway have wasted so much time, if I'd been you, on a hopeless case like Dawley. It's the women with the spark of possibility in them that we must focus on.'

'Yes but—' Miss Hewson began defensively. Suddenly, she felt a trifle indignant. But Mrs Herbert did not want to have an argument with her just then; so she cut in:

'If I were you, I'd forget Dawley for the moment. Instead, you might give a little thought to Dora Parsons—there's someone who really needs to be cheered up and given a bit of encouragement. Then there's Jessy Smith—you might try and buck her up a bit too, get her prepared for her release. I've noticed she's got gate-fever very badly.'

'I'll try and see what I can do, Mrs Herbert,' Miss Hewson assented humbly.

'Yes, well, thank you, I'm sure you will,' Mrs Herbert replied. She began to rustle among the papers on her desk. Miss Hewson realized she was dismissed.

Later, she wondered why Mrs Herbert had made no comment on the information she had reported to her. She might have given her some inkling of the steps she intended to take over the matter. She could at least have commended her for being conscientious. It seemed impossible ever to win anyone's approval. Perhaps, Miss Hewson reflected bitterly, she had picked the wrong job and ought to resign.

After Miss Hewson had gone, Mrs Herbert stopped rustling among her papers. She leaned forward on her desk, doodled in a notebook, and thought hard. If she acted on Miss Hewson's information and proceeded against Lorry and Jan, this would amount to a breach of confidence with Lorry, inasmuch as Lorry herself had previously told her all about the affair with Jan. At least, this was how it was likely to strike Lorry; even though of course she would know that Miss Hewson must have reported what she had witnessed. Lorry was unlikely to react rationally (few prisoners did). If punished, she would look for a scapegoat—and it was sure to be her, Mrs Herbert. She would lose Lorry's confidence for ever; and probably, at the same time, the confidence of a number of other women on the wing who had always assumed (with justification) that she had turned a blind eye on their lesbian affairs.

So she nearly decided to ignore what Miss Hewson had just told her. Then, as she cogitated further, she realized that Miss Hewson could get her into trouble if she did nothing. Perhaps she should not just now have castigated Miss Hewson quite so severely. She was bound to want to get her own back; and what better way of doing so, supposing she took no action about Lorry and Jan, than by complaining to the Governor about her?—accusing her of negligence and encouraging the women to break prison rules? This could lead to serious consequences for her.

The best thing—the only thing—to do, she eventually decided, was to report the matter to the Governor. She would recommend simply separating Lorry and Jan rather than by directly punishing them. This should prevent undue excitement and unrest on the wing, and she herself would run less risk of losing everyone's confidence. The Governor would quite likely take her advice.

Lorry, she decided regretfully, was the one who would have to go; for it was she, not Jan, who might cause trouble. Hurt and indignant because she felt her trust had been betrayed, she was quite capable of causing a minor riot on the wing. And if not this, she would be bound to set everyone against her. She could tarnish her image indelibly; at one blow shatter all the fragile relationships she had painstakingly constructed over such a long period with the women on her wing. This must be avoided at all costs. She would ask the Governor to transfer Lorry to one of the open or semi-security prisons.

She did not foresee any particular difficulty with Jan. Once Lorry was gone, she would probably retire into herself. It would be beneath her dignity to make a fuss or cause trouble.

As soon as she had worked all this out, Mrs Herbert went to the Governor. Lorry, they decided, should be sent to the Towers, the open prison for recidivists, as soon as there was a vacancy there. But the Governor did not agree with Mrs Herbert that this was enough. She insisted that Jan and Lorry must be directly punished too. It was decided that they should both have all their meals in solitary and lose their evening and weekend association for the next three weeks, or, in Lorry's case, until she went to the Towers.

23

MAVIS WAS NOT ONLY SILENT AND WITHDRAWN THESE days; she was also becoming heavy and slow. It was as though the fuel within her were drying up and she were gradually grinding to a halt.

Like Rose, she too was always hungry. She stuffed herself with bread in a vain effort to appease the pangs, which seemed to drive through her stomach like knives. As she no longer put any energy into her work —frequently breaking off and standing still for minutes on end doing nothing—she started to put on weight. Her face coarsened and puffed out slightly, losing some of the bony delicacy that so attracted Lorry. To move at all became an effort. Great chains seemed to be attached to her ankles, and had to be dragged everywhere she went. But curiously, although she was perpetually hungry, all the time it felt as if a heavy lump of rock were weighing down her stomach.

Believing at first that it might be due to the chronic constipation she had recently developed, she started booking regularly for the MO and asking for large doses of laxative. But this did not succeed in purging her of the lump of rock.

Then she began to fancy she was pregnant. She could not be really, otherwise it would have been revealed at her initial medical examination. Nevertheless, she persuaded them to re-examine her, with the same negative result. But even after this, she still felt in some odd way as if she were pregnant, impossible though it was. She developed bouts of morning sickness, and bought oranges with her weekly earnings instead of tobacco.

The Star Wing Governor was not observant. Neither she nor the other officers on the wing discerned Mavis's deep gloom. The MO was not given to making psychiatric diagnoses. In his opinion, Mavis was simply silly, fussy and tiresome. Miss Foster, however, eventually noticed how lethargic she had become in the garden and demanded her removal. She was sent back to the Work Room.

Nobody there cared whether she worked or not. She would sit, slowly and painfully poking her needle (which nowadays felt as heavy as a blunt steel bar) through the coarse mail-bag material. Sometimes the cloth would appear as thick and weighty as a densely-woven tennis net. Mavis would feel momentarily smothered, and would thrust and jab the needle frantically at it like a clumsily-wielded weapon, trying, so she imagined, to force an aperture large enough for her to escape through herself. Then, breathing hard and jerkily, she would recover. Her dulled eyes would come back to life and see the objects before her as they really were—or more or less as they were.

For long periods, she would sit doing nothing at all; just gazing before her with a glazed, apathetic expression. As she sat out of sight in the back row, the officers in charge seldom noticed that she was idle.

Mavis's depression took a sharp turn for the worse when one day Miss Davies brought her bad news about her family.

'It's dreadful having to tell you this, Mrs McCann,' she said, 'but I'm afraid I've got bad news for you. Your husband has gone off—with another woman, so the neighbours say.'

'Oh,' was all Mavis could bring herself to respond.

'And then, more bad news I'm afraid,' Miss Davies went on. 'The children's granny has decided she can't cope with them any longer—it's on account of her rheumatism. So they've had to be taken into care. They're in St James'—the big local authority home. I'm sure they're happy there. It's quite a nice home I believe.'

'In a home are they?' Mavis mumbled. Miss Davies could get little more out of her, and soon retired discouraged.

From then on, Mavis's gloom became broad, deep and enveloping. It smothered all her other thoughts and feelings like a rug—like the heavy, close-knit tennis net she so often imagined she was sewing in the Work Room. The gloom was so thick and impenetrable that it was insulating, and actually protected Mavis from much conscious suffering. She was shielded by it, not only from contact with the world immediately around her, but also from intolerably painful thoughts. Her mind was prevented from straying on to the sufferings of her children at being wrenched from home and thrust into an institution. Her imagination was not allowed to wander on to Tom. Any speculation about where he was, with whom, and what he might be doing was

176

firmly suppressed. Above all, her guilt, confusion and dread about the future were all, for the moment, successfully pushed down out of sight.

She came and went, following the day's routine like an iron robot. Her tummy still felt stuffed and perpetually weighed down, but the interior of her skull felt light and empty, almost a vacuum. Her lips, which she licked more persistently than ever before, turned, first dry, white and flaky, then red and raw.

One evening, the smothering gloom was pierced. An excruciating shaft of light penetrated the inner chamber of her mind, and, with the abrupt brilliance of lightning, revealed all her thoughts and feelings. They stood out deeply shadowed in sharp relief, like monstrous carvings in a medieval abbey; like dreadful gargoyles. The light gradually dimmed, and the objects faded into faintly adumbrated contours, but the scene in all its clear-cut brilliance lingered imprinted on Mavis's recollection.

This stabbing ray of light was injected unwittingly by Olive.

Rose had soon spread the story of Jan and Lorry getting caught by Miss Hewson with their pants down. Scandal travelled fast in Collingwood, so it was not long before Olive heard the tale. Although Mavis was gloomy and unapproachable these days, Olive had no idea how profound and all-pervading her depression was, nor what had caused it. She knew nothing of Mavis's latest bad news about her family, and assumed she was still worried and upset on account of her muddled feelings about Lorry. She might feel better—be able to get Lorry out of her system—Olive thought, if she knew Lorry had been carrying on with someone else. It might cure her of her unnatural affection for Lorry. So, after dinner, she approached Mavis, who was just then leaning over the landing rail outside her cell, gazing vacantly out over the wing.

'Know what I heard in the Laundry today, Mavey?' she said, laying a motherly arm across Mavis's shoulders. 'They was all on about that Lorry you used to go with when you was in the garden. She's carrying on now with someone on her own wing—some toffee-nosed piece, lady something or another—real Lady Muck, they say—a junky or something. Anyway, they was caught in bed together by the Governor—by Madam herself. Actually caught right at it, their fingers right up each others' whatsnames.' She paused to see what effect this news was having on Mavis; but Mavis said nothing. She just continued staring off into space as though she had not heard.

'Well, I just thought you'd be interested to know,' Olive went on, deflated and a trifle aggrieved by Mavis's apparent lack of interest, 'seeing as you two—you and that Lorry—used to be so thick. Shows the type she really is, don't it?' She hoped the question might provoke some response from Mavis. It did.

'Go away and let me alone,' Mavis said harshly. She shook off Olive's arm, and turned to face her for a second, glaring at her with such ferocity that Olive recoiled in amazement.

'Well, you needn't take on so,' she said, recovering from her surprise. 'I was only telling you for your own good.' She retired, injured and indignant, into her own cell. She had no idea what a brilliantly searing effect her words had had on Mavis.

To all outward appearances, Mavis's mood remained unchanged. But throughout the afternoon, as she sat still and expressionless at the back of the Work Room, her mind was turbulent with puzzled anguish. For the past week or two, her feelings had been so muddled and muffled that she had not realized how much Lorry still mattered to her. She had done her best to ignore her, before she was sacked from the garden, while all along she had been wanting her more than anything or anyone else.

Now, as she seemed to be staring round her own mind, examining and trying to comprehend what was in it, she found she could not understand it at all. Why, being so in love with Lorry, had she been persistently avoiding and rebuffing her? It was absurd—especially in view of the recent news of Tom's desertion. For, after all, it was he who had let her down, not she him through having an affair with Lorry, as she had previously thought.

Her mind was so busy that afternoon, trying feverishly to make sense of itself, that she was completely oblivious of her surroundings. Today, her needle was not a hefty steel bar; she was not conscious of holding a needle at all; nor did she even see the coarse mail-bag cloth before her. During the entire afternoon, she made only three laborious stitches.

Then, by degrees, as the afternoon and evening wore on, the protective shroud began to re-form over her mind. Her feelings were gradually dulled, and her thoughts grew less agitated.

After tea, there was the painting class. Usually, Mavis's productions were cramped, wishy-washy and finicky: flat little pallid single-sided houses stuck right down at the bottom of the page; or minute, childishly sketched cats and rabbits bristling with exaggerated whiskers. She never tried to paint people. This evening, however, to the teacher's surprise, she attempted a large, bold picture in all the colours available of a stiff man and woman standing holding hands.

'That's interesting, Mavis,' the teacher remarked. 'I'm glad to see you're branching out and trying a new style. It's good, now and again, to have a go at doing people.' She looked wonderingly at Mavis, noticing that her expression was a little brighter than usual, although still unfathomable.

Mavis felt a trifle better after she had finished the picture. Painting had somehow enabled her to come to terms with herself—or, at any rate, to feel more at ease for the moment. But then, as soon as the class was over, the agonizing light flooded into her for a second time that day. As she was queueing up with the others for her final mug of watery cocoa, Miss Davies entered the wing. She came straight over to Mavis and said:

'I've some news for you, Mrs McCann—good news. Let's sit down at the table over there for a moment.'

Mavis left the cocoa queue, and sat opposite Miss Davies at one of the small dinner tables.

'Well, Mrs McCann,' Miss Davies began, with a cheerful smile, 'I'm glad, very glad, to be able to tell you that we have been able to get your little Doreen fixed up with ever such a nice couple. Her child care officer took her there two days ago, and she's settled down nicely.' She paused expectantly. Mavis looked blankly at her and echoed:

'My Doreen fixed up with a couple.' She had not yet quite taken in what Miss Davies was saying.

'Yes,' Miss Davies went on, 'we've found her a nice foster home.'

The brilliance shone abruptly into Mavis's mind again. Transfixed with horror and misery, she simply stared back at Miss Davies, speechless. Miss Davies misinterpreted her expression. She chattered on for a few moments about Doreen's new home. As Mavis said nothing, she concluded all was well and that she was pleased by the news.

By the time Mavis had recovered enough to mumble:

'Yes but—' Miss Davies was ready to go. Mistaking Mavis's inarticulate words for 'Goodnight', she looked at her in mild surprise. She would have expected her to show some interest rather than simply bid her farewell. Still, if that was all she had to say, perhaps it would be best to leave it at that for the moment. After all, it was Mavis's bed time. She might be tired, even though, by outside standards, it was still so early. She could seek her out in a day or two and re-open the conversation at a more auspicious time. So she rose from the table.

'Well, we'll talk some more about it tomorrow or the next day then, shall we?' she said. 'And there'll be one or two things to discuss about the boys as well.' She left the wing. Mavis returned to the cocoa queue; then, forgetting to fill up her water jug, retired to her cell for the night.

She sat bolt upright on the edge of her bed for an hour and a half. She did not hear the officer on duty making her final round, nor respond to the clockwork, 'Are you all right? Goodnight.' She sat quite stiffly, the only bits of her to move being her tongue rubbing her raw lips at regular intervals, and the tips of her fingers involuntarily playing repeated scales down in her lap.

Her mind was in turmoil, teeming with jarring thoughts and grating feelings. Sometimes, it seemed to seethe like a heap of microscopic, stinging ants; at other times, it became again the shadowy chamber revealed by the piercing shafts of light: a vast, stone hall, crammed with grotesque carvings—hideous statues that leered maliciously at her.

Now and again, her thoughts and feelings became more coherent. She would allow her mind to fill with misery over Tom's desertion, and jealousy over Lorry's betrayal; or worse, she would be struck by bitter shame and remorse. All her misfortunes had been entirely her own fault. Had she not flown into an irrational rage that night in the pub, she would never have suffered the disgrace of being imprisoned. . . . She had been a nagging, irritable wife, so who but she was to blame for Tom's desertion? If she had not, for some incomprehensible reason, rejected Lorry, then Lorry would not have been forced to look for affection elsewhere. . . . And there must be something basically wrong with her: she must be emotionally twisted in some way ever to have let herself get involved with a lesbian in the first place. If she had had any willpower, she would have resisted Lorry from the outset. Acute longing for Lorry collided in her mind with extreme revulsion and self-loathing for wanting her. The feelings cancelled each other out; and, for a moment, Mavis felt empty.

Then the worst thoughts of all, which till now she had held at bay, entered the foreground of her mind—thoughts about her children. She felt more guilty about them than about anything else. She was unworthy to be their mother. The most terrible event in her life had been the awful occasion when they had come and dragged her, as a little girl, screaming from her home and mother and put her into an institution. It had been the most desolating, frightening thing that had ever happened to her; more frightening even than being sent to prison. And now here she was, responsible for making her own children suffer in the same way.

As she thought of Doreen and the boys enduring similar misery to her own as a child, it was as though she herself were re-living it. She became her own child. She became again a small, terrified girl being wrenched from home and left all alone among a crowd of strangers in a huge, frightening building. For Doreen and she were almost the same person, surely—Doreen was herself reborn.

But it was even worse than this. She allowed herself to remember that Doreen was not in a big, impersonal children's home any longer. If she were, it would not be quite so bad. It would be possible to recover her. She might be in the care of the local authority, but she would not be another person's private possession.

At last, the most anguished thought of all forced its way to the front of Mavis's mind. She had lost Doreen for ever; for Doreen had become someone else's little girl. She would never get her back, and it was all her own fault.

She punished herself by picturing Doreen being petted and cuddled by a stranger. She saw her, in her mind's eye, going through a whole day: being dressed, washed, fed, taken for a walk, played with, tucked up in bed and kissed goodnight. And this new mother of Doreen's was a much better mother than she had ever been; never cross with her; never shouting impatiently at her or slapping her, as she herself had from time to time, despite her love.

The consoling cord that, in early days before Lorry came to occupy all her thoughts, had seemed to unite her with Doreen, had dissolved so gradually and imperceptibly that Mavis had continued more or less to believe she was linked by at least a very fine thread to her daughter. But now that Doreen had been given away to new parents, even this thread was surely snapped, and snapped irreparably. Doreen was gone for ever; and because in some mystical way it was as though she and Doreen were one and the same person, or nearly so, now Mavis herself seemed to be distintegrating and evaporating.

The seething ant heap of her thoughts began to cave in and fall apart. Then, as her mind became again the vast, shadowy hall, the images and masonry seemed to loom ever larger, then start to crumble. The grins on the faces of the gigantic gargoyles stretched till the stone began to crack. The statues, she now saw, were precariously balanced and swayed slightly. Any minute, they would crash over on top of her.

Mavis got up from the bed, and began to move agitatedly about the cell. She needed to prove that she was still vital and mobile. But the fantasy that she was falling to pieces gradually dominated her, till she reached the point where she almost wanted to disintegrate. Her misery, jealousy and self-disgust became so unbearable that it was essential to dispel them, even at the cost of destroying herself. In any case, by now, she herself, as a separate entity, barely seemed to exist any more. She was just shifting sediment lying at the bottom of this overwhelming ocean of suffering. If, in getting rid of the suffering, she incidentally got rid of what was left of herself at the same time, it would not matter. For, if any trace of her remained in existence, inevitably it would have to endure the same torture again at some future date.

Still pacing rapidly up and down the cell, Mavis decided she must somehow detach the misery from herself; amputate it and throw it away, even though this meant there would then be nothing else left— or only some volatile substance that would soon be dispersed.

She picked up her dinner knife. She stared at it as she waved it vaguely to and fro. It would be difficult actually to amputate anything with it. She pondered for a moment. Surely it would serve no useful purpose to cut off her hair. This would not get rid of her agony. Cutting off a part of her body might; only now, as she studied the knife, she was doubtful whether it was sharp enough to slice through a thick layer of flesh, much less saw through bone. But might she not puncture a hole in herself? Then her misery could simply flow away. This, surely, should be simple enough?

She sat on the edge of the bed again and managed to pierce through the skin into the big vein first in her left wrist then in her right. The healing stream started to ooze, then trickle out. She watched with satisfaction as the bright moisture seeped out of her stabbed wrists, then ran down over her hands on to the floor. She felt better at once; as though she were relaxing in the aftermath of sweating out a fever, or enjoying the instant relief of passing water. All the wretchedness and poison were draining out of her.

The sense of warmth and content presently began to turn to weakness; the weakness to dizziness and fear. All at once, it was her first night in Collingwood again, and, somehow, at the same time, her first night in the children's home long ago. Abruptly, it appeared to be getting darker. The cell walls were closing in around her. She tried to scream, but her larynx had gone rusty. She tried to rise from the bed, but her muscles had seized up. Even her dried tongue could no longer lick her lips. When she attempted to move, she flopped forward and collapsed on the floor.

Now it was pitch dark, and she could no longer see the encroaching walls. Instead, she was aware of the monstrous statues, expanding, growing ever more immense, then slowly starting to topple over on to her. She felt the helmet enclose her skull. It began to tighten.

24

MAVIS FAILED: SHE DID NOT MANAGE TO GET RID OF HER misery; nor did she destroy herself.

Olive had been disturbed by the noise she was making next door as she paced up and down her cell. She ruminated about Mavis for a while, then decided there must be something seriously wrong with her. She had behaved strangely that day and had looked unusually upset at cocoa time. So she rang her bell. When eventually the night officer arrived, Olive told her that she thought Mavis was ill or in trouble. Mavis was discovered just in time and taken to the prison hospital, where she remained for many weeks.

When Lorry heard what had happened, she felt almost as miserable and desolate as Mavis herself had been. She in her turn would pace to and fro in her cell, suffering from bitter remorse, combined with an agonizing sense of loss. She had loved Mavis more than anyone she had ever met, and now she had gone. Probably she would never see her again. Somehow, Lorry felt it was her fault: mightn't she have won Mavis back if only she had tried a little harder and had not slid off into a degrading affair with Jan?

To get her own back on Rose for grassing on her and Jan, Lorry sent her a series of threatening, anonymous letters. She hoped in the end to be able to carry out the threats—or at any rate those that did not involve actually killing Rose.

Rose herself was having a bad time. She had been sent to Coventry by the entire wing. Any group she approached would at once fall silent. The women would glare balefully at her and resume their chatter only after she had departed. Rose was deeply humiliated and even a trifle alarmed. Her wretchedness and fear turned to terror when the anonymous letters, signed with skull and crossbones, started to appear on her cell table. They could only be from Lorry. They warned Rose never to talk to a screw again or her head would be cracked open; never so much as to glance into anyone's cell, or her eyes would be gouged out.

The letters steadily grew worse. Warnings turned to announcements of what was actually in store for her. The letters stated that one day, when she least expected it, she would be attacked from behind as she was at work re-painting a cell. She would be knocked out, and her brains beaten in. Or else, some evening when she was sitting quietly alone in her own cell, a horde of enemies would descend on her, beat her up, and cut her throat. The letters then began to outline, with sadistic relish, the most ingenious tortures that were shortly going to be inflicted on her.

The threats were so extreme that sometimes Rose only half-believed them. Still, this sort of thing could happen, she knew; and she would debate in her mind whether or not anyone was really likely to do these horrible things to her. Indeed, how could Lorry carry out her threats, Confined To Cell as she was most of the time nowadays? How did she even manage to deliver the notes? Perhaps, after all, it was not Lorry who had written them. Whoever it was, how were they actually going to attack her? Just where and when would the attack occur? Would she be beaten up, knifed or what? And so Rose would repeatedly and compulsively go over and over all the possibilities.

The more she speculated, the more nervous and uncertain she became. She was on edge all day. She never dared sit alone in her cell after tea. At work, she tried to avoid ever standing with her back to the door of the cell she was painting; and when she was obliged to, she would be taut and trembling with fear the whole time. She felt so embarrassed and ashamed at meal times, seated among stony-faced women who ignored her, that she lost her appetite and could no longer bring herself to eat more than a few mouthfuls at a time. Miss Hewson reported this to Mac; but Mac, who knew Rose had been sent to Coventry and approved of the fact, merely grunted and remarked jocularly:

'Serve her right. Can afford to lose a bit of weight, that one—big fat grass.'

So Rose grew pale and thin. Dark shadows appeared beneath her eyes, as she could not sleep properly. She would lie awake at night, tense with fear less somehow or another they broke in and killed her while she was asleep. When at last she did drop off, she was constantly disturbed by nightmares.

She did not like to show the letters to an officer. This would be grassing and therefore probably precipitate the dreaded assault. Eventually, however, she became so frightened that she decided anything would be better than living in this perpetual state of terrified suspense. She went as unobtrusively as possible to Mrs Herbert's office and showed her the letters. Mrs Herbert at first pretended to dismiss them lightly.

'You shouldn't let yourself take this sort of thing too seriously you know, Dawley,' she lied (actually she knew the threats could be genuine). 'In any case,' she continued coldly, 'you have rather brought it all on yourself, haven't you?—it never did anyone any good to go telling tales about their friends. It rather serves you right, doesn't it?— and you of all people should know all about anonymous letter writing!'

Rose mumbled some reply. She felt aggrieved. Looking closely at her, Mrs Herbert could see she really was exceedingly tense and frightened.

She might even be on the verge of a breakdown. She must prevent this. It was her duty to see that none of the women on her wing came to any harm. Speaking slowly, she said:

'I could, if you like, Dawley, arrange for you to go into voluntary solitary for a while till the business has died down. The Governor has permitted this on previous occasions at a prisoner's own request when she had some grounds for believing she might be physically harmed by someone.'

Rose readily agreed to the suggestion. She was transferred that same day to a special cell on the Punishment Wing.

If Lorry had been able to carry out any of her threats, it would have siphoned off some of her rage and frustration. As it was, pacing to and fro now, deprived of her prey, she felt positively distended with pent-up fury.

One evening, anger combined explosively with her misery over loving Mavis, a sudden irrational hatred of Jan, and general disgust with herself and everyone else. She just must do something violent to relieve her boiling feelings.

All at once, she badly needed to punish Mrs Herbert. She was the worst offender of all. She had betrayed her trust; she had gone and got her banged up away from all the others for hours on end. What was more, Mrs Herbert was one of *them*. She was the boss. She was also normal, respectable, one of those hundreds of people who despised and hated her, Lorry, and everyone like her—who were out to get her: to punish her and lock her away out of sight. They had been down on her from the start. They would like to extinguish her, annihilate her. And Mrs Herbert was the worst of all. She had pretended to be understanding and friendly, even sympathetic. Then she had gone and shopped her.

So Lorry wanted to kick and hit Mrs Herbert. As she could not, she did the next best thing: she hit and kicked Mrs Herbert's property— for that was how she regarded the contents of her cell just then.

She had a smash-up. She kicked the furniture, then hurled it about bodily till some of the legs of the chair and table were broken. She crashed and hammered at the tin washing utensils until they were dented and bashed out of shape. She tore the pages out of the Bible, and pulled the magazine pictures off the walls. She tossed her bedding all

186

over the floor and tipped her bucket of water and the contents of her chamber pot on to it. She squatted down on the floor for a few moments and stuffed a great wadge of sheet into her mouth, chewed it violently, then tore at it with her teeth. She shattered her china mug—the most gratifying action so far. She looked about for something else fragile to smash to smithereens. She wrenched a bar off the remains of her chair and thrust it violently through each window-pane in turn. Soon, a mass of glass splinters was added to the chaos all over the floor.

Rage instilled so much energy into Lorry that it did not take her long to wreck her cell. After about fifteen minutes of hectic activity, she had finished destroying everything she could, and subsided panting on to the wet bedding.

Mac was on duty that night. She was so engrossed in writing her report that she did not at once hear the noise coming from Lorry's cell up on the third landing. By the time she did, and had arrived on the threshold of Lorry's cell, Lorry had finished and was recumbent on the floor, breathing hard and staring with a fixed expression at the ceiling.

Mac knew she should send for Sister, but decided not to. If she did, Lorry would almost certainly be sent to the Hospital, where she would probably be put in the 'Strips'. Mac did not approve of this bare, cold cell where the women were padlocked into a canvas robe and usually put out with a shot in the arm. Besides, she liked Lorry; and at the moment she was sorry for her. She did not approve of the way she and Jan had been deprived of Association, and would sometimes herself, when on duty, come and chat to them in their cells to help relieve their boredom.

'This is a fine way to finish your days here, you damned fool!' she said, trying to sound as cross as possible. 'You know what you could get for this, you bloody idiot?—the "Strips" and the needle from old Doctor What's it.'

Lorry did not know what she meant. She had not yet heard that she was going to the Towers. Mac made her immediately clear up as much of the mess as possible, then ordered her to get into bed, wet though the sheets and blankets were.

'Serves you right. Stew in your own juice, and I hope you get pneumonia,' she said fiercely. All the same, she returned presently with a couple of fresh sheets and blankets.

Mac was obliged to report the matter to Mrs Herbert, who decided there was no point in taking it any further or inflicting any extra punishment on Lorry. At last, she had been notified of a vacancy at the Towers; so Lorry would be leaving Collingwood at the end of the week. When Lorry was standing before her next day, she just said:

'Well, Lorry, you're lucky. I'm going to be very lenient. By rights I ought to put you on report to the Governor. That would probably mean the Punishment Cells, also, probably, some loss of remission. But I'm going to let you off, as you do seem to have taken rather a lot of punishment lately.' She paused, expecting a grateful response; but Lorry just grunted. She hated Mrs Herbert and everyone else too much just then to notice any flicker of kindness. She did not care what happened to her. Mrs Herbert sighed and added sadly: 'In any case, Lorry, I've decided there isn't much point in punishing you, as, on Friday, you will be leaving for the Towers.'

25

EARLY IN THE MORNING, THREE DAYS LATER, LORRY SAT in the bus waiting to set off for the Towers. The bus was parked in the yard, and Lorry stared out of the window at Collingwood.

The prison, with its castle walls, loomed squat and sinister; like a scraggy hunchback; secretive, as though concealing something, at the same time crouched and ready to pounce. Lorry had mixed feelings about the place: a curious blend of hatred, contempt and affection. Here, she had been punished, berated and humiliated. Yet here she had been accepted for what she was, even respected, much more than she had ever been in the outside world. And she had had some good times.

Mingled with her sorrow (now a trifle nostalgic) at leaving the place that still contained Mavis, was a sense of relief. She had lost Mavis, and that was that. Now she felt glad in a way to be getting away from them all. It was time to start afresh. An open prison should make a pleasant change for a while. Besides, she could easily abscond if she wanted to. By the time the bus at last left the prison yard, Lorry's mind was already happily occupied working out an escape plan.

That same day, Miss Hewson also began a new life—over on F Wing. She too was glad of a change. For here, among short-term recidivists, she was not expected to try to be anything but a mere wardress. This was a closed wing, so her job was almost entirely custodial. In a way, she found it a relief just to be opening cell doors and clashing them to; herding prisoners off to work, then hustling them straight back into their cells as quickly as possible. She was not expected to attempt any casework; for the F Wing women were considered past redemption. She just had to bark out orders and bustle the prisoners about.

All the same, by the end of the day, a nuance of doubt and dissatisfaction had sidled into a corner of her mind. This job might be easy, but wasn't it pointless? Worse than useless, in fact? Perhaps she ought to give it all up and hand in her notice, she reflected morosely, as she paced along the endless landings that evening, checking that each door was securely locked. Or should she give it a little longer? What other job could she do anyway? And how could she face her family, especially her father, with such a confession of failure? She would allow herself a bit longer—a couple of weeks, say, or a month—she decided, before making up her mind finally about resigning. After all, perhaps she could do something to change the approach and methods on the wing? Surely it was her duty to try?

Mrs Herbert slept badly that night. She tossed and turned, wondering over and over again whether they had done the right thing with Lorry. It dawned on her at last that she had become fonder of Lorry than of any other prisoner who had ever been on her wing. She was going to miss her badly. It was really herself she was punishing, not Lorry, by sending her to the Towers. In some unfathomable, indefinable way, she had allowed herself to become emotionally involved over Lorry. But this knowledge was as unacceptable as it was baffling, so she soon pushed it out of sight in her mind. When at last she fell asleep, she dreamt about Noel and the day his plane crashed.

26

AFTER DINNER, A WEEK OR SO LATER, JAN WAS TRYING TO read the paper. The incessant chatter going on around her made it difficult to concentrate. Her thoughts kept wandering. She would recall times with Lorry and wonder how she was, what she was doing, with whom she was having an affair now? Was there any chance of Lorry sending her a note via some prisoner returning to Collingwood from the Towers?

She had been tempted, at first, to write Lorry a letter and get one of the weekly batch of prisoners going to the Towers to smuggle it out and give it to her. Then she decided not to, for fear someone else would read it first. Besides, what was the point of writing to Lorry? She was almost certain not to answer. Most likely she was knocking on with someone else already and had quite forgotten her. They would probably never meet again, or, anyway, not for years. Theirs had been a typical prison affair, transient and insubstantial. She would just have to wait for someone else to turn up.

Mac wandered over to her. She noticed how dispirited Jan was looking and felt sorry for her.

'Buck up now, Jan,' she said jovially, standing squarely before her so that Jan was obliged to attend. 'It'll work out all right in a bit. There's plenty of fish in the sea. She was a nice kid, that Lorry—but another one'll soon turn up.' She chuckled and moved off, having done her bit to cheer Jan up.

No doubt she was right. In time, someone else would turn up. Meanwhile, life was insufferably boring. Jan stared away down the wing, grey in the dull light of a cloudy afternoon. The wing was infinitely long and dismal; the far end in the gloaming barely visible. Her sentence stretched before her.

Also by Pat Arrowsmith:

JERICHO
Written during a six month prison sentence for CND activities,
Jericho is that rare creation, a successful blend of fiction and politics,
concerned as much with the problems of everyday life as with the
larger issues of the planet.

A blow-by-blow account of a picketing campaign against the Nuclear Weapons Establishment, it details the divisions and conflicts
within the peace movement itself as they converge on Iris, a young
typist who throws in her job to join the pickets. Set in the late 50s,
the novel carries with it a positive and confident message of non-violent resistance that is just as relevant to today's protests.

"*Jericho* makes it clear that the peace movement has a past which
today's movement can gain strength from" — *The Observer*
ISBN 0-946097-08-9   £3.95 pbk

Titles of lesbian interest, from GMP:

Michael Baker
OUR THREE SELVES: A life of Radclyffe Hall

Radclyffe Hall remains today the most famous of British lesbians - above all for her novel *The Well of Loneliness*, which was banned as "obscene" in a sensational court case in 1928. Her life story, however, is less well known, though she was a leading figure in the colourful homosexual subculture of the 1920s and 30s, and widely connected in the literary world. This comprehensive biography draws upon such unpublished material as letters, diaries and essays, as well as on her novels and poems. Baker throws fresh light on this remarkable woman, and on her two major love affairs with Mabel Batten and Una Troubridge, who together with Radclyffe Hall made up the "three selves" of the title.

ISBN 0-85449-042-6 £6.95 pbk

Kay Dick
THE SHELF

"The Shelf" is a repository in the coroner's office where Cassandra's letters to Anne had first been lodged — as well as that other, unposted letter found in Anne's handbag. It was all so long ago — back in the 1960s — but Cass has not been able to forget the passion Anne engendered in her; their brief affair; and the mystery that surrounded it.

"A tour de force, powerful in its evocation of relationships and the gradations of passion. This work places Kay Dick in the same category of sensibility as Jean Rhys, Katherine Mansfield and Ford Maddox Ford" — Gillian Freeman

ISBN 0-85449-002-7 £4.95 pbk

Lorraine Trenchard
BEING LESBIAN
In this insightful, unpretentious guide, Lorraine Trenchard explodes
the myths surrounding lesbianism, and encourages her readers to
embrace their sexuality with a positive mind. Drawing on her
experience as counsellor and activist, she examines the needs and
realities of loving your own sex, and in practical steps, explains how
to encourage self esteem and enjoy a successful lesbian lifestyle.

"Contains information that's helpful regardless of one's residence or
nationality... Besides coverage of relationships, parenthood, health
issues... *Being Lesbian* touches on subjects that many books miss"
— *Washington Blade*
ISBN 0-85449-113-9 £3.95 pbk

Titles of lesbian interest,
from ALYSON PUBLICATIONS, USA.
(distributed in the UK by GMP)

Nancy Toder
CHOICES
Lesbian love can bring joy and passion; it can also bring conflicts. In this straightforward, sensitive novel, Toder conveys the fear and confusion of a woman coming to terms with her sexual and emotional attraction to other women.
"Choices is a classic lesbian love story. It has everything required for a good read: plot, characters, action, erotica. I suspect that it may be the most popular novel since *Rubyfruit Jungle."* — *On Our Backs*
ISBN 0-932870-619 £5.95 pbk

Wendy Borgstrom
RAPTURE AND THE SECOND COMING
A proudly unashamed reflection of the new wave of lesbian writing flowering both in the States and the UK. Fleeing to New York to get over a failed first romance, Gwen buries her anger by acting out all her sexual fantasies, in a city where the women are never in short supply and anything is possible.
ISBN 1-55583-166-4 £5.95 pbk

Pat Califia
DOC AND FLUFF
The first full-length novel by the author of the cult classic *Macho Sluts*. Doc is a freewheeling biker who meets Fluff, a cute and kinky young girl, at a wild biker party. Unknown to her, Fluff turns out to be the property of the bike club's president. A raucous adventure of lesbian S/M ensues.
"Militant kink without compromise" — *On Our Backs*
ISBN 1-55583-176-1 £6.95 pbk

Carol S Becker
UNBROKEN TIES
"An important addition to the lesbian literature and community. Becker presents a fascinating account of the diverse experiences of lesbians as they break up, rebuild their lives, and develop varied relationships with ex-lovers. Every lesbian can profit from reading this book." — JoAnn Loulan, author of *Lesbian Passion: Loving Ourselves* and *Each Other*
ISBN 1-55583-106-0 £5.95 pbk

Titles by Brigid Brophy from GMP:

THE FINISHING TOUCH
Hetty Braid worships the lovely but selfish Antonia Mount, co-proprietor with herself of the most exclusive finishing school on the French Riviera. The girls they teach are quite remarkable, though hardly for academic distinction. But trouble looms when Antonia announces that "Royalty is coming".

Originally published over twenty-five years ago, this witty comedy is reissued with a new introduction by the author, explaining its background and the unexpected identity of its main character.

"You are presented with the idea of a very sensible woman sitting on a high desk and concocting an exquisitely mincing piece of high camp, which romps even *Cold Comfort Farm* under the daisies" — *City Limits*
ISBN 0-85449-059-0   £4.95 pbk

IN TRANSIT
A classic crisis-of-identity novel set in an airport transit lounge in which we reflect on Pat's confused identity and gender. Both a philosophical odyssey and a literary game of hide and seek, *In Transit* defies explanation; it's a puzzle and a transexual adventure — with a heroine who may turn out a hero...

"The best prose writer of her generation (of either gender) in Great Britain today. *In Transit* is the best argument I know for claiming that the novel is alive and doing well" — *Life Magazine*

ISBN 0-85449-100-7 £4.95 pbk

GMP/Alyson books can be ordered from any bookshop in the UK, and from specialised bookshops overseas. If you prefer to order by mail, please send full retail price plus £1.50 for postage and packing to: GMP Publishers Ltd (BL), P O Box 247, London N17 9QR. (For Access/Visa/American Express give number and signature.)

In North America order from Alyson Publications Inc, 40 Plympton St, Boston MA 02118, USA.

Name and Address in block letters please:

Name —————————————————————

Address: —————————————————————

—————————————————————

—————————————————————